BLUE
RIVER
and RED
EARTH

ALSO BY STEPHEN HENIGHAN

NOVELS
Other Americas
The Places Where Names Vanish
The Streets of Winter
The Path of the Jaguar
Mr. Singh Among the Fugitives

SHORT STORY COLLECTIONS
Nights in the Yungas
North of Tourism
A Grave in the Air

NON-FICTION
*Assuming the Light: The Parisian Literary Apprenticeship
of Miguel Ángel Asturias*
*When Words Deny the World: The Reshaping
of Canadian Writing*
Lost Province: Adventures in a Moldovan Family
A Report on the Afterlife of Culture
A Green Reef: The Impact of Climate Change
*Sandino's Nation: Ernesto Cardenal and Sergio Ramírez Writing
Nicaragua, 1940-2012*

BLUE
RIVER
and RED
EARTH

Cormorant Books

Canada Council **Conseil des Arts**
for the Arts **du Canada**

 ONTARIO ARTS COUNCIL
CONSEIL DES ARTS DE L'ONTARIO
an Ontario government agency
un organisme du gouvernement de l'Ontario

 Canadian Patrimoine Canadä
Heritage canadien

The publisher gratefully acknowledges the support of the Canada Council for the
Arts and the Ontario Arts Council for its publishing program. We acknowledge
the financial support of the Government of Canada through the Canada Book
Fund (CBF) for our publishing activities, and the Government of Ontario through
the Ontario Media Development Corporation, an agency of the Ontario Ministry
of Culture, and the Ontario Book Publishing Tax Credit Program.

LIBRARY AND ARCHIVES CANADA CATALOGUING IN PUBLICATION

Henighan, Stephen, 1960–, author
Blue river and red earth / Stephen Henighan.

Short stories.
Issued in print and electronic formats.
ISBN 978-1-77086-517-4 (SOFTCOVER). — ISBN 978-1-77086-518-1 (HTML)

I. Title.

PS8565.E5818A6 2018   C813'.54   C2018-900026-0
                        C2018-900027-9

Cover art and design: angeljohnguerra.com
Interior text design: Tannice Goddard, bookstopress.com
Printer: Friesens

Printed and bound in Canada.

CORMORANT BOOKS INC.
10 ST. MARY STREET, SUITE 615, TORONTO, ONTARIO, M4Y 1P9
www.cormorantbooks.com

CONTENTS

I

THREE FINGERS

"NEVER GO WITH A married man."

When they were alone in the kitchen, Irina's mother struck a match. A ring of blue flame rose up on the front right element of the gas stove, the flames turning orange as they lapped around the base of the plain iron samovar. Since Ivan's departure, Irina had ceased to view her parents as a unit of authority, coming to see them as two people in a relationship that was complicated by her presence. The warning against married men — the first time her mother had recognized her as a woman — encouraged her to distance herself from this triangle. Before she could assure her mother that she did not think married men would be a problem since in the closed city men with wives were grey-faced science teachers, brown-uniformed checkpoint guards or security officers who had started their careers in the KGB, her mother said, "And when you are married, watch your husband's stomach. A man who has a family and responsibilities must have a belly. If your husband grows thin, some young hussy has met a married man, and you must put a stop to it. Feed him! His belly is your security."

All summer, in the mountains, Irina pondered this advice. At the beginning of the summer, when her father drove her up to where the air blowing in the windows of his wheezing Moskvitch sedan turned cool, she watched the bottomless vertical fissures of cliff faces narrowing as they funnelled towards dark lakes. Clefts of rock above the waterline glistened with snow until mid-June. This would be her last summer with her grandmother, carrying in firewood, collecting eggs from the chickens, eating halal mutton with thick noodles, and brewing tea over live coals in the copper samovar decorated with caliphate designs. Her grandmother spoke to her in broken Russian, but all other conversation was in Bashkir. In the Urals, the doubling of Russian and Bashkir, Christianity and Islam, valley and mountain, flat and hut, laboratory and livestock, samovars of iron and those of copper, tripped up the unitary right answers of her school.

Her summers spilled into the long inert days of Ramadan when her body was sapped by heat and hunger, then revived by nights of feasting around wood fires and cast-iron pots. Her grandmother taught her to prepare *besbarmaq*, "five fingers," the meal her village ate when sunset ended the day's fast. Irina learned to wield long Tartar knives to slice the boiled horsemeat into snippets, mixing it with noodles and onion sauce. As hot food aroused her body in the cool mountain nights, she tried to think about the blond boys in her classes. Dark, clean-limbed peasant lads watched her when she brought out the food. She knew better than to dream about boys who went to rustic schools. The closed city promoted discipline. It had taught her that in spite of her broad features and straight dark hair, she was not a Muslim. She and her classmates had been born Soviet citizens. She owed her education to the heritage of socialism, which, in contrast to capitalism, did not divide people by race.

Her city did not appear on any map. It was surrounded by walls topped with fences and a double row of checkpoints on the highway that led across a plain and into the forest. Only residents, and government officials on business, passed the checkpoints. Until the late 1940s, this site had been prairie, traversed by wayward horsemen. The city consisted of apartment blocks and huge, walled installations with no signs on the outside to reveal their function. There were smokestacks and cooling towers; a football field and a hockey rink; a hospital; school playgrounds, named in honour of heroes of the Great Patriotic War, with brightly painted swings and slides. Only the Orthodox church, built after Stalin died and Khrushchev had come to power, was made of brick to fabricate an impression of a venerable Russian presence in this spot unimaginably far from Moscow.

The scientists, soldiers, and police had washed-out faces; many were fair, with blue eyes. Few other families inside the city's gates were of Bashkir origin. No one talked about work because everyone's work was secret. Even after the Soviet Union collapsed when she was four, a time of hideous anxiety felt even by young children, the new government maintained the checkpoints. It continued the research projects that suppressed the city's existence from maps. Her social studies teachers pointed to her presence in the classroom as evidence of the social justice created by the Soviet Union, whose glorious heritage would provide the foundation for the rebirth of Greater Russia. In the city, as in the mountains, she was conspicuous. Her father was a physicist, her mother a biochemist; she knew from infancy that she was her peers' intellectual equal. They were all, their teachers said, of superior genetic inheritance; it was a compliment to live in a city where everyone was intelligent. The checkpoints around the city's borders cordoned them off not only from sabotage, but from people of inferior genetics. When she left the city's boundaries she saw peasants and nomads, cattle in the valleys and rambling sheep in the mountains. Skinny-spired mosques clung to wooded hillsides. From early childhood, the world divided into educated and uneducated, genetically superior and genetically inferior. Like any girl who had studied Chekhov's *The Three Sisters*, Irina yearned for Moscow. It was difficult to enter a good university in European Russia when you came from the east. If she did not succeed, she had the consolation of knowing that merely to have been born in the closed city was an achievement.

Failure to achieve was unforgivable. Irina, who did not expect to be forgiven if she failed, did not forgive Ivan. Two years after the Soviet Union collapsed her older brother fell behind in arithmetic. An educational specialist from Moscow told Irina's parents that they were stunting their children's development by speaking to them in Bashkir. "Does speaking different languages slow development?" asked her mother, who spoke Bashkir and Russian with equal fluency and read scientific articles in German and English.

The specialist stiffened. "Your son cannot succeed because he is trying to think in a peasant dialect. The gap between a dialect and a language is very great. From now on, you must speak Russian at home."

Two days later their building superintendent notified them that their flat needed repairs. Even at age six, Irina knew that listening devices were being installed. After Ivan's failure, she heard the Bashkir language only in the summers. She never learned to speak it fluently; lacking the language, she lacked the religion. As frightening articles about Muslims appeared in the news, Irina learned to say, "I'm not really Muslim." The phrase reassured people, gaining her admission where she needed it. Her infant admiration of her brother had long since faded. When they began to speak Russian at home, Ivan receded into a taciturn figure whose bed on the living-room couch, though it was where all older brothers slept, felt like a form of exile. His brown eyes avoided her. Even as she expressed every atom of herself in Russian, she could not forgive him for depriving her of the language in which her mother spoke to her grandmother. She was glad to get away from him in the summer, happy that his desire to be Russian ruled out stays in the mountains. In adolescence she found the courage, when they were outside on the street, to taunt Ivan for the crewcut he wore to disguise the silkiness of his hair. Irina, her mother and father were a trio of scientists, researchers, people who had or would study at universities. Ivan withdrew during their supper-table conversations. Irina welcomed his departure for a second-rate military technical institute, where he would receive a diploma while doing his military service, as a purification of the atmosphere in their flat, an intensification of her identification with her mother and father and confirmation of their research careers. No one could deny her stupendous exam results. She was one of the rare students from the east to be admitted to Moscow State University. She carried the closed city within her to the grand metropolis where all of Russia mingled. As she studied in her tiny student room, keeping herself alert with black tea from an electric kettle, her mind extended a circular hub around her brain and body. No one breached this enclosure, not even those who believed they had passed her checkpoints. Recognizing the necessity of disposing of her virginity, she did so in a way that avoided incurring the burden of a fiancé. She did not forgive the boy who tried to cling to her once she was finished with him. The Soviet habit of marrying at twenty was dwindling. Ivan, retrograde as always, had married at twenty-two after graduating into a job as a technician in a Siberian mine. Irina did not discuss the details of being a single woman with her mother who, having married at eighteen, had never been one. Yet, Irina was certain that her mother would approve of her intimate decisions. Above all, she would understand that intimacy was not the most important part of her life; it was not even her deepest intimacy.

The relationships that riveted her were crystallized by her self-discipline. In her work, communities of fact and theory writhed in symmetrical harmony. She studied the cold, in which all beings were preserved; she focused on the fact that the cold was warming. When she graduated from Moscow State, she was offered a post at an institute in Germany whose ties to the University of Potsdam would allow her to parlay her climate-change research into a doctorate. Arriving in Berlin, she recognized the familiar contours of a closed city. The remnants from the four decades when half of Berlin had been a microcosm of the West surrounded by the East likened it to her city turned inside out. Even today, her supervisor — her "Doctorate-Father," the Germans said — joked, "Every direction you drive in is East." Beyond the city's outskirts lay the traits of former socialist society: the faceless apartment blocks, gigantic statues, low-set trams that she knew from home, and, in the districts that had not been renovated, the same puckered, greying stucco. The first time she took the train out to Potsdam, she stumbled on a bust of Lenin and a plaque in Russian and German that thanked the Red Army and the heroic workers and peasants of the Soviet Union for liberating Germany from fascism. She took a photograph of the plaque with her new cellphone and sent it to her parents. *You should send one to your brother*, her mother texted back.

Irina's German colleagues gave papers in English at international conferences. Realizing that she, too, would need to do this, she took night classes in this language that she had not studied since secondary school. One night, walking home to her flat in Prenzlauer Berg, in the former East Berlin, where she heard Russian spoken every day, she was surprised by a conversation between two men walking in front of her: a conversation that was not in Russian or German or English, but which she understood without effort. She hurried forward. Ignoring the risks of a young woman approaching two men on a dark street, she asked, "*Bitte*, what language are you speaking?"

The men smiled. "We speak Turkish," the clean-shaven one said.

The geography of her life pivoted, the secret city sinking deeper into its valley and the Ural Mountains, whose contour lines maps highlighted, rising higher. Being Russian connected her to one Berlin diaspora; her grandmother's language, a component in the great sweep of Turkic speech that stretched from the Urals to the Bosphorus and sprawled deep into Central Asia, made her part of another diaspora. The longer she remained in Germany, the more these two heritages settled into an equilibrium. In Berlin, it no longer seemed like a violation of her Russianness to have more than one heritage. She blamed this misconception, now debunked in her mind, on her brother. His selfish failures had deprived her of a full command of her ancestral language. Her renewed awareness of her connection to the Turkic world sharpened her resentment of Ivan's decision to pretend he was Russian, with a spiky crewcut and a Russian wife; no matter how long he worked underground, his skin would remain brown. Berlin freed her to embrace her contradictions. When the Turkish girl in her building, whom she passed on the stairs, stopped one day to talk, Irina heard herself say, her German trembling, "My grandparents were Bashkir."

"*Memnun oldum*," the girl replied.

Irina understood, though she stumbled to reciprocate the greeting.

The dispersion of her life did not bother her because in Berlin everything was multiple and incomplete; it was acceptable because she spent her days contemplating the solidity of ice.

Ice called out to her in a letter of invitation to join a research team at Russia's Institute for Arctic and Antarctic Research in St. Petersburg. Her Doctorate-Father advised her to accept; she could spend summers in Russia and return to Berlin for the academic year. She had entered her doctorate as a social scientist with a strong foundation in the natural sciences, studying the adaptation of Arctic architecture to climate change. In offices in St. Petersburg's enormous Museum of the Arctic and Antarctic, dominating Ulitsa Morata from behind its white classical facade, half a block from the flat where Dostoevsky had lived, she joined a project focused on an island in the Barents Sea. The Soviet Union had built a fortified city on this ice-bound pan of rock as a forward line of defence against a NATO fleet that might invade around the north coast of Norway. The closed city had been not only a military base, but a listening post, a vantage point from which to observe the heavens, an Arctic research station. In the early 1980s, it had been abandoned; for three decades the city sat frozen in ice. Now, as government agencies competed to claim this terrain, the streets were opening again. The military wanted to restore the base's capabilities to defend Russia against resurgent Western hostility. The scientists wanted to establish a centre for the study of climate change. Realizing that they would need economic arguments to make their policy prevail, the team at the Institute for Arctic and Antarctic Research was developing a project to combine a research lab with high-end tourism. Nowhere in the world was the architecture and interior design of the 1970s preserved as perfectly as here. Wealthy foreigners could be flown to the island for adventure tourism; the buildings that had housed officers and their families could become a theme park of Soviet life and taste. At the beginning of the summer, Irina and her colleagues flew to the island and spent a week taking measurements and collecting data. Segments of the data, relating to the impact on these buildings of a changing climate, would nourish Irina's doctoral thesis. She was gratified to be back in Russia, where she knew intuitively how people felt and reacted, even though for the first time, she saw these reactions from the outside — with Berlin eyes? with Bashkir eyes? — as Russian rather than as the essence of humanity.

Knowing no one in St. Petersburg, she asked the Institute for help in finding accommodation. They put her in touch with a young environmental journalist named Olga whose family owned a flat on the western side of Vasilyevsky Island, across the Neva River from the city centre. "It's an expensive flat by Russian standards, but for you, who have Euros, it will be cheap." Olga shook her mop of short, thick brown hair. "And I can help you meet people." Olga's welcome, disarmingly Western in its breeziness, offset the flat's incongruities. It was a standard two-room flat in a six-storey apartment block surrounded by a dozen identical blocks. Seagulls combed overhead. When, at Olga's urging, Irina stood on a stool in the kitchen and looked out the window, she saw the enormous cranes of the docks. Yet, unlike most older flats, this one was unencumbered by the cargo of past decades. The wall unit was nearly empty, the only books were school texts and a handful of classics; there were no medals attesting to a grandfather's service in the Great Patriotic War; no Soviet-era diplomas or citations; no leather trunks with brass locks; and, instead of a samovar, there was a glass French press coffee maker. Rather than stern black-and-white photographs of departed relatives, the wall unit's central panel featured a single framed, colour photograph of a group of young women in shorts and numbered jerseys competing in a track-and-field event in a large stadium. The couch in the kitchen-sitting room folded out into the bed where she slept at night. It was a short walk to the concrete square around the Vasileostrovskaya Metro Station, where women from the countryside sold fruits and vegetables. As Olga gave her the tour, Irina realized that her hasty stride was designed to minimize a limp. Her baggy slacks concealed the fact that Olga's right leg was twisted, or perhaps shorter than her left leg. "Do you want to meet people?" Olga said. "Do you have a boyfriend? I know lots of single men."

"I'm going away on a research trip."

When she came back from the Barents Sea, the flat both soothed and unsettled her. She kept forgetting to ask Olga about the sprinting girls in the photograph. Her journey to the Arctic had been more of an ordeal than she expected. The small plane, buffeted by turbulence over a lunging grey sea aslosh with a soup of fractured ice, sucked the breath out of her chest. She withdrew into her measurements and the photographs she was taking to put up with sharing a one-room prefab hut with five colleagues. The farther she walked down the empty streets, the closer her fascination came to being revoked by despair. She reached the edge of town, where watchtowers stood waiting to fend off a once and future enemy. The grey Barents Sea pitched along the low, flat, lumines-cent horizon. Her closed cities stacked one inside the other like matryoshka dolls. The wind that lashed at her face and blew her

hair into her eyes could not release her from the feeling that she
was the smallest doll, immured inside the others. Her arms and
legs felt as though they were painted on curves of bulbous wood.
She thought: I am at the top of the world, I have walked away from
my team, this is not disciplined behaviour; if I am of superior genetic
inheritance, if I am a good researcher, I must understand what
is wrong.

She decided that she was experiencing a crisis of the nerves.

The muted sun never set; they worked until eleven p.m. barely
noticing the long hours they put in to document the conditions of
roofs and pipes, internal and external temperatures, the effective-
ness of the surviving insulation. She spoke little to her colleagues
over dinner and was the first to go to bed. She endured the flight
back over the Barents Sea and when she arrived in St. Petersburg
she felt she had returned to a home that made her restless, a
Russia unlike any Russia she had imagined, a city that had been
built on a network of rivers and canals opening to the sea, exuding
its essence towards Europe and sucking Europe into its arteries
with an obscene promiscuity that masqueraded as an ultra-refined
dignity. Jostled by sleeplessness, she woke up with the sun — in
St. Petersburg's white nights, the sun went down from two to
four in the morning — and burned off her restlessness by jogging
along the fringes of the harbour. As her feet carried her along the
waterfront and her mind ranged back over her previous day's
work, she felt her body and brain working together like Siamese
twins. After work, she strolled the banks of the Neva River. In
the afternoon breeze the whitecaps were wind-tousled. The sheer
volume of water felt uncontainable, as though it were about to
spill its formlessness over the city's sober lines of Germanic
stolidity and French precision as it did in Pushkin's poem about
the bronze horseman. The surging water tugged at the middle of
her body until she felt breathless. Once, she had thrown discipline
to the winds. The night after speaking with the two Turkish men,
she had turned the corner to find the clean-shaven one standing

alone. He spoke to her in Turkish. She was busy, she had to get home; her research team had a meeting in Potsdam at eight-thirty the next morning. She lingered long enough to let him persuade her to meet on this corner on Saturday evening. Three nights later, after sharing a bottle of red wine, they went to his room. His flatmate was out. Irina stripped off her clothes before his muddled courting could request it of her. He regarded her with breathless gratitude tainted with disapproval. More than a year had passed since her last boy in Moscow. Her previous lovemaking had been in Russian, with boys whose fingers had been softened, almost pruned, by hours spent enveloped in lab gloves. With Ezmir she had to explain her wishes in her workplace German, devoid of any register of tenderness. He replied in an exalted Turkish, as though she were the virgin bride chosen for him by his family. As he kissed her body, she grasped that he, too, had been prised out of his culture by immigration; like her, he was acting in accordance with customs that were unknown to the lover in his arms. The thought pierced her with tenderness for his puzzled brown eyes and the square, callused fingertips that rasped over her ribcage, leaving triple score-marks. She heard him murmur the word *"güzel"*; he was telling her she was beautiful. Having promised herself that she would leave by midnight, she stayed until six a.m. The paltry spasms of pleasure she had experienced before, she realized, had not been full orgasms. When Ezmir asked where she lived, she offered him her cellphone number and transposed the last two digits. By daylight, his denuded room, with not a book or a poster in sight, only a newspaper in Turkish with a photograph of a soccer player on the front, reminded her that he was a *Gastarbeiter*. He had breached the walls of Berlin, but he would not have been admitted to the closed city. She began to take a different route home from her English class.

She had made herself forget this encounter, as though it were possible to wipe it from her memory like information deleted from a hard drive. Feeling the pull of the Neva in the soles of her feet, she greeted the recollection's return with a tightening of her breath that turned the slapping of wavelets against the bridges into the promise of pleasure.

Two nights later she met Olga in a little Jewish restaurant on Ulitsa Rubinshteyna, where Aston Martins and Mercedes coupes were parked against the sidewalks, and young people ducked from café to café. Olga knew everyone. She remained seated, keeping her legs beneath the table, and let others come to her. Her cellphone never stopped humming as she spoke of the two years she had studied at Oxford University and the articles she now wrote in English, where she criticized government environmental policy more openly than was possible in Russian-language publications. She worked for a German NGO and taught a course in journalism at the university. Raising a glass of white wine with her, Irina felt herself plunging into St. Petersburg like flotsam swept into the canals by the tides of the Neva. Confirming her visibility in this Russia that thirsted for the world, she received two invitations to speak: the first at a conference organized by her Doctorate-Father in Berlin, the second, to her astonishment, from an institute in Prince George, British Columbia, Canada, that studied the adaptation of high-latitude building procedures to a changing climate. "I can't go," she told Olga. "It's too far."

"You have to go! It's important that you see the world and that they hear from you. It's the only way to find solutions." Olga was second vice-president of an association of young environmental journalists funded by the United Nations. She had spoken at conferences in Beijing and Lima, and Nairobi. Spurred on by her friend's enthusiasm, Irina applied to the Canadian Embassy in Moscow for a visa. She must do this quickly, in order to get her passport back in time to travel to Berlin. The embassy called her to Moscow for an interview. She took two days off work and went on the high-speed train. The man in a brown suit who interviewed her in English, wrinkling his brow, asked her about her surname. Wasn't it a Muslim name? "I am not really a Muslim,"

Irina said in a tone of practised dismissal. "That's why my parents gave me a Russian first name."

The man asked her about her research, perusing the letter of invitation from Prince George. "The Government of Canada," he said, "recognizes that there is no consensus as to whether climate change is happening."

She refrained from replying. He asked her to provide the names and addresses of her family members: her parents in the city that was on no map, her brother in Siberia. A week later she received an email informing her that her application for a Canadian visa had been denied. The email did not permit replies; it made no mention of the return of her passport. She phoned five times from work and finally got through to a female voice that spoke native Russian. "Your passport is being held pending further investigation," the voice said.

"But I need to travel. I have to give a paper in Berlin. When will I get it back?"

"We have no fixed deadline for returning passports."

This was the great international world Olga encouraged her to visit? This was the free, open West? She wrote a distraught email to her Doctorate-Father in Berlin. The next day a German research institute made a formal complaint to the Canadian Embassy in Germany. On Monday her passport arrived by courier at the Institute for Arctic and Antarctic Research. On Wednesday Irina caught the plane to Berlin. When she returned to St. Petersburg, the leader of her research team told her that he would like to publish her summary of her preliminary investigations in the Barents Sea in an English-language journal. By establishing an international identity for the island as a centre for research and tourism, he hoped to pre-empt the military's claim to the abandoned city. "You must find a good English translator," he said.

She texted Olga, who invited her to a party in a former bomb shelter near the railway lines from the Moscow station. Irina walked through streets of abandoned buildings until she found the small lot where trees and bushes had twined around a squat construction. She pushed through the foliage and went upstairs into an overheated bar. The music — house, with loud, clanging keyboards — was mixed by a DJ with a grey ponytail. She climbed another level and came out on the roof, where Olga and her friends were sitting in chairs with blankets draped over them. It was still light but the night had turned cold. Olga was getting to her feet to go down to the bar. "Take my seat, sit next to Angus." She explained in a rush that she had hung out here in 1999, when she was twenty-one. The bomb shelter's nineties DJ, Kolya, had come back for tonight's revival. Like Olga, most of her friends were a dozen years older than Irina and had danced here as students. "Olga is spending all her time down in the bar taking selfies with Kolya," somebody said. They all laughed. "She's so nostalgic!"

Irina took Olga's chair and blanket, and ordered a glass of Georgian white wine. The blanket-swaddled group contained journalists and people who worked in tourism and international business, and a younger woman Irina's age who was immigrating to the United States with her boyfriend from Maine, who had promised to introduce her to Stephen King. They were discussing the possibility that Vladimir Putin was deliberately deflating the ruble to make it unaffordable for people such as themselves to travel abroad. Putin wanted to crush the cities' cosmopolitanism in order to make all of Russia as backward and inward-looking as the regions that supported him. Irina, who had never heard this sort of talk in the closed city and had avoided it in Moscow, remained silent. Seeking an escape from politics, she caught the eye of the man next to her. Angus was Olga's age, with broad shoulders, a lean face, and a well-nourished beard. He spoke to her in English.

"You're not Canadian, are you?" she replied. "Because I do not like Canadians right now."

He assured her he was British. He told her an anecdote about two men attempting to pick his pocket in a tram. The way he told it, devoid of melodrama or fear of savage Russia, casting an ironic light on his own behaviour, warmed her through her blanket. "You must try to look more like a Russian, Angus," she said, leaning towards him. "You must stop smiling!"

"I thought my beard would hide my smile," he protested, observing her more closely.

"You found your translator!" Olga said, returning to resume her role as social convener.

"You speak Russian?" Irina asked.

"I don't speak it very well," Angus said in Russian with an English accent, "but I read it and understand it very well. I started coming here in the nineties, when things opened up and fell in love ... well, with the place. I spend a few months each year working here as a freelance translator. They give me six-month business visas that I have to keep renewing."

"At least you get your visa."

He asked her where she was living. When she mentioned the Vasileostrovskaya Metro Station, he said, "I know that area. I had a girlfriend who lived there."

Olga, who had been talking to a man who worked cross-border for a Finnish high-tech company, turned around. Her sharpness of gaze melted into an ambiguous smile. She turned her back on them. Irina grasped that Olga was matching her with Angus as more than a translator. At the same time, she perceived that Angus's words had violated a pact between them. This unwanted insight — the burden of being of superior genetic inheritance, her mother would say — made her feel as though the canals, and even the Neva River, were drying up. She did not want her open city to shrivel into an ingrown nook. She did not want to be the naive young girl received by a group of cynical older people as this summer's available meat; at the same time, the thought of being greeted as flesh and not grey cells made her hot and dizzy. Olga's reaction had surprised her. For all her ardent socializing, or perhaps because of it, Olga did not seem to have a love life. Some weekends she disappeared to dachas on the Gulf of Finland; Irina waited in vain for confessions from these stays in the country. Olga seemed to have no current boyfriend, no ex-husband, no murky past that she was putting behind her with her bright-eyed fraternization. A daunting privacy underlied her gregariousness. Irina found it easier to ask Olga about her bad leg — she had been born with this disability, she replied, her right leg was slightly shorter than her left — than to probe her love life.

Olga went back downstairs to the bar. Angus, after touching Irina's arm, followed her. Irina talked to the man who had learned Finnish to work in high tech, then set aside her blanket and got up to leave. She had found her translator; it was time to go home. Down in the stifling bar, Kolya was bent over the mixing board. Half a dozen people in their late thirties hurled themselves against blasts of dated house music. Olga was hopping in an unabashed off-kilter dance, her arm flung around Angus's shoulder. They waved her over. Irina met Olga's eyes, waiting for a prohibition that did not come; she slid beneath Angus's free arm. His lean muscles contracted around her shoulders. Olga tugged on Irina's free arm until the three of them were dancing in a circle. Irina's handbag slapped against her hip. A strobe light flashed red and green. Olga smiled at Irina with an intensity that made her forget where she was. She kissed Irina on the cheek. Startled, Irina kept dancing. She smiled at each of them in turn, gave each a hug, then stumbled out through the bushes that grew close to the bomb shelter's door. In the chilly luminescent night she pulled out her cellphone and called an Uber.

"You must tell us when you are getting engaged," her mother said on the phone, after filling her ears with news of Ivan and his wife that Irina ignored. Now that she was back in Russia, it was cheaper to call the closed city. "What are you doing for the end of Ramadan?"

Irina did not know how to reply. During her childhood, Ramadan had belonged to her grandmother and summers in the mountains.

Her parents, who spent their working days wearing lab coats, had not mentioned religion until Irina's second year at Moscow State University, when the checkpoints had been removed from the highway leading to the closed city. Her home remained a research centre. It was absent from even the most recent printed maps, though it appeared as an unnamed conurbation on Google Earth. Outside influences had streamed in. Her parents seemed puzzled by her failure to practise a faith they had never mentioned to her. She attributed her own changes to new cities and experiences; yet, her parents, whose lives had remained the same, had also changed, as though the sea of the outside world had spilled across the plains of Central Asia and engulfed them in St. Petersburg's cosmopolitanism or Berlin's rough-edged mixing.

Angus came to the Institute wearing a brown jacket and a red knit tie that was flat at the bottom, a detail that made Irina regard him with tenderness. In his meeting with their research team, his Russian, though accented, was correct. He signed the contract to translate Irina's article; the leader of the research team spoke to him of future projects.

"Do you like him?" Olga asked two nights later.

"Do you?" Irina replied, leaning over an outdoor table at a small bar on Ulitsa Rubinshteyna that specialized in German beer. "He said he had a girlfriend who lived — "

"That wasn't me." Olga broke off to speak to the owner in German. Turning back to Irina, she said, "You must see him again."

As Olga uttered these words, shaking her hive of short, straw-coloured hair, her liquid eyes coquettish, Irina felt that she did want to see Angus. The ice inside her had melted, releasing a compass-less disorientation that only her body, not her mind, could soothe. The canals branching towards the Neva demanded an irrigation of the flesh, a balancing of the claims of the patterns in her head with those of body and blood. Repression led to irrational behaviour; it led to Ezmir. As for love, her grounding in self-discipline had taught her the foolishness of exaggerated emotions.

Moscow, Berlin, and now St. Petersburg had each made a case for seduction. She met Olga's smile and said, "Yes. But not alone."

Olga sat up. Irina saw that she had given her friend a gift: a social occasion to organize. They drank another Heineken and planned her invitation to Angus. She explained the end of Ramadan to Olga. "Eid-al-Fitr," she said. "There's a Bashkir dish called five fingers that I make." As she spoke the words, she felt relieved to have an answer to her mother's question. She pushed Angus out of her mind and concentrated on her grandmother's recipe. During her jogs down by the harbour she had passed a butcher whose brightly painted Halal symbol defied the marauding skinheads. When she stopped there after work, the man addressed her in Kazakh; as with Turkish, she understood most of what he said. She attempted a reply in Bashkir, asking him for horsemeat. "There is no horsemeat in Vasilyevsky Island!" he laughed, suggesting she make her *besbarmaq* with mutton.

Back in the flat, with the slow brightness of the white night seeping in the window, she sliced the meat. None of the knives in the drawer was as sharp as the curved Tartar blades she remembered. She rummaged in the wall unit, opening drawers she had not touched before. Most were empty; none contained knives. In a bottom drawer she found a folded, short-sleeved sports jersey with the number "33" on it. She stood up. In the photograph, the girl running ahead of the others wore this number. She lifted the jersey, beneath it lay the black shorts from the photograph. She closed the drawer. Runner number 33, like all of the competitors, was very young. It was difficult to be certain, yet her half-defined face resembled Olga's.

She returned to her slicing, making do with the knives in the drawer. The noodles were almost ready to be mixed with the onion sauce when the buzzer rang. Listening to Angus's voice as he uttered his accented, "*Privet*," she wondered whether Olga had abandoned her to leave the two of them alone. Was this her fear, or her longing? She pulled a bottle of Georgian wine out of the fridge and poured herself a glass. She took a sip before the elevator clunked to a halt. Looking out through the peephole when he knocked, she saw the leanness of his face, the wiry athleticism of his shoulders. He came in carrying a bottle of French wine. Without having intended to, she hugged him. They lingered with their arms around each other. "I haven't eaten Muslim food in ages," he said.

"I'm not really Muslim — "

The buzzer rang. Olga came up in the elevator and entered the flat wearing baggy batiked slacks and carrying a bottle of German wine. As Irina mixed the onion sauce into the long, flat noodles, Olga and Angus spoke of Kazakh restaurants. "They're cheap as long as they have old Kazakh men smoking outside them ..."

"Then people discover them," Angus said, "and the prices triple."

"And the old Kazakh men have to go somewhere else," Irina said. The sight of their heads bowed together over their drinks made her want to kick out her friend and pull Angus into bed. She felt excluded, a Muslim outsider. They should ask themselves why Russians had no good food of their own. The popular restaurants in St. Petersburg were either Georgian or Kazakh, or else they were sushi bars. The other two continued giggling. "Why are you speaking English?" Irina asked, as she laid the plate of noodles on the table.

"When I started coming to St. Petersburg as a student," Angus said, "I was still learning Russian. Olga and I got used to talking in English."

As she sat down in the kitchen, where she had set places for herself and Olga on the couch that opened into her bed, and for Angus on a chair on the opposite side of the table, wariness trickled through her, its keenness dulled by her second glass of wine.

"One of our first conversations," Angus said, "was right in this kitchen. In 1998 or 1999."

Irina glanced at Olga, wondering about her denial of having been Angus's girlfriend. Olga dug into her noodles and mutton. "Three fingers!" she said.

"Five fingers," Irina amended. "It's called five fingers because we eat it with our hands and if we were in the Urals you'd be eating horsemeat."

Olga's wince made Irina feel that she had gained a tiny, effective vengeance for the suspicion, which grew stronger with each irresistible sip of wine, that these two people presented her with a puzzle that logic could not solve. Having discarded the snowflake patterns in her mind in anticipation of feeling the soft chest hair that curled over the top of Angus's shirt on her breasts, she struggled to concentrate the analytical powers of her superior genetic inheritance. She could work this out! Yet, it was precisely the need to understand events as a logical sequence that she must relinquish in order to answer the blood in her veins. If she thought too much, she would paralyze herself as she had in the Barents Sea. She caught Angus's glance across the table. His brown eyes settled her disquiet, reassuring her that it was she that he had come to see. As Olga lounged at her side, wriggling her gaudy batiked legs, Irina flung her arm around her in an attempt to hold her friend apart from the man they had agreed that she, not Olga, would seduce tonight. Olga laughed and rolled against her. "I'm so glad we met, Irinushka."

"Eat your five fingers."

"Three fingers! I'm going to call it three fingers!"

Olga was drunker than she had realized. Just as Irina resigned herself to the fact that this conversation was descending into nonsense, Olga snapped into a lucid account of the building where the NGO she worked for was based. After the annexation of Crimea, the American NGOs had been kicked out of Russia. Their offices sat empty; her friends who worked for American organizations had lost their jobs. The Germans had been allowed to stay. "Putin is cautious with them," Olga said. "He knows that he must not be enemies with America and Germany at the same time."

Irina felt herself retreating. Putin was from the KGB; in the closed city, KGB men had been unmentionable. She glanced down at her cellphone. Her mother had texted her from the foothills of the Urals: *How are you celebrating Eid-al-Fitr?* If people in the closed city could now admit to being Muslims, could they also criticize Putin? Thwarted by Olga's complicity with Angus, she replied: *I'm eating besbarmaq with friends.* She left the dish's name in Bashkir, afraid that if she wrote it in Russian, she would put three fingers instead of five.

She glanced up from her cellphone, stretched out her arm, and swiped against empty space. The warmth of Olga's body, the gaudiness of her baggy slacks, had disappeared.

"Steady there," Angus said, getting up and slipping around the end of the table.

"Where's Olga?"

Angus was bending over her to straighten her posture on the couch, his hand firm on her arm. She realized that while her senses were in a blur, time had passed.

"Olga's gone, Irina. We're alone." He smiled at her. Had he and Olga planned this exit? "Try to stand up, won't you, love?"

She allowed him to haul her to her feet. She fell against him. She felt like sheer weight, nothing but a body. Somewhere in the high Arctic her mind continued to meander, demonstrating her superior genetic inheritance in obliviousness to Angus's lean torso. When they kissed, knowing that this was what she wanted, she closed her eyes until the Arctic vastness receded. His brown eyes refused to release her. She unbuttoned the front of his shirt, surprised that her fingers remained dexterous enough to do this. She took his chest hair in her mouth. "The sun still hasn't set," she teased him. "We can't undress until Ramadan is over."

"We've broken the fast by eating."

"Three fingers," she giggled, running her hands down to his waist. She pressed against him, the cellphone in her pocket reminding her of her mother. The matted hair on Angus's chest thinned to a glossy fuzz as it descended to his flat stomach. The leader of her research team, who was the same age as Angus, had a paunch. "I suppose you're married," she murmured, gripping his arm to avoid losing her balance.

"I spend my summers in St. Petersburg."

"You have a wife in England?"

"In Scotland," he gulped, his reluctance to confess making her feel guilty for pressing him. Never go with a married man, yet if a middle-aged man loses his belly he is seeing a young hussy. She had not expected the two pieces of advice to overlap. Her mother had set her a puzzle as inscrutable as the bond between Olga and Angus. Each had played its part in bringing her to where she was now. Her fingers, so adroit on Angus's buttons, fumbled to unhook her bra. Her head was both heavy and light as she clambered onto her bed on her knees. Her bra came off. The pull of the Neva tugged at the core of her body.

She awoke to the sun in her eyes and the sound of the door closing. The solution to her mother's conflicting pieces of advice, her first waking thought told her, was that she was the hussy. In spite of her headache, she felt secure in this victory over the paralysis that had painted her body onto the curves of a matryoshka doll. From the head down, she felt pliant and warm, revelling in her lasciviousness. She craned her head and peered with dried-out eyes, desolated by the thought that the closing door had sealed Angus's departure.

She was startled to see that the sound had heralded Olga's arrival.

Stepping around Irina's blue jeans on the kitchen floor, Olga limped to the side of her bed, her eyes clouded from lack of sleep. The coolness of the morning air as Irina lay on her back made her realize she was naked. A shock of vulnerability paralyzed her. Alarmed as though Olga were a strange man and not her best St. Petersburg girlfriend, she sought out her friend's eyes, which were roving over her in mixed sympathy and prurience, and thought how eastern, how Muslim, the dark lankness of her pubic hair would appear to Olga's pale blue eyes.

The hair on Angus's chest had been coarse and wiry, not silky as she had expected. The friction between their flesh had excited her. It had left fading, reddish score-marks on her breasts, as if his chest had been rasping her with a whisk as he moved inside her. Lifting her hands to cover herself, she realized that a T-shirt lay on top of her. Olga gasped. Sitting up, then regretting it, Irina looked down and saw that it was the sports tunic from the drawer.

"That's not yours!" Olga pulled the tunic away, leaving her naked.

Irina rolled to her feet, padded barefoot into the next room and pulled her jogging shorts and T-shirt out of the closet section of the wall unit. She returned to the kitchen, walked past Olga, who was holding the tunic and sobbing, and poured herself a glass of water from the one-point-five litre bottle on the counter. She drank in silence. She needed strong tea from a samovar. Her head was a disaster, incapable of comprehending Olga's distress; a residue of pleasure remained curdled in her thighs. Steadying her voice, she said, "I wish he hadn't left."

"He always leaves. I knew he'd leave. That's why I came to see how you were doing."

"How do you know he always leaves?"

"Oh, I sometimes help him find girlfriends."

Disdaining this as the lie it obviously was as her anger mounted at Olga's refusal to admit that she had been Angus's girlfriend from the Vasileostrovskaya Metro Station, she said, "You didn't tell me he was married."

"His lives are separate. He's a different person here than in the West."

As she knew, having two lives was no excuse for anything; a dual perspective should instill discipline, not irresponsibility.

Her head hurt.

Olga folded the tunic with the 33 facing out, carried it into the back room and restored it to the bottom drawer of the wall unit. Watching her return to the kitchen, Irina was aware of her lazy right foot. She poured herself another glass of water. Her composure cracked. "I don't understand why you're here and he's not. It's him I want to be with!"

By crying, she made it easy for Olga. Her friend stepped forward and embraced her with a tenderness that felt unnatural — or did she mean un-Russian? She wondered again where she belonged.

She hugged Olga and kissed her on both cheeks, then on the mouth. Olga looked startled, then at peace.

They sat down side by side on her ravaged bed. "Why were you so shocked to see the tunic?"

"It didn't look right on you."

"You've seen it on other women?" She laughed at the absurdity.

"Yes, sometimes they wear it."

A shiver ran up Irina's spine.

"On the others it made me feel good. But you're dark ..."

Irina felt angry on so many different levels that she could not express. "Why don't you just admit that you're the girl in the photograph? You weren't born with a bad leg, you hurt it and it ruined your career and lost Angus, and now you try to compensate by procuring other women for him. Why is it so hard for you to admit that?"

Her brain was clearing. She was starting to see things as they were. She had always been better at this than other people.

Olga shook her head. "No." She was quiet but seemed more upset than Irina had expected. "No, no ..."

Irina stood up. "This may be your flat, but I'm the tenant and if I ask you to leave, you must go."

She accompanied Olga to the door. Her head felt awful. She would have to find a different social circle for the rest of the summer. She would not forgive Olga — though she might sleep with Angus again. She drank more water from the bottle on the counter. She took a cold shower and stared at herself in the mirror, examining the tan colour of the skin that Angus had kissed, the black hair that fell so thick and straight it almost did not require a brush, the broadness with which her features spread out from the centre of her face, in contrast to the Russians' pinched-up noses and mouths. More obviously an outsider in St. Petersburg than in Moscow or the east, she was suffering from her estrangement. Last night, when she was drinking, she had forgotten that she had to work today. This morning the thought of the materials she must analyze, the meeting she had to attend, failed to set intricate intimacies whirling in her mind.

She was about to make a strong coffee in the French press coffee-maker when her cellphone peeped. The message was from Olga; she considered deleting it, then clicked with her thumb. A photograph filled the screen. She saw Angus, younger, rangier in the shoulders, with long hair. His arm was draped around the girl in the track-meet photograph, who was not quite Olga. Another buzz; another photograph appeared. This time the two girls, achingly similar, stood with Angus between them. *They were both runners*, Olga had written. *He fell in love with my sister Masha, but I was always with them. Except when they ran.* Another peep; another message. *She was diagnosed with a brain tumour. It seemed impossible. We were sure it was a mistake until the day she died.*

Irina waited for the next buzz. *I can't stop trying to bring the three of us back together.*

She sat down on the bed. If Olga's sister, the owner of this flat, had lived, she would be Angus's wife. Sisters in experience, she, Olga and Masha had all slept on this bed — and with Angus? Irina's thumbs trembled on the keypad. *My poor little love*, she wrote. *I forgive you. We'll talk on the weekend.* The phone hummed again. *Did you make besbarmaq? Did you wait for sunset before eating it?*

She could not imagine what it felt like to have a sister, much less to lose one. A brother, if he embarrassed you, could be ignored. Calling up a number she had barely used, she sent Ivan a photograph she had taken last night of her *besbarmaq*. Afterwards, she stared at the twisted bedclothes. She had expected to forgive Angus, not Olga and Ivan.

As she swallowed her first sip of coffee, the reversal in her feelings unsettled her. Her impatience to leave St. Petersburg grew.

She texted her mother: *I made three fingers!* She felt better once she had corrected the mistake: *I mean five fingers!* In a month she would return to Berlin, where her one life was two. She would ride the train out to Potsdam to her research group and return in the evening to Prenzlauer Berg, where she would walk the streets until she found the building she remembered, then press the buzzer and ask for Ezmir.

2

THE SECRETS OF VERONIKA

I READ VERONIKA'S MESSAGE cancelling our meeting at the Czech Embassy, then left the smoky basement internet café off Magheru Boulevard. Out on the quiet streets, snow covered the construction hoardings. At a phone booth on the traffic circle with the statue of Mihail Kogălniceanu in the middle, I rang Veronika's number. She answered me in a throttled voice. "*Sînt în pat. M-am îmbolnăvit.*" She was ill in bed. "Are you coming back to Bucharest after Transylvania?"

"No," I said. "I'm flying home from Vienna."

"Call me tomorrow. Maybe I'll be better." She laughed. "We've known each other's secrets for so many years and this is the first time I have spoken to you from my bed!"

⸻

THE FIRST SUMMER COURSE I took in Romania, after the country opened up in the 1990s, was in Sinaia, where the ring of the Carpathian Mountains swings around in a sky-high wall that divides the sweltering Wallachian Plain from the rambling hills of

Transylvania. Generations of aristocrats had summered among the chipped, grey peaks. The language and culture course for foreign graduate students, diplomats, and business people was housed in a Communist-era concrete-block hotel with access to glorious hiking trails. I was admitted on the basis of having learned a colloquial, Slavicized Romanian while teaching English as a Second Language in a city in the former Soviet Union. My roommate, like me, was a man in his mid-thirties; this was all we had in common. He had a wife and a career in the French diplomatic service, I had my editing and contract teaching, my expatriation and my search for romance.

I might have missed Veronika. Adrift and emotionally unattached, a state that I should have been old enough to recognize as being dangerous, I became fixated on a twenty-eight-year-old Central European reporter for Deutsche Welle who was in the same intermediate language class as my roommate and me. Between memorizing irregular plural endings and studying the rhyming couplets of the Romantic poet Mihai Eminescu, I stared at Klara. When I took her hand in the dark during a showing of the film adaptation of Marin Preda's *The Moromete Family*, I was confident that her fellow German journalist, who was seated on her left, would not notice what was going on because seated on his left was a Czech girl named Milena on whom he had a crush.

Everyone knew Milena, who was tall and flamboyant, had long, wavy hair, and spoke in a loud voice in Czech and German, and fractured English and Romanian; Veronika was Milena's roommate. Though tall, she was thin. Her square glasses recalled the days of socialist medicine. Her short, dark brown hair, and long bangs made her look like a schoolgirl. The difference that divided the two Czech girls, aside from Veronika's being five years younger and, at twenty, one of the youngest students in the summer school, was Milena's boyfriend. The fact that Milena had a boyfriend was the first information we learned about her. The day before the course began, Romania was paralyzed by a massive power outage. Not even the phones worked. While the rest of us, lining up to check

in at the candlelit reception desk, were chuckling over the headline in
the newspaper in the lobby — *Europe Cut Off from Romania!* —
Milena was in a rage that she could not get through to Prague.
"Europe doesn't know it's cut off from Romania," she repeated in
four languages. "Europe doesn't care."

After our language class and a lecture on literature or history,
a light lunch, and an afternoon hike in the mountains or a bus
excursion to a historic site, we ate dinner in the hotel dining room
in groups defined by nationality or language. I avoided the tables that
spoke English or French. I sat with Eastern Europeans or Germans. I
tried to sit close to Klara.

As we were eating our polenta or *piept de pui*, a uniformed man
from the reception desk would appear in the dining room doorway
and shout: "*Domnişoară Milena! La telefon!*" Milena would
jump up and cross the dining room like a competitive walker, her
head flung back. She held her arms high, her elbows pumping in a
movement that drew attention to her large breasts. Milena's phone
conversations lasted for the whole meal; Veronika finished dinner
by herself. I remarked to my roommate that the other Czech girl
seemed lonely. Having been promoted to an upper-intermediate
language course in which Veronika was one of the students, the
diplomat replied that the other Czech girl was highly intelligent and,
above all, independent. "Milena is *banale*," he said. "She will do
what everyone expects. But the other girl — she might do anything."

THE NEXT DAY VERONIKA'S flu was worse. "Can't you stay in Europe
a little longer?" she gasped.

I hesitated. I had moved back to Canada, convinced that I was
going home, only to discover that my emotions circulated in frag-
ments on other continents. Here I was travelling again; I needed
to go back and stay put. Reluctant to explain this to Veronika,
who was making a profession of being abroad, I responded with
an Eminescu rhyming couplet: "*Şi de când m-am depărtat, multă*

lume am umblat." Since I left home, I've wandered over lots of the world ...

"Yes! I want to hear about your trip to Bulgaria."

The summer school's grapevine remained intact. "That was three years ago."

"You see. We need to catch up —"

My phone card ran out. I had one card left. I used it to make another call. In the morning, I caught the train to Sibiu, the first stop on my way to Vienna. An adherent of summer schools, I had never travelled through Romania in the winter. When the mountains around Sinaia appeared out the window, their beauty in their white garb plunged a stab of cold air into my lungs. I jumped to my feet and rushed to the window, pressing my face against the glass as though winter could become summer and the past the present; the fragrances of that summer deluged my nostrils. The three women sitting opposite me, government architects on their way to Braşov, were startled. "*Sinaia e frumoasă cu zăpada,*" I offered. Sinaia is beautiful in the snow.

"These foreigners come here for our landscape," one woman said in a weary voice.

"He's right," another replied. "The snow is good. It covers up how dirty and poor Romania is."

WE WORRIED ABOUT OUR visas. They were difficult to obtain and never lasted long enough. I'd travelled for two weeks prior to the course; by my second week in Sinaia, my visa was on the verge of expiring. I went to the police station to ask about a renewal and was told I had to go to Piteşti, the capital of this *judeţ*, a once-industrialized wreck of a city in the hottest, flattest stretch of the Wallachian Plain. Having stocked up on multiple copies of all the documentation that any official could conceivably ask for, I caught a dawn train down to the lowlands. I spent the day being shunted from one building to another, standing on line for an hour or two to reach an official who grudgingly gave me the stamp I needed and mumbled directions to the building where I could exchange this stamp for an application form, which I must fill in meticulously in order for it to be stamped and exchanged for another form, which required a further stamp, which could be obtained in another building. After seven hours of walking and standing on line, without having stopped to eat, I ended up back in the building where I had started, where the officials were about to go home. Won over by the novelty of a Westerner who pleaded with them in Romanian, they relented and stamped my visa extension into my passport, then slammed shut the wicket on the wooden counter.

I returned to Sinaia to find Klara eating dinner with a pudgy young man from Dortmund. They mumbled to each other in colloquial German. Klara looked at me with an owlish smile. The next day, as we joined a hike led by a professor who lauded the Romanian royal family as a bulwark against Communism and stopped on sweeping hillsides to explain the history of the *stâna regală*, the royal sheepfold, from which the king had harvested his private quotient of wool, the guy from Dortmund remained at her side. He wheezed during the steep stretches. I suspected Klara of favouring him to stir up my jealousy — in which she was succeeding — or of using him as a shield because she wasn't sure what to do about me. I became aware again of her shyness, which heightened the audacity of her moments of daring. For the first half of the hike I slogged along at Klara's heels. I asked the professor questions, hoping that by advertising my Romanian, the currency in which we all traded, I would earn her attention.

I was wrong. The person whose attention I attracted was Veronika.

At a point where the trail narrowed as it climbed through the woods, the other Czech girl, whose name I hadn't absorbed, burst in alongside me with adolescent exuberance and began to question me about Canada. I was the first Canadian she had met and there was much she wanted to know! Her eyes were bright behind her glasses with an energy that promised more than she intended; she lacked Klara's seasoned awareness of the impression she made on men. Veronika's intuition for male-female dynamics might be untutored, but her intellect was not. Her questions were perceptive. When she ran out of words in Romanian, she switched to a schoolgirl French of impeccable grammatical correctness. As I replied to her, I saw Klara's head lift.

The trail broke out of the thick-set beeches and poplars into a rock-strewn meadow where reddish cattle, fitted with clapping bells, meandered through scraps of fog that broke up as they descended from the peaks above. Dressed in shorts, hiking boots, and T-shirts, we stopped to pull our sweaters out of our day-packs. Cool, fresh moisture came off the grass, seeming to mingle with the substance of Klara's body as she leaned close to me and murmured in English, "Are you going to spend the whole day talking to that little Czech girl, or are you going to pay attention to me?"

With a calculation I had not planned, I said, "I will pay attention to you if you drink a bottle of wine with me tonight."

Klara's brooding manner made her smiles, when they happened, twice as rewarding as other people's. "We will meet after dinner."

That night we found a little bar on the downhill side of the hotel-lined main street, ordered a bottle of red wine and exchanged stories of Eastern European adventures. We went back to Klara's room and necked on her bed until her roommate came home. Tugging Klara into the hall to kiss her good night, I told her a secret: my roommate's wife was arriving from Paris the next morning. I was moving out of our double room into a single room at the end of the hall.

"Stupid man! Do you really think I will visit you there?"

She visited the next night, and every night after that, and sometimes with furtive haste when desperation seized us, in the middle of the afternoon. Her orgasms were as startling as her smiles. Though we continued to go on bus excursions, sitting together as friends,

we arranged our own mountain hikes. We rode the chairlift up
to the peaks and roamed the chilly, threaded summits. Klara wore
a jacket over her sweater. Hand-in-hand, we looked down on the
whole world; lakes were shrunken to rounded visa stamps on
the valley floor. There were no cattle at those altitudes, only a
scattering of grey-coated sheep. Once we walked away from the
chairlift station, we met no one other than gasping members of
the Romanian Olympic team, which had built a high-altitude train-
ing camp on the bare rock.

At the end of the course, Klara and I drove away together
through Transylvania and Hungary and back to Germany with
her roommate, in her roommate's car. The next time I saw Sinaia's
peaks, ten years later, they were covered in snow.

THE NEW MILLENNIUM BROUGHT me home, but the graft did not
take. I was offered a contract to finish a book on the fall of Nicolae
Ceauşescu that a hard-drinking journalist had abandoned after
hitting the bottle. I asked for time and money to take a summer
course to revive my Romanian before beginning the project.

The course I found was in Baia Mare, a city whose name
resounded with the echo of bays and seas, but in fact meant "Big
Steam Bath." There was nothing steamy about this hard-nosed
mining town at the end of a railway branch line, squeezed up
against the mountains along the Ukrainian border. The smelters
and tower-block apartments were built on a flat plain; the hills
were the object of bus excursions rather than day-hikes. This was
Maramureş, home of the densest surviving folklore in Europe;
a place of half-pagan religious rites, ancient wooden churches,
intricate woven dolls, untutored peasant girls who sang immemorial ballads with a vocal range that made opera singers stare, and
no-nonsense farmers who gave matter-of-fact instructions on how
to bring a man back from the dead. There were no tourists, fewer
diversions from study than in Sinaia, only thirty students and a

more rigorous academic program with classes that lasted all day. I revelled in the spot's glorious grimness. My roommate, Taras, was the only professor of Romanian at the University of Ukraine. He saw us as fellow confirmed bachelors, a definition from which I demurred in silence.

The morning after I checked in, I ate breakfast in a gloomy little back dining room. Groggy from the marathon train journeys that had brought me here from Paris, where my plane had landed, I took in, but did not register, the woman at the next table who was explaining to two young students how summer courses worked. I sipped my coffee and browsed the local newspaper, *Graiul Maramureşului*. The unconscious part of my brain repeated the name "Veronika," while the conscious part tried to slap down this irritation as though it were a buzzing fly. As I finished my breakfast and stood up, the older woman called my name.

We shook hands. Veronika had assumed the authority that descends early in life on educated women in Eastern Europe. She wore her hair long and swept back off her forehead. Her round glasses slid down her nose. Since we had last studied together, cultural differences had dwindled: in contrast to Sinaia, seating arrangements at dinner divided by generation rather than nation. In lieu of aging male professors who were nostalgic for the King, the Baia Mare coordinator was a busy professional woman in her thirties. Veronika adopted the coordinator as a role model; she made Veronika her unofficial deputy. My conversation was halting; my Romanian having slipped in the last seven years. Veronika had continued to study the language. Two years after Sinaia, she had taken another summer course in hot, humid Craiova; a year later she had secured a one-year contract as the Czech language assistant at the University of Bucharest. As she told me this, a girlish smile emerged, reminding me of the day she had questioned me in the woods. "Do you remember Milena? She's married now."

"To the boyfriend who was always phoning her?"

"No, to a German guy she met in Sinaia!"

I remembered Klara's journalism colleague flirting with Milena during the movie.

Veronika was finishing a doctorate in Romanian literature in Prague, where she shared an apartment with her mother and her boyfriend. She intimated that her father had died, that her boyfriend was older than she, and that she perceived a link between the loss of her male parent and her attraction to an older man. Taken aback by this naked psychological revelation, I asked, "How old is your boyfriend?"

"Forty." Her playful smile returned. "That must be about your age, no?"

I ATE DINNER WITH Taras, Veronika, the coordinator, and the professors, but in classes and on bus excursions I sat next to Tereza. A thin, ironic young Bulgarian woman with long dark hair, she studied philosophy, theology, and Balkan languages. She loved the writing of Mircea Eliade, spoke Turkish and some Albanian, was proud of being "*foarte amestecată*" — "very mixed" — and believed that the sooner Balkan people celebrated their mixtures the sooner invidious nationalisms would retreat. She was twenty-two; suddenly I was twenty years older than the object of my idle desires. Tereza's well-nourished brain drew me into conversation, but her long legs and taut hips did not vanish. Achingly single, I became her courtly escort, like a gentleman from the royalist past. My desire for Tereza moved through me in a hollow wave, unimaginable to act upon, like the longing I had felt for girls when I was thirteen. As we browsed in second-hand bookstores or visited Baia Mare's smoke-drenched internet café, where a two-line email could take ten minutes to open, I adhered to the boundaries of a fraternal friendship. The fact that this brilliant young woman had chosen to spend time with me was a compliment that sated a variety of hungers. Tereza told me about her relationships with her mother, with whom she shared an apartment, and her boyfriend, who was

Turkish and lived in Istanbul. Her father was dead; information that I received as a crushing verdict, accepting that after forty the only young women whose attention a man will attract are those who are tormented by the absence of fathers.

In Sinaia I had spoken French to my roommate and English to Klara; in Baia Mare, I spoke to Taras, Tereza, Veronika, and everyone else in Romanian. Only Georgi, Tereza's compatriot, who had been educated at an American school in Plovdiv, spoke to me in English, telling me about his career as a hard-rock guitarist. One afternoon, between two classes, Tereza, Veronika, and I converged in an awkward trio that made me feel as though two parts of my life that belonged apart were being plaited together. Tereza related a bad experience with a Romanian policeman. Veronika countered with a good experience.

"When I was working in Bucharest my boyfriend came to visit me. We were in Cişmigiu Park and a police officer approached me in a very courteous way. 'Is everything all right, *Domnişoara?*' A real gentleman."

"Why did he ask you that?" Tereza said.

Veronika hesitated. "*Ne-am certat.* We had a fight. He saw us fighting and came to help me."

"Were you breaking up?" Tereza's interest in this subject caught my attention.

Veronika's mouth was firm. "We were having problems. Since I returned to Prague, everything is fine. We are good now."

The smile with which she sealed this statement caught my eye. The next afternoon, as our group was boarding a bus to visit a Stalin-era prison on the Ukrainian border, Veronika suggested that she and I sit together.

The bus rolled past the wooden fence-lines of the bright green fields that climbed towards matted forest. "Who are you in touch with from Sinaia?" Veronika asked.

"Mainly Klara."

"I forgot you were friends."

Her words were so offhand that I didn't know whether to accept them as being as ingenuous as they sounded. The bus went up a hill and around a curve; sturdy wooden huts came into view. "Klara and I fell in love in Sinaia," I said, unable to find a more worldly way to phrase this; "*ne-am îndrăgostit*" sounded excessively romantic. "We stayed together for a year and a half after the course."

"Oh! Oh, really? I don't believe it." Her astonishment was muted yet profound, as though tectonic plates were shifting beneath the subsoil of her perceptions. "I never would have guessed that of you." She shook her head, and said, "Oh, oh, oh." She looked me in the eye. "And now," she said, her voice dropping, "you spend your time with Tereza. Maybe your life is going to change again?"

"It's completely different. Tereza and I have intellectual conversations —"

"It's not just about ideas. I've seen how you look at her."

"I'm too old for her. And she has a boyfriend."

Veronika smiled. "So did Milena."

⁓

SHIVERING IN THE SNOW, I gave up on Veronika and used my last phone card to call Tereza. She answered at once. "Are you having a good trip?" she said. "How I envy you! It's been so long since I've been to Romania."

We had discussed my return to Europe on email. Tereza had said she might meet me in Romania; we had talked about which regions of the country we would visit. I had allowed myself to indulge in this fantasy for just long enough to be disappointed when it didn't work out. "Where are you?" I asked.

"I'm in Sofia. In a car, driving around with friends."

During the course in Baia Mare, Tereza had told me I offered her a canvas for sounding out the teeming world beyond Bulgaria's borders, a world she was barred from exploring because she came from a poor country, had no money, and required a visa to

go almost anywhere. She asked me about each of the countries
I had visited. "You are a grotto without end!" she said, a compliment that sounded elegant in Romanian. In the final days of the
course our conversations reached a pitch of intensity. The last day
she broke all the rules — her own rules of propriety and respect
for her boyfriend — and came to my room when Taras was out.
Rocking back and forth on her long legs, her unexpected freckles
glowing on her pale face in a sheen of sweat between the smouldering wings of her dark hair, she said, "*Nu ştiu când ne vom
vedea din nou*. I don't know when we are going to see each other
again. She handed me an enamelled wooden plate covered with
an engraving of Alexander Nevsky Cathedral. Our hug was chaste,
yet trembling. Two hours before her scheduled departure, she
cashed in the Baia Mare-Bucharest-Sofia train ticket provided by
her scholarship for a third-class overnight ticket to Iaşi, a student
city that was home to the country's best second-hand bookstores.
She would wander home over the next few days in a succession
of third-class trains. I understood this as her way of mourning the
end of the course, the snapping shut of her glimmering opening on
the world. She wrote me long emails each day of her trip home.
She was swarmed by Roma boys twice, yet managed to cling to
her scarce belongings. When she got home, four days late, her
mother was so angry that she nearly forbade Tereza from seeing
her boyfriend the next time he came from Istanbul to visit her.

The next year, when a contract took me to Athens, I finished
my work, then boarded the overnight train to Sofia. I stayed in a
cheap room in a widow's apartment; at times Tereza and I recap-
tured the effortless understanding of our summer in Baia Mare. Yet,
my fitful reabsorption into Canadian life had put up walls between
us. In the photographs I'd emailed her of my life in Toronto, some
of the friends who smiled with their arms around me were as dark-
skinned as the Roma. The tour Tereza gave me of her university led
through threadbare classrooms whose little wooden desks looked
as though they belonged in a nineteenth-century primary school. In

this impoverished physical environment, she had studied difficult works by autocratic cultural arbiters in the original languages. On the fringes of the university area, she pointed out a dormitory that had housed African students during the Communist era. "Bulgarians hated Communism because it brought black people to our country," she said. "Even today, Bulgarian students refuse to live in those buildings."

Her vehemence cut short as I stared at her. Her pride in being *foarte amestecata* was restricted to Balkan lineages. Her Levantine loyalty to her boyfriend rendered impossible stops in restaurants, or even cafés. Tereza had no money, but would not let me pay. At last, half-starved, I sat down for lunch — five dollars for a three-course meal. Tereza helped me order, then sipped a glass of water and watched me eat. Over the next three years' emails we overlooked these obstacles, fooling ourselves that we could travel together.

As I stamped my boots in the snow, her voice faded. Darkness gathered around the statue of Kogălniceanu. "What's going on?" I asked.

"My friends are laughing at me. They think Romanian sounds funny."

The phone cut out.

⁓

HALFWAY THROUGH THE COURSE in Baia Mare a black limousine, coated with dust from the roads of Maramureş, pulled up in front of the hotel. A big-bellied man in a bulky suit and a woman in a garish dress got out of the back seat; an anonymous man in a black suit followed two steps behind them. Trailing in their wake was a tall, soft-bellied boy who didn't know what to do with his hands. The man ordered the hotel receptionist to find the course coordinator. He addressed her in a language that Taras identified as Russian. Announcing that he was Poland's new ambassador to Romania, the man explained that he wished his son to be ready to study at the University of Bucharest by the autumn. "I asked for the best summer language school in Romania, and they told me it was the school run by *you*." A smile of avuncular disbelief appeared beneath his grey moustache.

"Not even the best language school can take a boy who knows nothing and prepare him for university," the coordinator replied in Russian, in Taras's rendering. "Especially," she added, "when he starts late. But we will do the best job that can be done."

The Polish delegation stayed for one night. When the ambassador and his wife departed, they left their son behind. Adam smiled at everyone from his round face, topped by the shaggy thatch of a crewcut that was growing out in uneven tufts. Smiling was all he could do, for he spoke no language but Polish. The coordinator placed him in the lowest-level language course and excused him from the literature and history lectures, which were given in Romanian. At dinner he sat not with his own generation, but with us, the elders. A message from a government office in Bucharest had enjoined the coordinator to look after this boy. She, Taras, and Veronika all spoke Slavic languages that were mutually comprehensible with Polish. As Czech, in Veronika's explanation, was the language most closely related to Polish, she assumed the bulk of the translating responsibilities. Watching her take on this role, I observed her authority and maturity. I thought how different this Veronika was from the girl of the impetuous questions in the mountains above Sinaia.

The younger students mocked Adam, referring to him as *băiatul*, "the boy." Without Veronika's protection, he would have become an object of ridicule. I saw how much she enjoyed tutoring him. Adam learned little Romanian, but the other younger students accepted him, mustering whatever phrases of Polish, Russian, or Ukrainian they might know to make him feel at home. At the end of the course, a group of younger students, led by Georgi, planned to get off the train to Bucharest in Sighișoara to spend two days at a rock music festival. They invited Adam along. As we gathered on the station platform with our luggage, I was surprised to bump into Veronika. "You're going to Sighişoara?" I said.

Before I could ask about her interest in rock music, she replied, "Yes, but this isn't goodbye. We can see each other in Bucharest."

"So, you are going to Bucharest?"

She looked at me as though this were obvious, then murmured, "I thought you would go to Iaşi."

"Iaşi? My research on Ceauşescu is in Bucharest."

"It wouldn't hurt you to get there a few days late." I felt as though everyone else had disappeared, leaving Veronika's face and mine confronting one another against the clattering confusion of the railway platform. "*Prostule!* Don't you see what you've done?"

"I—"

"She changed her ticket because of you! She thought you would go with her. Don't you see? It was the only way she could get you alone without her boyfriend finding out. And you abandoned her."

"I never thought—"

"Tereza would have changed your life. Unlike that German reporter, who was never to going to settle down with anybody. Did you really not understand? Oh, don't tell me you were so insensitive that you didn't understand when she changed her ticket!"

"Maybe I'm too old." I peered into a widening chasm of loss. Was Veronika right? Could I have been on the train to Iaşi with Tereza? Beseeching her as I would the old friend she almost was, I said, "How can I make it up to her?"

"You're old enough to know you only get one chance in love. If you miss it, it's gone."

She turned away to organize the younger students. At four o'clock in the morning, awoken by my Baia Mare classmates stumbling off the train in Sighişoara, I realized that whatever I might know about Veronika, she knew me far better.

⌒

AFTER MY PAINFUL MEAL with Tereza, I left Sofia, but not Bulgaria. Georgi had sent an email saying that he was playing a concert in

Plovdiv two nights later. Tereza and I phoned him together. She walked me to the bus station, where I hugged her with all my strength. I caught a bus from the capital to the country's second city, where the Rhodopes Hills stood out in low, criss-crossing horizons. Stocked with markets, eighteenth-century houses and mosques, this city built around a Roman amphitheatre felt more lively than Sofia, with its vacant plazas and denuded monuments. Georgi loped up to me at our rendezvous point on a pedestrian street in the city centre. We took in the sights, speaking in English. Georgi had no objection to my buying him a meal; he would repay me with a ticket to his concert.

The only other diners in the tackily lavish restaurant were a middle-aged man in a dark suit whose receding hair was drenched in gel, and his date, a dyed-blonde woman who wore makeup as thick as stucco. "Is Tereza really going to marry a Muslim?" Georgi asked. He brooded over her boyfriend in Istanbul, then said, "You know that Veronika's married, right?"

"It's not surprising," I said. "She had been living with her boy-friend for a long time."

"She didn't marry her boyfriend. She married Adam."

"Adam? *Băiatul* Adam?"

"They were always talking ..." He laughed. "Kind of like you and Tereza except with different results."

"But she's ten years older than him!" The sound of English made the businessman look up from his dinner.

"When we got to Sighişoara the town was packed. Adam's parents had reserved him a room, but the rest of us didn't have any-where to stay. We went to Adam's hotel. The room next to his was free. Six of us had to share it, most of us on the floor. Nobody was able to sleep. Somebody said that Adam was selfish and should share his room. Veronika said, 'I'm going to go see him.' We thought she was going to tell him to share the room. Then we heard the noises. Everybody tried not to laugh." He looked at his plate.

The restaurant was silent, its brocaded tablecloths gathering dust. I thought of Veronika making love in the knowledge that she would be overheard by her acolytes. Now I understood her harangue on the railway platform. You only get one chance in love. Veronika had taken her chance. She had embraced the future in the body of a boy.

⁓

THE ARCHITECTS GOT OFF the train in Braşov. All along the flat run to Sibiu, the snowy cushions of the Făgăraş Mountains gleamed on the lefthand side of the train. I had come this way before in summer, aware of the mountains but unable to see them in the heat haze. In winter they stood revealed like facts that emerge in a crisis. I added up my journey through Romanianness, ticking off three years since I had seen Tereza and Georgi in Bulgaria, four years since Baia Mare, more than a decade since Sinaia. When I wrote to Veronika after my visit to Bulgaria I feigned ignorance. *Cred că ştii ce s-a întâmplat la Baia Mare*, she replied. *I think you know what happened in Baia Mare.* She would not accept that I had been unaware of her lovemaking with Adam, as she had been of mine with Klara. As our correspondence flourished, I learned the rest of the story. After the festival in Sighişoara, Veronika had taken refuge in Bucharest, sleeping on the couch of our course coordinator and her husband. Back in Prague, her mother had supervised her boyfriend's removal from the family apartment. Veronika had stayed in Bucharest that fall. Adam's parents having insisted that he start university, no matter how poor his Romanian, she sat in lectures with him, taught him, helped him read books page by page. Her self-abnegating devotion shocked me. My life with Tereza would have required similar sacrifices — sacrifices I had been unwilling to make. Only now was I beginning to understand about myself what Veronika had grasped about me on the platform.

I got off the train in Sibiu and walked into the old Saxon town. Roma women in bright headscarves stood in the snow selling flowers. Teenage girls strolled arm in arm like staunch allies. In the frigid air of the foothills, with the Făgăras still visible, I felt the distance I had travelled from Kogălniceanu's statue. While coaching Adam, Veronika had finished her doctoral thesis. During the next three years, she had married Adam, given birth to a daughter, joined the Czech diplomatic service, and wangled a posting to Bucharest in time to help her husband through his final year of university. My steps crunched the packed snow that covered the medieval street. I wandered into the past, realizing that if I went back to Canada and stayed there, I might not speak to Veronika again. If I didn't go back to Bucharest she would be simply an acquaintance, someone who had been a classmate in two courses. In my search for love and belonging, was I undervaluing friendship? The cold air scoured out my lungs. Having balked at trading authority for love, I was left with neither. Veronika had taken that risk and I had not. Nothing else I knew about her was as important as that.

~

I GOT AS FAR as the tile roofs and slant-eyed windows of Sibiu's old town before I turned around. I went back to the train station, bought a ticket on the overnight *acceleratul* and went back the way I had come. If I flew to Vienna from Bucharest, I could wait out Veronika's flu and still make my flight to Canada. Or cancel it, if I decided to stay. That morning, boarding the train, I had worried about not fitting in at home; now I worried about losing my moorings in Europe.

Three mornings later, Veronika and I had coffee at the Czech Embassy. She wore a dark-red cotton dress and a black jacket; her hair was shorter, and her glasses more fashionable. In a framed photograph on her desk, she and Adam smiled at a banquet, the difference in their ages barely discernible. The photograph next to it was of her daughter.

"You haven't seen Tereza since your trip to Bulgaria?" she asked, almost before I sat down.

"*Nu.*" Our cups of coffee, brought in by a woman in an apron, sat untouched between us. I recounted our futile plans to travel together, culminating in Tereza's last words on the phone: *They think Romanian sounds funny.*

"If you had gone to Iaşi with her, love would have given you the patience to work out how to be together in spite of the economic differences. If you'd acted then ... Now she's going to marry her Turk because it's the only way she can get out of Bulgaria."

I stared at her. Veronika was like a stranger after all these years, yet this stranger had my life figured out as I did not. "You acted when you fell in love," I said. "You didn't worry about what people would think."

"I recognized that Adam would follow me. My boyfriend refused to leave Prague. He was older, he set the rules. When I came to Bucharest for a year, we fought and almost broke up. When I met Adam, I saw the possibility of a different dynamic. I would get a job before he did and, coming from a diplomatic family, he expected to move around."

"That's what your love boiled down to? Seeing you could have your own way?" My disappointment was as cavernous as the valleys below Sinaia. This was a different Veronika than any other that I had known.

"Even love has its motives," she said. "By choosing Adam I freed myself to become the person I am today."

I didn't reply. In my mind, I was already walking down Magheru Boulevard to the internet café to plan my trip home.

3

MY SOUL WILL BE IN PARIS

EVERY NIGHT A DREAM that was half a nightmare, shaken by the creak of wagon wheels on dirt roads, transported Castillo to Chimaltenango. He heard himself utter polite banalities at family lunches at his uncle's coffee plantation; he listened to the clucking speech of Mayan Indians in the market. Between a form of language he despised and a language he did not understand, he feared that he would never be a poet. The trip to Europe by boat, even his years as a law student in Guatemala City, vanished from his nocturnal memory. Nothing remained but his youth and his present: Chimaltenango and Paris. He woke elated each morning as the gurgle of plumbing, the mingled odour of baguettes and Gauloises, the self-confident assertions of French voices, rescued him from hopelessness.

His hotel was on a side street that crossed Boulevard Montparnasse, far from the intersection with Raspail. His first morning he had walked to a café called Le Jockey, where he had stood dumbfounded at the sight of a man in a blue smock, whom he knew at a glance to be Pablo Picasso, defending his vision of the female nude against a crowd of howling antagonists. The argument ended when Picasso caught a young woman's eye and asked her to model for him. From that moment, Castillo had known that Paris would give him art and romance.

He had come of age as the Great War was ending in Europe and the dictatorship was teetering at home. The time was ripe to throw off the influence of Rubén Darío, with his poems full of nymphs, princesses, and Greek gods; he would write about modern men and women in clipped, accessible verses. In Chimaltenango, he had been unable to write; in Guatemala City, he had been a provincial poet; only in Paris could he be a Latin American writer. Yet, while he revelled in meeting Argentines, Peruvians, or Venezuelans, savouring their accents and expressions while learning all they had in common, he had failed to make the acquaintance of the two famous Guatemalans in Paris: old Gómez Carrillo, whose newspaper columns were syndicated throughout Latin America, and the young Mayan Idol, said to be a writer of divine promise, who had been two years ahead of him in law school. Of the four cafés on the corner where Boulevard Raspail cut slantwise across Boulevard Montparnasse, Castillo preferred La Rotonde. He found La Coupole's high ceiling sepulchral; Le Dôme and Le Sélect were full of loud Yanquis. Most Latin Americans went to La Rotonde at night, but Castillo got his best work done there in the early morning. One morning during his second year in Paris he came in at seven a.m. and they were all there: Gómez Carrillo, his much younger French mistress, the Mayan Idol and the Czech cabaret singer who was his mistress, and another woman Castillo didn't know. Valéry Larbaud, who was making the Mayan Idol famous by translating his short stories into French, sat with them. Castillo saw that they had been carousing all night. A wince wrenched his stomach. He hated himself for sitting down at the next table rather than having the confidence to introduce himself and join them.

Gómez Carrillo, dressed in a suit like Clemenceau's, was telling the story, which Castillo had heard from others, of his seduction of Mata Hari. Larbaud laughed out loud. "You are all primitive creators!"

Opening his notebook to the pages containing his hexameters, Castillo despaired of becoming primitive. His worn jacket, its dowdy lapels the badge of the *métèque* surviving on an allowance, ruined his claim to the exotic. If only he looked like the Mayan Idol! He watched his compatriot stretch his long back. He had shaved his beard since being told by his professor at the Sorbonne that he had the face of an ancient statue. The Idol's father, the Supreme Court judge, had saved his son from the dictator's prison by giving him a ticket to Europe and an allowance. Castillo observed his fellow countrymen, the old sophisticate and the young primitivist, who were rumoured to despise each other across the generational divide. His gaze strayed to the woman who sat between the Idol and Larbaud. The stranger had pale skin and long, heavy dark hair, features that could have been Spanish but equally Greek. Her face was bright and her body was shapely. He longed to be with her, or simply to be like her; an outsider who had penetrated the inner circle. She waved away the waiter's suggestion of coffee and ordered a glass of red wine.

He looked down at his poems. In spite of having promised his uncle artistic glory in return for a monthly stipend from his coffee plantation, he had failed to attract anyone's tutelage. Late at night, when his hexameters refused to ring with effortless music, despair seeped through him as he listened to the drunken Yanquis cavorting on the sidewalks of Boulevard Montparnasse. His mother urged him in letters to pay more attention to the *familias distinguidas* from Guatemala who maintained residences in Paris. She reminded him that these families had daughters, and that he must think about his future. Eligible young women would be more susceptible to his charms, she wrote, if he tempered his poetic rashness by resuming his study of the law. Perhaps he could take courses at the Sorbonne like that young Guatemalan who was always in the newspapers ...

The spectre of life as a lawyer drove him to audacity. He stood up and crossed the café. Gómez Carrillo was telling Larbaud about Josephine Baker's dancing, "That woman's primitive strength —!"

Larbaud, noticing Castillo, delayed replying. Castillo turned towards the great Gómez Carrillo, begging to be noticed. Ordering a second espresso, Gómez Carrillo described his seduction of Isadora Duncan.

Castillo felt his slightness, the dinginess of his mixed-raced complexion. His father and uncle, brawling dark-skinned men, had emerged from the tumult of the nineteenth century with a small, hard-won plot of land on the outskirts of Chimaltenango. As social advancement required, they had married women whose complexions were lighter than theirs. Gazing on the Mayan Idol's beauty, Castillo felt his forebears' exertions mocked. What crazed zigzag of heredity had decreed that the Mayan Idol's mixed heritage should give him the body of a white-skinned giant, retaining only the facial imprint of a Mayan lord, while he remained not only darker, but also shorter, than many of the women who passed him on the Paris streets?

"They say you write poetry," a slow voice said.

Leaning forward to kiss her hand, he wondered where her chaperone was. Never, in Chimaltenango, Guatemala City, or Paris, had he spoken to a young Latin American woman of good family without her mother, father, brother, aunt, or governess being present.

"Lidia Corvina," she said, "from Buenos Aires."

Larbaud tugged on her arm and spoke to her in rapid French. No one invited Castillo to sit down. He left the café to the sound of their laughter. A week later his mother wrote to him that she had arranged for a distinguished Guatemalan family to give him permission to visit their youngest daughter on Thursday afternoons. As his French improved, his explorations of Montparnasse's nightlife grew more daring. That spring, for the first time, he spent a whole night in bed with a Frenchwoman who had joined him without asking to be paid. The sensation was almost as sweet as the squeeze of his heart at the sight of his poems printed on a mimeographed sheet produced by a friend of the distinguished family. Absorbed in his tiny Chapin circle, he forgot about his famous compatriots until the morning he read that Gómez Carrillo had died.

The master had succumbed at sixty to complications from a life of late nights and gourmet food. All of Latin American Paris accompanied him to Père Lachaise Cemetery. The *señoras distinguidas,* who had learned how to dress by reading Gómez Carrillo's fashion columns in the drawing rooms of their haciendas on the outskirts of Buenos Aires, Mexico City, or Caracas, climbed the narrow paths supported on the arms of their sons and husbands. As the *señoras* sobbed, their husbands looked sombre, mulling over the great man's powerful, often intimate, influence on their wives. The crowd filtered through the trees at the top of the hillside cemetery, lowering their heads as they stepped over stones and loose gravel. Castillo felt a woman seize his arm; it was the aunt of the girl he visited. She stationed him next to her niece, who shot him a quick smile.

A gasp went up as the coffin was brought out. A voice shouted, "Why is it draped in the Argentine flag?"

Castillo heard the grating of the coffin bearers' boots on the gravel. The man following the coffin was the Argentine Ambassador.

"He took out Argentine citizenship," the girl's mother hissed. "He renounced his Guatemalan nationality!"

"Can you blame him," the aunt said, "for being ashamed of a country where half the population have the faces of monkeys?"

The girl brushed her fingers across Castillo's knuckles. Her blushing brown cheeks bunched into a furious smile. Castillo clasped his hands behind his back.

"Remove that flag!" a voice commanded. The Mayan Idol loped down the incline. His brushed-back hair accentuating his stela-like profile, he stepped in front of the coffin bearers. "Remove the flag," he repeated.

The Argentine Ambassador hurried forward. "What a lack of respect —!"

"What a lack of respect for the Guatemalan nationality with which *Señor* Gómez Carrillo was born and with which he died!"

The two men faced each other, rocked by the grumbling crowd. The coffin bearers hesitated.

"He chose Argentina, *che*!" shouted the Buenos Aires poet González Tuñón.

The girl clasped Castillo's hands behind his back. She ran her finger down his spine. Behind González Tuñón, Castillo spotted Lidia Corvina. Her thick hair descended in a restless swoop. The willowiness of her body arrested his attention almost as forcefully as the fact of a *señorita decente*'s being present without a chaperone. The realization that she was returning his gaze made him wish that he was as tall as the Mayan Idol. He ventured forward, escaping the pressure of the girl's finger. They stared at each other across the clearing, separated by the tall men standing toe to toe on the gravel.

"A Guatemalan's homeland is Guatemala," the Mayan Idol said, "and when we speak of Guatemala we must speak of the Maya."

The distinguished families, having applauded his opening words, caught their breath at the second half of the Mayan Idol's pronouncement. The Argentine Ambassador, sensing the momentum turning, waved the funeral cortège forward. As the coffin went past, the Mayan Idol took a disparaging swat at the blue bands of the Argentine flag.

Lidia withdrew into the trees.

⁓

PARIS CHANGED AFTER GÓMEZ Carrillo's death. The young writers spent more time with the French. When Castillo spotted the Mayan Idol with his new friends — the pale-skinned Venezuelan Uslar Pietri and Carpentier, the burly Cuban music critic who spoke French like a Frenchman — their group was surrounded by the Surrealists André Breton and Robert Desnos. The Mayan Idol had left his

Czech cabaret singer to live with a thin French girl. Not the kind of girl one met in *boîtes*, but a girl from the suburbs whose parents disapproved of her living with a man. The Yanquis disappeared from Paris amid rumours that some of them had been writers. Castillo's Thursday visits became uncomfortable as the girl's family stressed that her education was nearly complete.

He was drinking his third espresso of the morning at La Rotonde, remembering the firm hips of last night's Frenchwoman (he must ask his uncle for an increase in his allowance), when the pages of *Revista Parisiense* fell open to a selection of Surrealist poems by Marcel Riquewehr — a member of André Breton's outer, rather than his inner, circle — translated into Spanish by Lidia Corvina. The mechanistic modernity of Riquewehr's poems put Castillo in a bad mood. The poem that he was trying to write, a description of a man climbing a volcano, mocked him by emerging in old-fashioned Alexandrines.

A crisis was brewing in Surrealism. The Peruvian Surrealist César Moro, sitting down next to Castillo, laid a hand on his thigh as he unfolded a newspaper photograph of the writers known as "Surrealist dissidents." Blond Marcel Riquewehr, whose body bulged until it threatened to tear through his clothes, stood in a pugnacious stance that suggested he was challenging Breton to fisticuffs. Two women were visible near the back of the group. Flattening the page between his forefinger and thumb, Moro said, "That one's Lidia Corvina."

"The Latin American *señorita* in Paris," the girl's aunt said that Thursday, "must take special care of her reputation."

"As must a *señorita* anywhere," Castillo said, regarding the girl perched on the scarlet cushion of the Louis Quatorze couch.

"Exactly so, sir. But especially in Paris. There are rumours that *señoritas decentes* are behaving in ways that do our nations no credit."

"We are not our nations," Castillo said. "It is to ourselves that we are answerable."

"We are answerable to God," the aunt said. "I would not expect a man of your distinguished surname to forget that — even," she added, "if you did not grow up in the capital."

The girl stared in alarm. In his mind, Castillo heard the sound of wagon wheels.

The aunt brandished a newspaper. She opened the paper to a photograph showing: *The Alsatian poet Marcel Riquewehr and an unidentified woman leaving the apartment of André Breton, the "Pope" of Surrealism.* Lidia Corvina looked strained, the pallor of her face accentuated by cheap newsprint.

"You know this woman, don't you?" the aunt said. "She is immoral, no?"

"I do not know her that well, *señora.* "

The aunt told the girl to leave the room.

The girl resisted. "Will *Señor* Castillo visit me next week?"

"Yes, I will," Castillo said, before the aunt could reply.

When the girl left, the aunt said, "You have been visiting my niece for two years, *Señor* Castillo. If we do not announce either an engagement or a rupture, her reputation will be stained. The example of that wanton Argentine makes this matter more urgent." She circled on the Persian carpet whose luxuriance recalled articles by Gómez Carrillo that Castillo had read in Chimaltenango at a time when Paris was a mere phantom in his fevered imagination. "If my niece does not marry you, she must return to Guatemala with a reputation that is immaculate."

A vision of the church in Chimaltenango surrounded by the horse-drawn carts that blocked every street of the dusty city crowded Castillo's mind. "I'll write to my uncle," he said, playing for time. "I must be certain of my position."

The aunt looked relieved. Castillo left the family's rooms in the Marais. Desire for Lidia Corvina congealed around a stark feeling of having been abandoned by poetry. He crossed the Seine and wandered through Saint-Germain-des-Prés. When he reached Boulevard Montparnasse night had fallen and the bare shins of the French girls on their bicycles flashed like luminous fins as they paddled through the shadows extended by the gas lamps. The sidewalk tables outside La Rotonde were full. The Mayan Idol sat with Carpentier, Uslar Pietri, and Valéry Larbaud. The men were passing around a paper placemat and taking turns writing on it. Castillo sat down between Larbaud and the Mayan Idol.

Lifting the placemat and adjusting his glasses, Uslar Pietri read, in a voice full of Caribbean music: "The most startling meeting does not take place on a dissecting table, as Breton maintains, but at a café table, and it is the meeting of one Latin American with another in Paris, which is the capital of Latin America."

"We're supposed to be creating original imagery," the Mayan Idol complained.

"That is an original statement," Carpentier said. "As such it has resonance, as the themes of a symphony create resonance, even though they are not themselves poetic or musical images."

"I write my poetry in cafés in the mornings," Castillo said, fingering the sheet on which he had written *Dear Uncle ...*

"What sort of poetry do you write?" Larbaud asked.

Castillo held his breath. "Modern poetry. Modern poetry influenced by the Maya."

The Mayan Idol's almond-shaped eyes gleamed with hatred. He leaned towards Carpentier. The sight of their massive, impeccably garbed bodies stooping together plunged Castillo into darkness; he heard the clatter of wagon wheels. A book of the Mayan Idol's stories was being published in Madrid; he was writing a novel about a dictator. Carpentier spoke of editors and journalistic assignments. What had he to show in return?

On the other side of the sprawl of outdoor tables, he saw Lidia Corvina.

Larbaud followed his glance to where Lidia was talking to Marcel Riquewehr. In the candlelight her face looked bloated, her hair too long for current Parisian fashion. "They think they're plotting the demise of Surrealism," Larbaud whispered. "But if their plotting were important our friend Carpentier would be at their table."

"How can a decent woman become a Frenchman's mistress?" Castillo replied in the French he had refined while making mistresses of Frenchwomen.

"She came here chaperoned by an elderly aunt. When the aunt died, she remained here."

"She will never be able to go home," Castillo said. "She's not a *señorita decente* now."

Larbaud asked about Guatemala. To each reply, he said, "Your countries are drenched in marvels!" Marcel Riquewehr and Lidia Corvina got up and left. Castillo watched the night close around the tail of Lidia's dress.

IN THE MORNING, PACING his room, he harangued himself. Any writer with the most minimal respect for his art would have asked Larbaud to read his manuscripts. Feeling unworthy of poetry, he spent the day finishing his letter to his uncle.

He avoided the corner of Raspail and Boulevard Montparnasse. The papers reported that André Breton had expelled many of his followers from the Surrealist movement. The dissidents, led by the passionate Desnos, had responded with a pamphlet in which they denounced Breton as a living corpse. A familiar name jumped out of the list of those who had signed the denunciation: Carpentier had entered French literary history.

Castillo fell into inertia. Others, not he, would be remembered. His uncle's next letter, confirmed that there would be no increase in his allowance. Early in the new year his uncle wrote to draw Castillo's attention to the crash of the stock market in the United States. It would be helpful if Castillo could earn money from his writing like that other talented young Guatemalan in Paris who contributed so many articles to the newspapers.

Distinguished families began to close their residences. The girl's aunt insisted that they had no plans to leave. Castillo's visits had grown stale. The girl was nineteen now, heavier of limb, lewdly knowing in the innuendos she insinuated into their conversations. He expected lascivious conversation from a mistress; in a fiancée it was off-putting. She turned her cynical Parisian eye on his frail build, his long bachelorhood. Her frank assessment of his potential as a lover frightened him. Yet, having gone to such lengths to retain this link to respectable society, he could not give it up now, when life had sunk into the slow desperation of trying to salvage a shred of the destiny that had once seemed his by right. To break off his visits would produce a letter from his mother expressing a disappointment deeper than he could bear. He plunged into his poems every morning. Immersed in his inner world, he missed the changes that were transforming Montparnasse.

Weeks later he trawled the cafés until he saw Larbaud at Le Dôme. Next to him the renegade Desnos, an expression of perpetual debauchery hollowing out his features, was engaged in a furious argument with Carpentier about the differences between African and Afro-Cuban drumming. When Castillo sat down, Larbaud looked puzzled.

"I'm the Guatemalan poet," Castillo said. "I draw my art from the heritage of the Maya."

Larbaud sat up. "We spoke about Lidia Corvina — before she left Riquewehr —"

"Left Riquewehr?" Castillo tried to absorb the news. "How does she live?"

"She receives money from home, as you all do. She was distressed, so I suggested her as an editor for *Revista Parisiense*. You should send her your poems."

A hot chord thrummed in Castillo's chest. "Will my poems be translated into French?"

"Publish in Spanish, then we'll see about French."

In the morning Castillo folded the best of his hexameters into an envelope and wrote Lidia Corvina's name across the outside. He included a painstakingly worded letter in which he emphasized that he was submitting at Larbaud's recommendation. When he knocked on the door of the cramped second-floor apartment that served as *Revista Parisiense*'s editorial office, an old man answered. "Is this a submission?" he said, glancing at the envelope.

"It is for Lidia Corvina," Castillo replied.

He went home in agonized frustration. Two weeks later three of his poems were filling a page of a crisp new issue of the *Revista*. His euphoria was hobbled by disappointment at the thought that she had not asked to meet him after reading his poetry. That Thursday the aunt announced him to her niece with the words, "The distinguished poet has come to visit you."

He asked the aunt if they could speak alone. In a back parlour, he said, "I apologize that my financial situation has not clarified ..."

"Whose financial situation is clear now? We may all be back in Guatemala soon enough. Go! Enjoy the company of my delightful niece."

THE TELEGRAM ARRIVED ON a winter morning. Marooned in bed by a hangover, he had decided to give himself a day off. The message was from his uncle. *Plantation ruined. Return home.*

He looked around the hotel room. For nearly five years this had been his home; he could imagine no other. He could not live in Guatemala. The dust churned up by the carts of Chimaltenango would suffocate him, the constipated rectitude of decent Guatemala City society would drain his mind of creativity. And under the new, harsher dictatorship of General Ubico, where would he publish? He shaved with a trembling hand, pulled on the jacket with the worn lapels and walked into the bright blue morning like a man unable to see the generous breadth of Boulevard Montparnasse. On a side street, he went up a staircase to a second-floor apartment.

She looked up from the desk. Her hair brushed her shoulders, as it had the day of Gómez Carrillo's funeral. "You haven't changed at all," he murmured.

"Castillo, no?" she said. "I read your poems."

"I have to leave. My uncle's plantation—"

"We all have to leave," she said in her slow Argentine drawl. "It is a tragedy for Latin American art."

"Come out for a coffee with me. All my years in Paris I've wanted to sit at a café table with you. I think I wanted that more than anything, more than writing poetry ..."

Her smile was hesitant. "This is my last issue of the *Revista*," she said. "But I suppose it can wait."

The chill air pierced his hangover, clearing a path for a deeper pain. Lidia's self-confident stride reminded him of the night he had seen her leave La Rotonde with Riquewehr. He did not understand how her passionate darkness could have found satisfaction in Riquewehr's fine-haired Teutonic arms. On Boulevard Montparnasse he laid his hand on her elbow, glorying in the solicitude with which she turned to him as he said, "Let's not go to the usual places. We'll try Le Jockey. Once I saw Picasso there ..."

When they reached Le Jockey Picasso was not there but, to Castillo's astonishment, Carpentier sat consoling the Mayan Idol, who was blubbering and slurring his words. As they ordered coffee — cheaper here than at Le Dôme — Lidia Corvina said, "We all have the same problem."

"The same problem?"

"Don't you read the newspapers?" she said with a practicality that startled him. "Coffee, cotton, sugar — they're all worth a fraction of what they were. Everyone in Paris who's living on the revenue of a plantation or a hacienda has to go home ... You thought you were the only one?"

"This is the death-agony of Montparnasse!" Carpentier cried.

"If he goes back to Cuba," Lidia whispered. "They'll put him in jail. He's going to have to stay and earn his living. He'll be alone. But the Mayan Idol's family has called him back." Her voice dived lower. "He's going to leave his French girl; her parents won't let her go to Guatemala with him."

Castillo glanced at the Mayan Idol. His compatriot's tie was undone, his stela profile was smudged. "I would have been famous," he sobbed. "My short stories published in French, my novel completed ... it's all gone. I can't publish a novel about a dictator if I'm living in Guatemala!" The waiter came over to ask if he could help. "My soul will always be in Paris!" the Mayan Idol said in French.

Castillo pushed his face closer to Lidia's dark eyes. "I didn't think you could go home."

"Because I've had lovers?" she said, startling him with her frankness, and with the plural. "Buenos Aires is a city of two million people. It's not Guatemala City." Her disdain hit him harder because she didn't seem to notice that she was expressing it. "Unlike you, I am returning to the Paris of South America."

Castillo lifted his hand and laid it on hers. His mahogany skin contrasted with her shining whiteness. She removed her other hand from her mug and with it lifted Castillo's hand from hers. Four hands curled on the table, two light and two dark, facing each other like opposing football squads. She looked him in the eyes with an expression in which the sympathy he had glimpsed in her office was corralled by more uncompromising feelings. Behind her Carpentier laid his hand on the Mayan Idol's shoulder.

He murmured, "I wanted —"

Lidia cut him off. "Life in Guatemala is going to be hard, Castillo."

He stumbled to his feet, apologizing for leaving her. "There's a family I have to visit ... before they go ..."

He ordered the words of his proposal, knowing it was the last poem he would write. As he started towards the door, Picasso entered the café in a burst of bright-blue confidence and spotted Lidia sitting alone. Stepping onto Boulevard Montparnasse, Castillo saw Picasso's face stretch into a hungry smile.

4

BLUE RIVER HOTEL

THE FIRST TIME HE shared a room at the Hotel Río Azul with a woman, he was young and the country was at war. The government celebrated the new year by announcing that the war had ended in a victory for the Army. On New Year's Day the UNGR guerrillas struck back, blacking out the electricity in eleven cities. The war ground into its thirty-fifth year. In the morning, when he caught a rattling Bluebird school bus north from the market in Chichicastenango, the edge of town was rimmed with soldiers. At each roadblock, the passengers opened their documents, then stood by the side of the road while gaunt, dwarf-like teenagers in skin-tight uniforms clambered into the bus's interior and prodded the barrels of their Galils at the dark green upholstery.

The regularity of the seasons guaranteed pellucid blue January days. He drank down the clarity, even though he felt ill and exhausted, and on edge from the checkpoints. A frigid hotel in Chichi had left him with a blood-sapping cold. As they approached Quetzaltenango — the country's second city, high and remote, and only a fraction of the size of the capital — he blew his nose on toilet paper from the roll in his pocket. On the hillsides above the city the papery off-yellow of corn stalks and the dark humus colour of earth tilled for irrigation channels marked out the tiny plots of Mayan farmers. Dark green conifers clung to the upper reaches of the hillsides. The Bluebird bus dropped him at the Minerva Bus Station, a chaotic field outside of town. He took a taxi downtown and stepped out of the cab below the park's Roman pillars and fountain. He sweated and shivered in the chill mountain air. Every other town he'd visited had been either a tourist trap or a garrison under military lock-down. Quetzaltenango, busy yet venerable, offered a Guatemalan normality.

He picked his way along crowded streets of close-packed shops dominated by battered second-hand cars, teenagers in tracksuits and blue jeans, men in open-necked shirts and pressed slacks, women in traditional Mayan skirts and *huipiles,* or sweaters and long dresses. He turned uphill on Avenida 12, entering a district where the shops were interspersed with nineteenth-century mansions that had been converted into hotels. All along the street there was graffiti on the walls, signed by the UNGR guerrillas. *El pueblo maya lucha con valentía* — UNGR ("The Mayan people fight with courage — UNGR") was splashed on the front of a hotel. The owner of a hardware store had spray-painted the stucco next to his front door with the words *Se vende concreto* ("Cement for sale"), and some wit had added UNGR to that as well.

The Hotel Río Azul stood at the junction of two narrow, steep streets. Inside, split-level floors were conjoined at unexpected angles, as though geological strata had been shaken, sliding together epochs and continents. Balconies hung over each of the down-plunging streets. There was a bright enclosed lounge on the third floor and an elevated courtyard at the back of the fourth floor that was open to the elements. The only signs of a blue river were the navy-coloured plastic rectangles that were attached to the keys. The cheapest rooms were in the courtyard at the back; narrow twin-bed cubicles with the toilet located across the cold tiles of the outdoor landing.

The hotel was full. They gave him a bed on the condition that he share the room. The external courtyard looked out past the roof of the hardware store and the fall of the street at the distant snow-covered peak of the Santa María volcano. The cold bored into his bones. As he lay sneezing on his bed, he heard Doña Bendición tell a young gringa she would have to share the room. "With a *muchacho*?" the girl said as the door opened.

Scrubbed and blonde, she carried a backpack of no-nonsense compactness that lent her an air midway between that of an intrepid NGO worker and a hygienic Christian missionary. She confirmed both of his guesses by introducing herself as the representative of a Catholic NGO that followed up on adoptions of indigenous children. She dropped her pack on her bed and left. He lay there reading an article in a newspaper he had found in the lobby that explained that in the Mayan calendar January 2, 1995 was the date 12 baktun, 19 katun, 1 tun, 13 winal, 17 k'in. At night he rolled under the covers, relieved to discover that the blankets, which Doña Bendición said had been woven in the village of Momostenango, were heavy enough to protect him from the cold. The idea that this was a country where two calendars overlapped soothed him. As darkness fell, the girl returned. He saw how young she was, only twenty or twenty-one. She was too terrified at sharing a room with a strange man to speak to him. When she got into bed, taking off only her hiking boots, she sat up in vigilance. "Is it all right if I turn out the light?" he said. Her response was a nervous whimper. He got out of bed in his woollen pyjamas and flipped the switch. As the light went out and he returned towards the beds, the girl whimpered out loud. All night she murmured to herself as though praying. Each time his stuffed-up nose awoke him, the whispering was continuing. In the morning she stood by the door. "I left fifteen Quetzales on the table for my share of the bill." She opened the door, confiding a glimpse of the snowy peak of Santa María high in the thin blue sky. He knew he would never think about her again.

COUGHING, HE ENTERED THE hotel through the door at the top of the steps. The reception desk and the dim lobby were decorated with black-and-white stills from the surrounding mountains: close-ups of the summit of Santa María, the Fuentes Georginas hot springs, corn growing in terraced plots cultivated by Maya in traditional dress. Don Miguel and Doña Bendición explained that the hotel was full because a group from the capital had booked two floors for a New Year's party. They signed him in by hand in a huge ancient register where they listed his *procedencia* — where he was coming from — as Chichicastenango, and filled in his *destino* as Guatemala City because anywhere farther away was beyond human imagination. It was only the next day, after the girl departed, and he staggered out to a pharmacy and bought cold pills, that he began to speak to them. The couple's three children capered around the reception desk. Don Miguel was a bony man with a solicitous grey moustache, his woollen waistcoat and dark jacket mirroring the hotel's austere decency. His wiriness and yellowish skin made him look southern European; Doña Bendición's dark hair curled and her face was a pale tan. Their three children, with their long eyes, high cheekbones, and straight black hair, were much darker than their parents. The inconsistency was obvious and unmentionable. It was only ten years later, when he had booked a student group into the hotel and they invited him to share a sweet, potent coffee, that he asked the question. He had allayed their discomfort with his perpetual singleness by revealing that he had a fiancée, a confession which drew sharp looks from their elder daughter. María was a short, willowy teenager whose curiosity about relations between women and men drew reprimands from her parents. Doña Bendición's curls were grey now and Don Miguel cleared his throat more often. "God did not intend us to have children," Doña Bendición said, her index finger sliding down the thin gold cross suspended from her neck. "We were devastated by this until we understood that His plan was for us to provide a family for three children who did not have one."

The children were adopted through the Catholic Church from a Mayan village in the mountains. "Are they siblings?" he asked.

"Possibly cousins," Don Miguel said. "Their families were connected."

The past tense confirmed his suspicions. The children came from a village on the banks of a river in the mountains to which the UNGR had retreated in the mid-1980s, when it began losing territory to the Army's helicopter gunships. The Army had entered the village, accused the inhabitants of supporting the guerrillas, and forced them to dig a pit in the muddy village square. The adults were divided into male and female. One by one, each of the village's women was stripped naked. The soldiers led each woman to the edge of the pit and raped her, then shot her in the head and threw her body into the hole in the ground. Between noon and four p.m., jeering at each other as they unbuckled the belts of their tight uniform trousers, the soldiers raped and killed all of the village's women. They started with the grandmothers and ended with girls who had not begun to menstruate. Then, more briskly, they seized each man in turn, shot him in the back of the head and threw him into the pit. Once the village's adults were dead, the soldiers slaughtered their chickens and burned their houses, their corn, their stacked firewood, and the beehives at the back of the village where two families produced honey. Later the soldiers and their officers would return to build houses for themselves on land that had belonged for centuries to a community that had ceased to exist. As homeless bees buzzed in the air, children were piled into the backs of Army trucks. Their culture was eradicated; as they grew up, they would forget the Quiché language. But, if given decent homes, they would become obedient citizens who were respectful of authority and the Army. Don Miguel and Doña Bendición did not speak these words; others had spoken them in his hearing. He understood that this couple had been chosen to adopt because their household exemplified values which would ensure that subversives' children integrated into society. And, ten years after sharing a room with her, he understood what the blonde girl had been doing at the Blue River Hotel.

~~~

ON HIS FIRST VISIT he asked them why they had named their hotel after a blue river.

"To remind ourselves of the river of life that carries us to eternity," Doña Bendición said.

"But to signal the joy that we experience in passing down the river of life," Don Miguel explained, "we chose the colour blue."

The next time he stayed there, they didn't remember him. Their business relationship began when he started booking student groups into the small double rooms that surrounded the interior lounge on the third floor and inviting representatives of local community organizations to give talks there. He was older, less skinny and unsettled, with a decent haircut. The country was no longer at war. It was the time of building democracy and implementing the Peace Accords — or, as his speakers pointed out, of failing to implement the clauses pertaining to indigenous rights. He now spent half of the year in the tourist town of Antigua, close to the capital, where he managed student excursions and provided English-language services, and the other half at home in Ottawa, working on short-term government contracts. His parents, who had emigrated from Central Europe to swampy, boulder-strewn Ottawa Valley farmland, had called him Trevor, a name popular among Scots-Irish farming families in the region, to encourage him to integrate into their new home. At fifteen his imagination had been ignited by dreams of Latin America. He gazed at picture books in the school library, read about Mayas and Incas and conquistadors, plotted routes across the map of South America with his finger, sought ways to learn Spanish at a high school that taught only French. His imaginings isolated him from his classmates, making him believe that his emotions were unique. The conviction carried over into his relationships in university and beyond. "Why can't you

meet a girl who is like you?" his mother complained, convinced
that his happiness depended on marriage to a woman whose parents
came from the old country. At a superficial level his mother was
so obviously wrong that only after a decade did he concede that in
a deeper sense she was right; there was an intimacy he had not
allowed himself. He wouldn't expect anyone to display total
understanding of the cross-stitching of rural Ontario and Central
America that dominated his imagination, certainly not Jasmin,
whom he called his fiancée when he was in Guatemala, and sometimes, also in Ottawa. Her parents had emigrated from Asia; her
career was in finance. She was in Ottawa on an eighteen-month
government consulting contract when they met; then moved to
Toronto to work on Bay Street; and was often on a plane to Hong
Kong, Singapore, or Shanghai. They spent weekends in the same
city for a few months each year and went on vacations together.
Each time he feared that their relationship was little more than
a source of reliable sex after stretches of intense work, their sen-
sitivity to each other's needs surprised him: the lack of fuss with
which a rare Saturday afternoon together was sacrificed to ensure
that a report was finished, the acceptance of each other's single-
professional quirks and tyrannical agendas, but also how she
suddenly became more caring than he could have imagined when a
contract slipped through his fingers, the warm reliability she pulled
out of him when her uncle died of a heart attack and he spent two
days at her side during funeral rites in Markham in a language he
didn't understand. Working in different places didn't mean they
couldn't be sensitive or nurturing; it didn't mean he wasn't growing
as a person. Even when weeks passed during which his only glimpses
of Jasmin were the sweaters, parka, toque, and scarves that she left
hanging in the closet of his Lower Town condo, or the photograph
of her that he propped up on the counter of the colonial stone
cottage that he rented in Antigua, he was sure he knew her better
than his friends knew the wives they had lived with for a decade.

RHEA SAT NEXT TO him at a workshop in Ottawa. She was slight and fine-boned with a feminine delicacy of skin and perception; a youthful irony; wavy, dark hair; and a deep, commanding voice. He chatted with her during lunch and the Styrofoam-cupped coffee breaks without realizing that she was an undergraduate. She was more mature and definite than the students whom he led on excursions. She had travelled in all of his favourite countries: first in pursuit of Latin American theatre, then to rescue giant turtles, and now in search of gender definitions. She was applying for funding to develop programs for drag queen prostitutes in Buenos Aires. When, not quite believing her tales, he spoke to her in Spanish, she replied in an Argentine drawl, telling him that her boyfriend was flying in to visit her. He mentioned that his fiancée was in Taipei on business. After the workshop ended, they had coffee in the Byward Market and exchanged email addresses and phone numbers. Only then did he notice that they used the same phrases: "do you not" for "don't you," "laneway" for "driveway," "it doesn't care" for "it doesn't matter." "Where are you from originally?" When she told him, his heart went still. Her village was five kilometres from his; they'd attended the same high school, years apart. He asked her surname and recognized its local provenance. "How did you get interested in Latin America there?"

She smiled. "They had a few books in the school library."

Two weeks later, on Saturday night, leading his jet-lagged fiancée around a corner in the Market after dinner, he swerved to avoid a young couple who were kissing against one of the pillars that held up a portico where stalls were set out during the day. Jasmin's high heels danced a brief tango as she skirted the couple. He saw Rhea's white cheeks pull back from a tall, dark youth's embrace. Neither of them spoke. The next month, when she emailed to invite him to coffee, he was relieved to reply, from an internet café down the hill from the Hotel Río Azul, that he was in Quetzaltenango.

"WHEN I WAS SIXTEEN, my father died and left me money. I knew what he would want me to do with it."

Trevor's palm grew hot against his mug of beer. His mother had left the old country at sixteen, also after the death of her father. Should he ask about her father's death? He decided to ask about his life. She told him that her dad had been a lawyer and rural township councillor, a serious Catholic who might have had a future in politics had he not passed away at forty-five. "My father was a Catholic, too." He, too, had died young, though not as young as Rhea's father. The harshness of the Ottawa Valley poured back like the icy spring runoff: everybody knowing everyone's business, the limitations of vision that shackled a place where time stopped in its tracks and turned in circles, as though Rhea and he *had* gone to high school together. She was in full flight, telling stories of situations her innocence had led her into and how she had got out of them. After her first bout of Latin American travelling, she returned to her village to finish high school. Nobody understood what she had experienced, her every divergence from accepted opinion was seen as a sign that her father's death had made her weird.

She grasped his hand across the café table, then released it. They were drinking Mexican beer in an Irish pub. It was their first meeting in six months. Her hair was longer than the last time he had seen her. In defiance of her small-boned delicacy, the picture window behind her, with the Sussex Drive traffic streaming past, embellished her silhouette to a shaggy grandeur. Over her shoulder, high up on Parliament Hill, the clock in the Peace Tower insisted that they occupied the same place and time, in spite of the generational discrepancies that reminded him that she was his protégée.

A protégée unknown to his fiancée.

"Are you all right?" she asked, when he failed to reply. "Are you afraid of me?"

"I'm amazed by you." That was too strong. He didn't want to give her the wrong idea; the Argentine boyfriend seemed to be out of the picture. "I think you're one of the most impressive young people I've met in my field."

"Oh, come on. Don't be so formal. I like to be close to people who are older than me." There was a silence, as though one of them might be about to mention the dead father. She sipped her Corona. When she had returned to high school, after hiking in Peru and rescuing turtles in Panama, she was no longer capable of dating boys her own age. "In my last year of high school my best friend had an affair with the drama teacher. He was fifty. But she said he was in great shape!"

The pleasure in her laughter told him that it was she, not her friend, who had slept with the teacher. "I've got to go," he said. "I'm setting up a meeting with a man in Guatemala."

⁓

HE GOT COMPAÑERO TINO's phone number from Don Miguel. The next group of students he was guiding were third-years with two years of university Spanish who were studying the history of the civil war. Trevor made an overnight preparation trip up the Pan-American Highway from Antigua to Quetzaltenango (he called the city Xela, as the locals did). Preferring not to divulge his legal name, Compañero Tino asked for his meagre honorarium in cash. They met at a stall in the market, identifying each other through an exchange of pre-arranged phrases, as though time had turned back to the war years of code words and underground activity. It was six years since the signing of the Peace Accords. The country was adrift under a corrupt government, influxes of gringo money, incursions by Salvadoran drug gangs, and unravelling Mayan cultures. Tino's view of these developments was that of a defeated warrior. A fine-boned man of peasant modesty, he led Trevor to the back room of the community radio station where he worked. On a creased red poster pasted to a damp stucco wall, the features of a bespectacled youth were defined in bold black strokes. *¡Oliverio Castañeda Vive!* read the lettering below. A brilliant student orator, Trevor knew,

Castañeda had been murdered by the Army after giving a speech.

The station's broadcasts were audible from the adjoining booth: 1970s political folk songs mingled with tinkling marimba-led ditties from the highlands and public service announcements from cooperatives and community groups in Spanish interspersed with Quiché. As Tino interrogated him, Trevor saw how, in the context of a different time, this subdued questioning could have been terrifying; how giving the wrong answers could have led to execution. Tino stumbled over his name, pronouncing it "Tre-borr," a sound that approximated *trébol*, the Spanish word for "clover." He told Tino to call him Trébol. Addressing each other by their *nommes-de-guerre*, they settled on a subject, a date, and a price for Tino's talk.

When he got back to Antigua, there was a message from Rhea. She was in Mexico City, researching gender among drag queen prostitutes in the Zona Rosa. Email flattened her anecdotes, but enough of her personality came through that he responded by writing her a quick reply. He had work lined up for five months in Antigua. Jasmin, who had never come to Guatemala, had promised to visit him this time. In the morning she wrote to cancel her plans for a January visit. He wrote back to settle a date in February or March.

He spent four days guiding twenty students through the highlands, visiting the vegetable market in Zunil, the weavers in Momostenango, and holding talks in the third-floor lounge of the Hotel Río Azul. Compañero Tino was the final speaker. He shuffled into the lounge and stood with his head bowed before the tall, fair students; nearly all of them young women. He said nothing. When the silence became uncomfortable, one of the students asked, in passable Spanish, "Why did you become a guerrilla?"

Tino looked down at his hands. "I became a guerrilla because when I am eleven years old I wake up, I open my eyes and see four soldiers drag my father out of our house. I will never see my father again …" In the spasmodic Spanish of a native speaker of a Mayan language, mingling past, present, and future tense verbs, Tino related how, after the murder of his father, a spokesman for local small farmers, he fled to the mountains and grew up among the guerrillas, eating two servings of rice and beans a day; sacrificing for his compañeros; and, as he grew older, suppressing his jealousy, in order to maintain discipline, at the relations some compañeros had with the few compañeras present. He spoke of sleeping out in the rain, being trained to make broadcasts on guerrilla radio, and mourning compañeros who died in combat.

"Are you happy with the Peace Accords?" a student asked.

"No. This isn't the Guatemala I want. My whole life, I dream of the day I will enter the capital with a revolutionary army."

"Did you ever go back to your village?"

"Yes, to bring to justice the men who killed my father." He paused. "Now I cannot go back."

Uncertain how many of the students had understood the verb *ajusticiar*, or realized that Tino was using this revolutionary euphemism to tell them that he had murdered the soldiers who had killed his father, Trevor tried to bring the talk to a close.

"Why can't you go back?" a girl in glasses said. Fascinated by meeting a real guerrilla, the students kept asking questions. An hour later than planned, Trevor took Tino down the street to an anonymous restaurant with tiny booths, where they ate rice and refried black beans and a leg of undernourished chicken with a slice of avocado. They drank Coca-Cola. Expressing a mournful gratitude at the students' interest, Tino told him that his village had been razed by the military while he was away in the guerrillas; the soldiers who had killed the inhabitants had occupied their land. Tino complained of the impossibility of explaining to his son why he had spent seventeen years as a guerrilla instead of earning a living. "My son and I live in different historical periods and cannot meet. Do you have children?"

"No. I have a fiancée. But when I come to Guatemala I don't see her for five months."

Tino shook his head. "Five months! I could not do that. Not anymore." For the first time since they had met, he smiled. "Compañero Clover, you are the last person in Guatemala who lives with revolutionary discipline!"

⸻

JASMIN CANCELLED HER FEBRUARY trip, then her March trip. She phoned him three times a week on the cellphone he'd bought in the market. "Don't worry," she said. "Five months'll be over before you know it."

At night he listened to the mice crawling through the rafters of his zinc-roofed stone hut on a cobblestoned colonial street with a view of the Agua Volcano. His body stored the heat of the sunny days and emitted it in pangs of nocturnal lust. Though not even easygoing Antigua was a good place to be out after dark, he met up with old acquaintances in cafés in the evenings to exchange stories of the civil war, gossip about local politicians, and talk about the customs of different regions of the country. Jasmin kept phoning, growing petulant when GuaTel's connection to Canada lapsed, or when she caught him at night in a place with music playing in the background. "I work hard!" she said, mentioning a swap, merger, or acquisition. "I'm beat. I need a beach. Are there beaches in Guatemala?"

"A couple." He was suppressing his emotional and sexual needs for the cause. Compañero Tino had done this for seventeen years. Yet, all the phone sex in the world — and Jasmin was good at phone sex, delighting in asking in a coy voice whether he was alone — could not soothe his restlessness. Why couldn't she just get on the damned plane?

"Give me a little time. I'm on the cusp of something big. I can't bail now or somebody else will get the promotion."

He gave her the space she required, as she did him. Their relationship, always open in this way, and in this way alone, continued at night, in the real time of cellphone conversations.

His communication with Rhea was consigned to the timelessness of email. Once a day, he ducked into a street corner internet café, sat among Guatemalan teenagers playing video games, tourists writing messages home, and drawling missionaries coordinating crusades for Mayan souls. Nothing obliged him to reply, or even open, Rhea's messages. When he had business to deal with, he left her words preserved under glass. Yet, he always replied eventually. How to identify the hour when he had begun to follow her misadventures in the Zona Rosa as though they belonged to a *telenovela*? The day when he had started to feel a punishing little stab in his gut if he opened his email to find no message from Rhea? The night when the abundance of her curls got tangled up with his fiancée's fine, dark strands in his lustful fantasies? The month when a communication that had been timeless elbowed its way into his daily schedule? She asked him for advice on grant applications. She was hoping to turn the drag queens into a Master's thesis. *Of course before I can do that, I have to actually finish my undergrad!* She pasted a draft of her project description at the bottom of an email. Set upon by chores, he put off reading it. When he went to the internet café later in the week, she had written again. *I'm sorry I did that! It would be so much easier if I could talk to you about it.*

He agreed this would be easier. An email agreement morphed into commitment, so perhaps that was the instant when the momentum shifted and *if* became *when,* and *when* demanded the assessment of possibilities, and the assessment of possibilities required that dates be chosen, and without knowing how this had come about, he found himself wanting, with a longing in which desire, loneliness, and an old-fashioned spark of traveller's adventure blended like the compounds that powered firecrackers during Antigua's Holy Week celebrations, to make this meeting happen. The crystalline air of December, January, and February had yielded to the wispy white clouds of March, then April, when cumulus built up like stealthy towers behind the mountains. The students he was guiding finished their semester and went home; a professor for

whose research project he had been doing interviews arrived in
Antigua, declared the project completed and left with his recordings;
and two Guatemalan accountants to whom he had been teaching
business English stopped coming to their classes. His flight home
was at the end of May, he had saved some money; his only remaining
commitment was to interview the Mayan mayor of Quetzaltenango
for a Montreal newspaper. Free time yawned; unexplored regions
of northern Guatemala beckoned. He could visit the remote north,
return via Xela and do the interview. If Rhea chose to come down
from Mexico, they could meet up north and go over her grant
proposal.

"Come and meet me!" he said.

"I can't, hon," Jasmin replied. "Not now. You'll have such a good
time in all those jungly places by yourself."

She knew the risks of their heading into the back of the beyond
together. She had heard him complain about how travelling com-
panions wilted under the heat, balked at local food, got sick, broke
out in grotesque rashes at the first insect bite, became constipated
because they were afraid to use the toilets, or embarrassed him by
stumbling over the language. He was happiest on his own: independent, fluent, resilient, and soaking up local cultures in great waves
of understanding that perpetually replenished his enthusiasm for
travel. Would he have been more forgiving if, back in the era when
his habits were being formed, he had hooked up with a woman who
shared his love of travelling rough?

He bit his lip and wrote: *I'm going to northern Guatemala.
A meeting could be a possibility* —

I agree about the meeting, Rhea replied an hour later. *That's very
important.* He thought of her riding buses from Mexico City —
thirty hours on buses? — and wondered what she was expecting.
For two weeks he travelled on his own in the Petén jungle. Returning
to civilization in Cobán, a small city in northeastern Guatemala
from where he would ride pickup trucks across the north, he
walked to an internet café. He looked for messages from Jasmin and

colleagues in Ottawa. His most recent message was from Rhea: *I'm running like a happily mad thing. On my way to the bus ...*

⌒

AS THE DUST-DRENCHED pickup bounced out of the arid mountains and down into the fringes of Huehuetenango, he saw that he had entered a zone that was not Mexico, yet was no longer entirely Guatemala. Here two histories coiled together. The men in the central park wore thick black moustaches and broad-brimmed white straw hats; when he objected to the truck driver charging him twice as much as the other passengers, the man reviled him, with Mexican-tinged venom, as a *pinche gringo*. He walked to the cheap hotel where they had arranged to rendezvous, took a shower, and lay down on his bed. Two hours later Rhea knocked on his door.

She was taller than the woman he had refashioned in his mind. She wore sandals, white three-quarter-length slacks, and a black tank top. He leaned towards her in greeting. As he followed her down a narrow, raised sidewalk to a restaurant, his eyes hungered for the shape of her legs. They were mopping up the last of their refried black beans with tortillas when the restaurant's power went out. "This used to happen all the time," he said, "when the guerrillas blew up the pylons."

"I know there was a war here," she said, "but I'm not old enough to remember it."

He was sitting in Huehuetenango with the girl he used to run into in the Byward Market.

After supper they walked through the crowded, rundown streets of the Mayan market, where plastic bags and wrapping paper gusted along the sidewalks and burnt food simmered on ashy embers in the creeping dusk. They emerged onto the steps that looked out over the Minerva Temple. As large as a city block, the building was a replica of a white, Doric-columned temple in ancient Rome. "The dictator at the beginning of the twentieth century put up fake Roman ruins and shrines to Minerva. He figured that if you imported Roman gods to replace Mayan gods, Guatemala would jump historical periods and become a developed country." They sat down on the steps to look at the deserted temple in the fading light. "He forgot that histories with different starting points end up in different times."

"I have nothing against inter-generational relationships," Rhea said.

Was that what he had been referring to? He wasn't used to being with someone this intuitive. As he stared at her, she asked him if he rode a motorcycle; she was always getting involved with men with motorcycles. Touched by her willingness to tease him, he shook his head. "No motorcycle?" she said. "That reduces your chances."

In the hotel, they exchanged a Latin embrace before going to their rooms. He was unable to sleep. Over breakfast, feeling that it was his duty to do so, he told her in a stilted voice how his relationship with Jasmin worked. He felt relieved when he had finished.

Rhea reached for her day pack. "Can I show you my proposal?"

They went to a café and worked on her application. Her prose had a purposeful lack of flab. Familiar with the committee that would assess her proposal, he suggested points that she might emphasize to increase her chance of getting the grant. By mid-afternoon, they were finished. "I guess that's it," she said. "Time for me to be getting back to Mexico."

She slid the folder into a woven bag. She was already on her feet when he said, "Why don't you come to Xela with me?"

⁓

THEY STAYED AT THE Hotel Río Azul.

He wondered whether he could pass off Rhea to Don Miguel and Doña Bendición as his fiancée. Had he told them that Jasmin was Asian? Rhea's youth would give them pause. To his relief, the owners were out when they arrived; the children were at the reception desk. The oldest girl, María, already had a daughter of her own, though her parents never referred to a husband. She sat on a chair with her toddler, while her adolescent brother and sister examined the register with serious gazes.

"Is a room on the third floor all right, Don Clover?" the boy, Alberto, asked.

He nodded. Alberto assigned them to one of the little double rooms around the lounge where the students had been billeted.

As he signed in and paid for three nights, María, hefting her infant, said, "Is she your fiancée?"

"Is he your brother …? Your dad?" Alberto asked Rhea, his voice shrill.

"We're going to get married," Rhea replied.

The youngest girl, picking up on the game, said, "Is he your grandfather …? Your uncle …?"

Giving him a concentrated look from beneath her eyelids, María handed him the plastic rectangle with the dangling key. Her little sister's mockery pursued them out of the lounge. On the trip down from Huehue in the recycled Bluebird school bus, he had been squeezed against the window with Rhea next to him and a man in a broad-brimmed hat on the aisle. After an hour, the man got off and a girl in a Mayan *huipil* and skirt, about thirteen years old, grabbed the place for herself and her baby daughter. The baby screamed; the girl laughed and swung her around, singing to her in Quiché. He and Rhea, pressed shoulder to shoulder, murmured together like teenage classmates riding the bus to their Ottawa Valley high school. They passed rock faces, smouldering under-growth, and ragtag streams of people walking along the roadside. Rhea told him that her father had died of a hereditary genetic disorder. If she had male children, they, too, would die at forty-five, though girls would have normal life spans. "That's another reason I keep travelling. Why settle down if my children have a fifty percent chance of being born with a death sentence?" She leaned into him as the bus went around a steep curve; this time he took her hand. For a shuddering, bone-rattling moment, they remained linked. "How old are you?" she murmured, with a naughty smile.

He told her. He had her doubled: forty-two to twenty-one. She was the same age as the students who had listened to Compañero Tino.

The beds in their room were set against opposite walls; there was enough space at the foot of each bed to prop up a backpack. An interior room, it had no windows, though there was a small bathroom and a transom of wavy glass over the door that trapped the flat light of the lounge. "My body aches," Rhea said. They went to bed early, after taking turns changing in the bathroom. In the morning, she was no better. "I think it's my kidneys." Her deep voice drowned her moan. "Too many long bus rides."

He phoned the mayor's secretary to confirm his interview. Rigoberto Quemé Chay was Guatemala's first Mayan mayor, elected by urban indigenous neighbourhoods in defiance of a racist city where Mayan people were banned from sports clubs and good restaurants. Trevor left Rhea, who wanted nothing to eat, walked down the hill and crossed the square to the nineteenth-century city hall that looked out over the Roman columns in the park. The interview took place in the mayor's office at the back of the second floor. Quemé Chay, dressed in black, was an urban Maya who had grown up without the Quiché language or traditional culture; he was considering running for president. Trevor asked him whether he would help rural Maya by implementing land reform. The mayor shook his head. "The land issue belongs to the past. Young people don't want to sow corn. Our future is in the cities, as entrepreneurs."

Once he had turned off his recorder, he asked the mayor if he knew the Hotel Río Azul. Quemé Chay seemed surprised that he was staying there. "Those children will inherit a business; other Maya will create them." He flexed his lips. "You know why it is called the Hotel Río Azul."

"Doña Bendición said the river of life ..."

"For the river that runs through the village from which their children were adopted." Quemé Chay stood up. "Give my regards to Don Miguel."

He returned to the room to find Rhea in pain. He went down

to the lobby, where Don Miguel was bent over the register, and transmitted the mayor's greetings as a prelude to broaching his need for a doctor's phone number and a taxi. Don Miguel lifted the receiver of the phone at his elbow and made the arrangements. "Where is Doña Bendición?" he asked.

"She is busy." Don Miguel shrugged his shoulders. "She knows that girl is not your fiancée."

"We're only frien—"

"Do not trouble yourself, Don Clover. I am a man." Trevor had never seen him look so old.

The taxi honked at the door. He went up to the room. "I'm so sorry," Rhea said, dragging herself out of bed. "Me, the great traveller … you'll never believe my stories again."

He helped her down the stairs and into the taxi. They rode to a nineteenth-century building past the lower end of the park that housed a private clinic. Rhea inched her way along the hall, leaning against the wooden panels of the vast corridor with its marble floors and twenty-foot ceilings. She was ushered in to see the doctor, who told Trevor to wait outside. When she came out, she said that the doctor had remained seated behind an enormous desk; crammed bookshelves rose behind him. She felt like a *señora* from a distinguished family consulting a physician about an embarrassing complaint. Diagnosing exhaustion, the doctor prescribed pills. They rode back to the hotel. Trevor ran around to three pharmacies to collect the medicine. They spent the rest of the day in the room. In the afternoon he went out to eat rice, refried black beans, and chicken. He brought her soup.

"I've never had a man look after me before. I feel like crying."

They talked about their childhoods in the same clutch of swamp-encircled villages: his parents' desire that he marry a girl "like him," how her father's death had expelled her from the arc of her generation's experiences. "I've crossed over to the other side. That's why I'm here with you."

She was so tired that he doubted she would remember her words in the morning. That night he slipped out of the room, went out onto the balcony, and waited for a pre-arranged call from Jasmin. In the cloudy darkness, the Santa María volcano was invisible. "I've been offered a really great job in Australia," Jasmin said, "and I feel I can't take it because of you."

"You said you were coming here!"

"Give me time, baby…"

He hung up and paced the lounge. When he returned to the room, Rhea was asleep.

"PUT ON YOUR BATHING suit under your clothes," he said, as she stepped towards the bathroom. She had woken in the morning announcing that she felt five hundred times better. "Since you're feeling better we can visit the hot springs."

She stopped, her exuberance contracting into watchful wariness. "I'm not used to men telling me what to wear." He remembered the blonde girl taking off her boots. Rhea hesitated, then burrowed in her pack and emerged with a cream-coloured, two-piece bathing suit. They ate a pancake breakfast at a gringo restaurant off the park. It was mid-May. In the implacable chronometer of the seasons, the rains were approaching. The air was damp and grey, like the unwashed, uncarded wool sold at market stalls.

He took her on the tour he gave to students. They caught a bus from the corner of the park to the village of Zunil. The vegetable market, which fascinated development students, bored Rhea. They hunted down the village's saint. San Simón, a replica of a man in garish plastic, was carried from house to house. After asking around, he tracked down the saint in a house where a family had surrounded him, begging him to petition God to give them the money to buy the land they needed to feed themselves and keep their sons at home. "All we want is the land our people used to have before the war." The father supplicated before the saint in a sibilant, anguished voice that went on and on without halting for breath, while the mother and grandmother sat on their knees before him, planting lighted candles on the floor. The sons emptied bottles of hard liquor down Simón's plastic throat.

As they left the house, he sensed her mood lightening. She gloried in the ride up the mountain in the back of a pickup truck. They gripped the metal frame fixed to the half ton's box. As the pickup climbed, the valleys filled with mist that streaked across the road and prickled their eyebrows with cold dew. "This is like the cloud forest in Costa Rica," Rhea said. He saw that, at least for part of the year, this was a cloud forest. He had brought student groups here, but always in the dry season. Only now, seeing through her eyes, had he grasped the mountainside's rainy season identity.

The hot springs were nearly deserted. They floated, lulled to the verge of sleepiness. Their fingers, bobbing side by side, grew wrinkled. They were basking in the soupy, sulphurous water beneath the black overhanging cliffs when the soldiers arrived.

There were thirty of them; tiny, tight-uniformed youths whose arms looked too spindly to wield their Galils. He gripped Rhea's shoulder, seeking her substance, afraid that he had carried her back to the era of his first visit to Guatemala.

The young men laughed and clowned around, returning him to the present. An officer imposed order: half of the soldiers stood at ease in the mist, their Galils level at their waists in a phantas-magoric recollection of the war, while the other half stripped to their underwear and waded into the springs. Rhea was shocked by the military presence; Trevor felt oddly reassured. At the time of his first visits to Guatemala being surprised in a swimsuit by the military could have meant death; now it was an irritation.

They dried off, dressed, rode down the mountain in the back of a truck, then walked across the village to catch the bus back to Xela.

"I said I'd stay for three nights," Rhea said. "I'll leave tomorrow. I have to get back to my drag queens."

They ate supper at a Mexican restaurant. Rhea's banter about the Zona Rosa oppressed him. Afterwards, they rambled through the silent park in the darkness. The morning newspaper had announced a lunar eclipse. To their astonishment, high above the Roman columns, they saw cloud sliding by curved degrees over the moon until the lunar surface was blotted out: celestial bodies born at distant points fell into alignment. As they climbed Avenida 12, she slid her arm through his. At the reception desk, Doña Bendición handed them their key in silence. They climbed to the third floor, entered the stuffy room and lay down on their beds.

"You look pensive," Rhea said. "What are you pensing?"

His breath hurt his chest.

"Whatever I'm pensing," she said, "I'm going to come and pense it over there." She crossed the room and lay down on his bed with her back to him. "I know this is wrong because of Jasmin," she murmured, "but, I know when someone is like me."

He clasped himself against her back. They adjusted their hug, then adjusted it again. At long intervals they gave each other chaste, close-mouthed kisses on innocuous body parts. He kissed her shoulders, her elbows. Their bodies clambered together with infinite slowness, as though wallowing through a zone where time had been suspended. After forty minutes he reached under her low-cut black T-shirt and caressed her back; he ran his hands down the backs of her legs. He was back in the Ottawa Valley, in a grade twelve class where they were studying *Wuthering Heights*, except that this time he understood what Cathy meant when she shouted, "I *am* Heathcliff." Each caress peeled away layers of concealment; each stripping stroke brought the merging of their essences closer. He pressed down harder on her flesh as he slid his palms over her back. Rhea's breathing quickened, synchronizing with the motions of his lightly sweating hands.

"What I'm pensing now," she gasped, "is that I've intruded on a lot of situations and caused a lot of problems." She rolled over. "That's what happens when you're attracted to older men who already have lives." She sat up, the corners of her eyes glistening. "This time I'm going to keep my clothes on. I'm sorry."

His breath caught in his chest. "There's no doubt," he said, "that in moral terms you're doing the right thing."

"That's a first. Me doing something moral in a relationship!"

"Just my luck to run into you when you decide to be moral."

Having intended these words as a joke, he heard their bitterness cut the night. Rhea became angry. "You're the one who laid out every detail of your relationship with Jasmin over breakfast in Huehue. How do you think that made me feel, after I'd ruined my health coming all that way to meet you? I wanted to be welcomed, not pushed away."

"You know I had to do that."

"Did you? Did you really? She's here in the room with us!"

He bowed his head.

"It would have been so much better," she said, her voice faltering, "if you had let me pretend that this high-flying career woman wasn't going to out-compete me for you. Then I could have fallen in love with you, and if you'd gone back to her afterwards, we would have had our moment ..."

They spent the rest of the night, dressed in makeshift pajamas, sleeping in each other's arms. Now and then they woke to run their lips over each other with pursed affection. He felt the compactness and burning heat of her body. Near dawn, he dreamed that he was embracing the adoption girl and felt a lurch of revulsion at her scrubbed blondeness.

In the morning they took a taxi to the Minerva Bus Station. The bus to Huehuetenango was parked in a muddy trench. Rhea watched the *ayudante* load her backpack onto the roof. He kissed her on the lips. She opened her mouth until their lips met around an oval-shaped space that was locked between them. She turned away, then veered towards him again and gave him a hard kiss on the neck. She disappeared into the bus. And that should have been the end of that story.

IT WAS INEVITABLE THAT they would flirt on email, she suggesting that he visit Mexico City that summer, he inviting her to call him when she was in Ottawa. Then, equally inevitably, the tone of her messages changed: *I have a lover, a lover who loves me and who I can love every night ...* She danced around the specifics of her relationship until just before her return to Canada. Then what had been implicit was made explicit: Rhea's lover was a middle-aged woman. Her fleeting backpacker affairs, her long-distance relationships with older men, the absence of a serious boyfriend in her life, fell into place. She had been able to acknowledge the inter-generational dimension of her desire before the same-sex dimension. One night she phoned and they met for coffee in the Byward Market, in an Eastern European place on a side street concealed from the Peace Tower, where the maps on the walls depicted vanished national borders revered by Trevor's parents. He expected Rhea to bring her lover, a woman from rural southern Mexico, but she came alone. She seemed just the same; her hair tousled, her virile voice vying with her soft-toned sensitivities, her mind continuing to nourish itself on Latin American politics and literature. With the help of her grant money, she had finished her undergraduate degree by submitting independent study projects long distance. She was going back to Mexico to live. "To Mexico City?"

"No, to Tabasco. That's where Guadelupe's from. Her whole family's there."

He wanted to say: Tabasco's too rural, nobody will accept you. Realizing that any objection he made would be suspect, he asked, "What does your mother say?"

"She says Guadelupe's too old for me." She smiled. "Focusing on generational difference is her way of not dealing with lesbianism." She scrutinized him. "Are you still with Jasmin? Are things the same between you? Was I right to say no?"

"Yes, yes, and no," he said.

"Which, from my point of view, means yes, yes, and yes."

Her emails stopped. Sometimes, in the middle of the night, when Jasmin lay naked beside him, he would wake and hear himself saying, in a voice inside his head: No, Rhea. Not Tabasco. Not those endless swamps, more water than land, Mexico's Ottawa Valley, as ingrown as the Ottawa Valley fifty years ago and much, much poorer; you can't live a same-sex life there — or any life you'd want to live. Who was he to make such judgments? After a point, time and understanding fused. What his mind ruled to be impossible, might be feasible in her reality.

He stopped spending part of the year in Antigua. He found a desk job in the civil service, on contract at first, and then permanent, and had an affair, which felt stupid even as it was occurring, with a woman in another department. This gave Jasmin the pretext they both sought to end their relationship. Within six months, she was engaged to a Chinese-Canadian banker from Toronto; he heard later that she had a daughter. Trevor settled down as an Ottawa bureaucrat, one of countless stolid men who came off farms in the Ottawa Valley, shed their overalls for ill-fitting suits and landed government jobs. He was comfortable, yet resented his job security even as he clung to it. Unlike other men he knew, who struggled to pinpoint the moment at which their lives had declined into ordinariness, he knew exactly when and where his nerve had failed him.

⁓

A DECADE LATER THE phone on his desk rang. The call-display screen showed a cell number of which he had no record. He sweated as he heard the tones that had responded to his passion. "I'm in town," she said. "Could you meet me in the Market for a coffee?"

He left work and walked through the construction and the Rideau Street traffic. On the maps on the café's walls, the national boundaries from bygone eras were fading. She sat at a table at the back, petite yet well nourished, looking fresher and more beautiful than he could have imagined after all these years. "Oh, you're all grey!" she said, lifting her cheek for a kiss.

"You look great."

As Jasmin smiled, an alertness to her body combed his skin. He observed her shape, sheathed in her blue pantsuit and high-necked white blouse. They had been together for seven years, and he remembered little about their conversations. In the middle of telling him about her daughter, who was eight, she asked, "Are you still with her?"

Thinking she meant the woman in the other department, he said: "No, that didn't last—"

"I knew you weren't going to stay with *her*. I mean the other one, the young girl ..."

"I don't know what you're talking about."

"Come on, Trev, who ever knew you better than I did?" Her eyes refused to release him.

"She fell in love with a woman," he said, hoping this would put an end to this subject.

Jasmin laughed. "Oh, Trev, that was really bad luck!" She sipped her coffee. "Are you in touch with her?"

"The last time I wrote to her, four years ago, I got a reply telling me that she had promised her lover not to communicate with anyone from her past."

"She was looking for a mother, not a father." Jasmin savoured her coffee, regarding him with an expression that rankled him. He didn't remember her showing any interest in personal psychology. He wondered what her husband was like. Or was it her daughter who had changed her? "Listen, I'm not here to make you feel bad. I actually wanted to ask you a favour. I have the most incredible mother-in-law ... a rich lady who collects art. When she decides she wants something, there's no stopping her. She used to get on planes and go and buy whatever she wanted. But she's too old now. She's gone crazy over Mayan weaving. She has to have blankets —"

"There are a couple of good import stores —"

"My mother-in-law only uses middlemen she appoints personally.

The village she's been reading about is called Momo —"

"Momostenango. Yeah, that's one of the best weaving villages."

"Could you go there for me, Trev? We'll pay your expenses and a finder's fee. I know you'd do a great job and make my mother-in-law happy."

"I haven't been to Guatemala in years."

"Maybe it would do you good to go back. We'll make it worth your while."

Mergers and acquisitions. Their merger had ended, but he remained her acquisition. Straightening his shoulders, he said, "I always thought you were going to be the person who would make me stop going to Guatemala. I never imagined you paying me to go back again."

Jasmin smiled.

HE RETURNED TO QUETZALTENANGO in a downpour. It was December 10, 2013, the date 13 baktun, 0 katun, 0 tun, 17 winal, 14 k'in. Time's order lay broken. It rained in the dry season, rain falling nonstop at the coldest time of year. The Santa María volcano was invisible. The Mayan farmers on the hillsides above the city — those who still had land — faced hunger as their crops washed away, along with the immemorial order of their calendars. Trevor got out of the tourist minivan from Antigua next to the park and sat down beneath the Roman pillars. He wheezed with fever. A decade's absence had drained his body of its Guatemalan immunities. Having allowed his vaccinations to lapse, he had renewed them all at once. His body ached, he was popping immodium to keep his bowels under control, his stomach felt bloated, his breath short, his head throbbed from the altitude. Remembering an eclipse he had watched from this park, he wondered whether he had the strength to carry his backpack up the slope of Avenida 12.

The climb exhausted him, reminding him that he was fifty-one. Would Don Miguel and Doña Bendición remember him? In his feverish weakness all he wanted was a bed. He crossed the street and went in the door. Instead of opening into the wood-panelled lobby, the steps funnelled him up a narrow staircase to a landing at the top. He was on the third floor, but it was not the third floor he recalled; a wall ran through it. A tired young woman and an adolescent girl sat behind a makeshift counter. He asked for a room and was shown a box where the single bed occupied most of the floor space. The carpet had been clawed away in patches and a film of brown water covered the bathroom floor.

"No?" the woman said, as he stared at the sight in confusion. "Gringos don't stay here."

"I remember when lots of gringos stayed here."

She snorted and turned away.

He stumbled towards the stairs, hesitating as he felt the woman peer after him. He walked down the narrow staircase and out onto the street. Crossing to the opposite sidewalk to get a better look, he saw that the Hotel Río Azul sign had moved. What used to be the main entrance was blocked off. The building looked dilapidated. He stumbled down the hill to the park, spotted two blond young people and trailed them to a new hotel called The Black Cat. He went in the door and asked for a room. Without thinking, he asked in Spanish. The ponytailed receptionist struggled to reply, then switched to Australian English. "It's chockablock, mate," he said, "but if you're up to sharing with another bloke we might squeeze you in."

He shared a room with an aging hippie from Washington State. "The Guatemala I know is gone," Trevor muttered.

"I hear you, man."

They went downstairs to the restaurant. The menu, in English only, featured pizza and chicken wings, hamburgers and huge salads. Trevor, wary of his stomach, ordered ginger ale and garlic bread. They sat at a table with half a dozen travellers from different countries who chatted in English. They had all come up from Antigua in tourist shuttles. They rode from one English-speaking hotel to another in transportation restricted to foreigners by U.S. dollar ticket pricing. None of them spoke Spanish; none of them knew that Guatemala had suffered thirty-six years of civil war or wondered why there were Roman pillars in the park. Events impressed them as spectacles, not as cause-and-effect along a strand of time. As he made a faltering attempt to tell the girl on his left about the civil war only to see her glance flicker away in boredom, he felt as despairing as the Maya he had glimpsed along the edges of the enlarged, four-lane Pan-American Highway trying to flag down buses that no longer stopped to pick them up.

After supper he paid to use one of the computers in the lobby. Calling up Rhea's email address, he wrote: I'm back in Xela. You and I shared more than we realized ...

He sent the message, knowing it was foolish. He read his other messages and answered some of them.

His breath cut short; Rhea had replied.

He clicked on her message: *Rhea ya no usa esta dirección. Guadelupe.* ("Rhea no longer uses this address. Guadelupe.")

What the hell did that mean? He typed: *¿Rhea todavía vive en Tabasco?* ("Does Rhea still live in Tabasco?")

He waited for a reply. At last one came: *Se fue.* ("She went away.")

He typed: *¿Adónde fue?* ("Where did she go?")

Quién sabe. ("Who knows.")

He sent three more messages without receiving a reply. He woke in the morning feeling healthier, though not five hundred times better, or fit enough to make the trip to Momostenango. Needing to talk to someone, he left the hippie snoring beneath a black eye mask, stepped out of The Black Cat and crossed the park. He found his way through back streets to a small door. He thought it was the right door, even though the gaudy, digital-looking logo overhead was unfamiliar. He stepped inside to find a reception desk. "I'd like to talk to Compañero Tino."

Giving him an odd look, the woman at the desk asked him to wait. He stood listening to a soundtrack of Mexican norteño music and *pop-en-español* ballads. After a few minutes a light-boned young man who wore a white dress shirt and a dark jacket came to the desk. He introduced himself as Oliverio Morales. "You asked for my father?" When Trevor nodded, he said, "My father is deceased."

"My most sincere condolences. I knew him a long time ago. Was it sudden?"

The young man looked uncomfortable. He opened the counter and led Trevor to a back room. "What's your name, *señor?*"

"Your father called me Compañero Clover." This was the room where Tino had interviewed him. The walls had been re-plastered and whitewashed; red tiles covered the floor. The same logo that hung over the front door blazed from between speakers on the wall.

"My father's life ended because of his drinking. He suffered badly during the internal armed conflict." Oliverio paused. "After he died I bought out the other members of the cooperative, then sold the station to this company from Miami" — he waved at the logo — "and they hired me back as manager." An elusive smile. "Of course the content had to change."

"But you cover local news? I used to stay in the Hotel Río Azul —"

Oliverio looked disconcerted. "That was a great tragedy. Five years ago Don Miguel and Doña Bendición were coming back from a shopping trip to the capital. They died in an accident on the Pan-American Highway. The children began to fight, María —"

María. The woman who had shown him the room had been María. "But they were all adopted from the same village."

"I see you know the family. And, though you are too polite to say so, I'm sure you know it's the same village my father came from."

"A village that was destroyed —"

"Joining the guerrillas at eleven saved my father's life. If he had been there during the events that followed, he would have been killed. Only very young children were spared. Like María. We're cousins. But Alberto and the younger sister were the children of one of the soldiers who killed my father's father —"

"Who were orphaned when your father and his *compañeros* executed the soldiers."

Oliverio winced at the verb *ajusticiar*. "Please excuse me, Compañero Clover, but nobody talks like that now." He caught his breath. "You know that when my father killed the soldiers who murdered my grandfather, he left the bodies on the riverbank where the whole village would see them? It is difficult for me to accept some of the things my father did." He shook his head. "When the children were growing up, they thought they were victims of the same tragedy. But in recent years, with all these people dragging out the details of this history, they learned that they came from families that had killed each other. When the parents died, María and Alberto got lawyers and the hotel was divided. History taught them hatred. That's why your hotel is falling to pieces."

"You hold history responsible for that?"

"That's why I was happy to get rid of the political programming." Oliverio leaned back in his chair, mouthing the words of love that sighed from the broadcast booth. "I'm finished with history and so are you. All you'll learn here is that love lasts forever."

⌒

"I KNEW YOU WOULD come back," María said the next night, when he walked into the Hotel Río Azul. All day he had roamed through the city, then the park, in dwindling circles that encompassed markets and shops, *huipiles* and school uniforms, bursts of Quiché and pseudo-classical architecture. A cold drizzle fell. He fortified himself with two Gallo beers before climbing Avenida 12, where the hotel's front walls were splashed with political graffiti he was too out of touch to understand. When he emerged onto the partitioned landing that served as a reception area, María stood alone behind the desk. She wore a baggy hooded sweatshirt that was too large for her. "You remember me, don't you?"

"I didn't recognize you the other night," he said, insisting on the formal *usted* even though she had addressed him as *tú*. "My most sincere condolences on the loss of your parents. They were an important part of my life."

"We haven't seen you in years," she said, in a strange hankering tone that made him wonder how old she was. Almost thirty? Was it possible that María was almost thirty? And that Rhea was thirty, too? As he regarded her with the curiosity owed to the last surviving thread of a vital seam of his life, she said, "I'm glad you remember my parents fondly. I no longer know what to think of them. They gave me a good life when I was a child. I was their beloved daughter until I got pregnant. Then I became a lascivious Indian who was unable to control her desires. They favoured Alberto, I knew he'd get the hotel, even before we learned we weren't brother and sister."

"You got part of the hotel."

"He got more of it. We're both in debt to lawyers and he's doing as badly as I am. The people who used to stay here — backpackers, decent, modest Guatemalans — those people don't exist anymore. All I get are drunks and whores. The people who travel now are rich. They want luxury hotels. The gringos want everybody to speak English. In a year or two Alberto and I will both be out of business."

She stepped out from behind the counter. He watched her lank, shiny-black hair spill over the thrust-back hood as she stepped past him and closed and bolted the door at the top of the stairs. She returned — she looked a foot shorter than he — took his hand and said, "When I was a little girl I used to listen to you talking about your fiancée in Canada and I dreamed that someday a man would make me his fiancée. Maybe even take me north." She led him down a hall, pulled a clutch of keys out of the pouch at the front of her hoodie and opened a door. They entered a windowless room where muted light filtered through a glass transom.

"Why didn't you show me this room the other night?" he said. "I would have taken it."

"I didn't recognize you. These days too many gringos with backpacks look around here then go to The Black Cat. I thought, 'Well, fuck him. If he's not going to stay here anyway, I'll show him a really terrible room.'"

They sat down on the right-hand bed in the gloom. "The time you came here with that girl —"

"Your daughter was already born then, wasn't she?" he murmured, yielding by addressing her as *tú*.

"Yes, I knew then that no man would marry me in church because I already had a child. And I knew that girl wasn't your fiancée. You confirmed for me the way the world really was. That men who had fiancées went to hotels with young girls."

"It was more complicated than that."

"Yes, it is always complicated, isn't it? If my mother were still alive she might not welcome you back."

He heard their breathing in the near-darkness. She had brought him to the room he had shared with Rhea. Or a room that was identical. It was shabby now, but less decayed than the room she had shown him two nights ago. The silence went on until María said, "I'll welcome you, if you like."

She reached up to kiss him. He closed his arms around her, feeling wrapped in her strong scent. He was aware of the rank milkiness of his own odour. Was she persuading herself that she was possessing the shining gringo of her teenage fantasies? He slid his hands down the brief space of her back. This was the second time he had caressed a woman's back on this bed, the third time he had shared a room at the Hotel Río Azul with a woman. As María stood up, slid her hoodie over her head, then shucked off her T-shirt and unhooked her bra, he thought that this would be the first time he had had sex with a woman in this room. He rolled alongside her onto the narrow bed, hauling her against his cushioned gut. "I'm glad you came back," she said. "These days the only men who are interested in me are men I don't want."

He slid his tongue over the tiny dents inside her collar bones. As he took her small, firm breasts in his mouth, his libido cranked up, his body stumbling in its wake. The headache from his cold, the immodium plug in his bowels, his queasy stomach, and unsteady breathing warned that his flesh was his antagonist. The torpor in his veins stoked moral qualms. As true as it might be, at a submerged level, that each of them was delving for compensation for emotional losses, that she as much as he would be gratified by their encounter, at a more blatant level he was a tall white man who was about to take advantage of a small Mayan woman, re-enacting a pattern of exploitation that had been recurring in Guatemala for five hundred years. Even as they kissed and he felt drawn into her body, his mind tripped on the assumption that his privileges were a match for her easy availability. Racial assumptions such as these underlaid the atrocities that had dispatched María from her village.

He fell back on the bed, almost nudging her onto the floor. "You're very beautiful, María, but I'm an old man now. *Ya soy viejito*. It's better if I keep my clothes on."

"Don't you want me?"

"Of course. But I don't think it would be right."

"You can't do it because you're thinking about that girl. She's here in the room with us."

"Then why did you bring me to the same room?"

As María's distrustful eyes observed him across the pillow, he wondered how she had known that this was the room he and Rhea had shared. She couldn't have remembered from all those years ago! Yet, he was almost certain this was the room. The thought released an access of tenderness towards her; they embraced like two survivors from a disaster. "Where's your daughter?"

"Playing video games in her room."

"Her life will be better. Now that the war's over —"

"The war is not over!" María sat up fiercely, as though unaware that the top half of her body was naked. "Never let anyone tell you the war in Guatemala is over. If the war had not happened, I would live in a village and I would speak Quiché. My village would exist, I would have my culture ... all these people floating around like bees in the cities, bees who cannot return to their hives, who cannot return to the village and are not accepted in the city because they have the faces of *indios*, who cannot be city people and cannot be peasants — that is the war continuing!" As she ran out of breath, he thought of Compañero Tino's son, of her former brother Alberto. "It is the same for my daughter. She belongs nowhere. That is the war continuing."

María slid off the bed. She put on her bra, т-shirt, and hoodie. "I will accompany you ..."

"I'm sorry, María." The words had never felt so inadequate. The apology required by María, by the hotel, by the country, was of cosmic proportions.

They stepped into the corridor. He had shared a room at the Hotel Río Azul with a woman for the last time.

They entered the partitioned-off lobby. She unlocked the door to the staircase. "You know she came back."

"Who?"

"Your girlfriend."

"She came *here*? To this hotel?" The thin air made him faint. "When?"

"Two weeks ago. She looked at lots of rooms before deciding where to stay. That's why I remembered ... she talks like a Mexican now," she said with a laugh. "On the day she left, she asked me if you still stayed here."

"Did she say where she was going?"

María stepped behind the desk and opened the large, hand-written register he remembered from her parents' time. She flipped through pages and pointed out a line with Rhea's name. In the register her *procedencia* and her *destino* were both entered as *México*. His wrist trembled as he took María's hand. Leaning over, he kissed her on the cheek like a brother or a cousin. He held her for a moment, then let her go and walked back to The Black Cat. Tomorrow he would go to Momostenango to bargain with the weavers. Once he had shipped Jasmin her purchases, he would cancel his flight home and get a bus to Mexico.

5

TERMS OF SURRENDER

THE CHIEF OF THE president's security staff left the palace for lunch. He crossed the square in the heat, ignoring the vendors waving limp reels of lottery tickets. Motionless men in baseball caps, Indians from the highlands, leaned back into the slender noonday shadow hugging the base of the statue. The conquistador reared above them on horseback, the letters of his name eroded by the elements. The fortune teller sitting at her wooden table with the hand-printed cardboard sign was exploring a man's palm. "You can remember clearly ..."

The heat spread across the shoulders of the security chief's black suit jacket. Passing the steps of the cathedral in front of old women in headscarves sitting listless in the sunlight, he enjoyed the warmth. Beneath his jacket, the grip of his shoulder holster supported the weight of his 50-calibre magnum Desert Eagle.

For fifteen years he had laid hands on Israeli pistols only when he stripped the bodies of government soldiers. In those days he was a legend, Comandante Ezequial, Commander of the Southern Front for the Guerrilla Army of the Oppressed. He had spent fifteen years in mountains and jungle, sleeping rough, eating rice and beans twice a day and nothing more, too famous to risk treading the militarized streets of the capital.

He entered the Central Zone, where pedestrians either shuffled single file through the channel of shadow separating the storefronts from the stalls built on the sidewalks in front of them, or took their chances in the street among the gusts of diesel fumes from packed American school buses. The smell of roast corn mingled with the blare from car-roof loudspeakers announcing sales and religious revival meetings. When, after the peace deal brokered by the Norwegians, he had joined the president's security team as part of the "integration of government and rebel forces" stipulated by the terms of surrender, the front page of every newspaper had displayed Ezequial's photograph. (Where were his *compañeros* today? Back in the villages they had come from, poorer than they were before they picked up arms.)

The newspaper photos had shown him with shoulder-length hair, a beret, a tuft of beard floating above the open neck of his combat fatigues. When he came down from the hills thousands poured into the streets to acclaim him. Now he was invisible, one more figure leaving the presidential palace in close-cropped hair, wraparound sunglasses, and a black suit. His only distinguishing feature was the size of the bulge in his shoulder holster. He had held out for a more powerful sidearm than those carried by his staff.

No one looked at him for more than a second when he entered the restaurant. His suit struck a note of quiet respect among the truck drivers, lottery-ticket salesmen, and backstreet muggers who came in for lunch. He ordered the special: a spicy highland soup, followed by rice, black beans, a roast chicken leg, and a Coca-Cola. It cost twelve pesos; the same food, on china plates, cost ten times the price in the casinos on the edge of town where his men gambled away their U.S.-dollar salaries. He sat facing the open door, his back to the room. He shooed away the street children who loitered before his table — was that the only homage a suit earned him?

Outside the door, the beggar swished his stump at the people peering at the newspapers piled next to his hips.

If he told the bypassers that he had been Comandante Ezequial they might not believe him. A few years from now, Ezequial would be forgotten. Only a man in a suit would remain. He chewed his black beans, hating the crowd's dull eyes.

The fortune teller came into the restaurant, ordered the special and sat down in the corner.

The security chief got to his feet. "Boss," he said to the owner. "Hey, boss!"

Stirring beans in a pot, the owner kept his head lowered. The security chief slid his hand along the seam of his jacket, peeling back the collar in a nonchalant gesture that exposed the Desert Eagle. He could hear the hush, see the muggers' eyes gazing at him.

"Yes ...?" the owner said.

"A beer," the security chief said. "Good and cold!"

"Yes, sir."

The owner brought him a beer in a paper cup. The chief sat down with his back to the room and inhaled the hot breath of diesel, corn, and black beans. He heard chairs being pushed back behind him. A rim of metal touched his temple and cancelled out memory.

⁓

THE MUGGERS' SOUP STEAMED on their abandoned table. The runt of a man on the right kept the tip of his 22-calibre pistol pressed against the rich man's temple after he had pulled the trigger. The engine of a souped-up school bus passing in the street outside almost covered the sound of the shot. The body fell in the direction of the other man, who stopped the black worsted shoulder with his knee. He reached into the jacket and pulled out his trophy.

The two men hurried into the street. For a second they stood in the sunlight, startling the women in wide skirts, the vendors and beggars and street children, as they held up the biggest pistol anyone had seen. The tiny man smiled at the crowd's fearful gaze. The fortune teller avoided his eyes. While the beggar stared, a boy stole a newspaper from his pile and threw it into the street. When the secret service agents arrived no one remembered their faces.

6

DODGING THE BULLET

THE FIRST TIME WE argued Leslie told me that at nineteen, in a riot
in Guatemala City, she had dodged a bullet.

She was a young contract instructor in charge of a huge class.
I was sent to give a guest lecture. When we introduced ourselves,
our courtesies produced instant conflict. We moved away from the
microphone to argue. The bullet came up in the argument. It was
years before I heard the beginning of the story: at eighteen, as the
first buds of her Latin American fascination were sprouting, she
had joined a church mission to build daycare centres in northern
Nicaragua. It was the last summer of the Sandinista Revolution.
In the cool highland air of Jinotega, where the morning mist took
half a day to burn off and the summer rains turned the roads to
mud-sluices, Leslie got her first taste of community organizing.
The miracle of people realizing their own strength won her over.
She learned Spanish, as an almost unconscious consequence of
her work, and she learned that it was easier to have a boyfriend
when she was on her own in Central America than when she was
the Lutheran minister's daughter in a town in the British Columbia

interior. She planned to return to Jinotega the next summer, but in February the Nicaraguan elections produced a result no one had expected, quashing the revolution. Guatemala beckoned: the generals held power; there was a struggle to be joined.

I heard this part years later, in a café in Antigua Guatemala. I was working in the cobblestoned colonial town beneath the volcanoes, supervising a semester abroad for Canadian students. Leslie passed through on a research trip with her husband. That morning she and I had gone into the market together. Leslie showed up with an enormous Nikon camera and a case full of lenses. As we wandered through the indoor market she pointed her lens straight into the faces of Mayan women in *huipiles*, peasant men and little boys, snapping photos without mercy. I had expected her to photograph the sapodilla fruit and the tethered chickens and the cones of the volcanoes, but it was the people's faces that fascinated her. The Guatemalans made no objection. Leslie would smile and exchange a few words with them, and in a second the Maya saw her not as an arrogant tourist, but as a friend. That afternoon, as we sat at a café table, I told her that I envied her gift. She replied, "So you've been here for eight weeks and your girlfriend hasn't visited you. What's going on? Are you breaking up?"

"No, she's just got a lot of work."

"Oh, come on."

"You know what she's like, Leslie. Unlike most people, when she says she's too busy to see me, it's because she really is too busy to see me. She's writing grant applications, she's presenting at four conferences —"

Leslie advanced her mug of highland coffee across the table like a rook in a chess game. "Tell her that if she doesn't visit you soon, I'm giving you permission to go out with a Guatemalan woman. You'd like having a Guatemalan girlfriend. I had a Guatemalan boyfriend."

"You told me that the first time we met."

"I bet I never told you how I dodged a bullet with him."

The bullet, in fact, had been mentioned. I had wheeled into

the classroom with the brusqueness of the tenured professor for whom a guest lecture was an obligation to be dispatched with curt superiority. All I knew about the course instructor was that she was a young woman whose husband had been imported from England as a research superstar; the university's concession to the multiple six-figure grants he brought with him had been to give his partner a one-year contract. Such people didn't get much respect, as the assumption was that they earned their jobs on the basis of whose bed they shared.

"Leslie Engel," she said, shaking my hand.

"Engels as in Marx and Engels?"

"Without the *s*. Similar ideology, but I'm going to be more famous."

"How can you be more famous than Engels?" I set down my briefcase next to the podium, then moved away from the microphone so that the students wouldn't hear us. "Engels was able to seduce women in twenty languages. What can you do?"

"I can dodge bullets. When I was nineteen, the Guatemalan army opened fire on me, and I dodged a bullet. That was when I knew I had magical powers."

Having come to talk about national identity, not magic realism, I returned to the microphone to face the students. Our spat laid the foundations of a friendship. I was a notorious scourge, my frank tongue a source of scandal on this polite southern Ontario campus that sought "synergies" and discouraged debate. I respected people who stood up to me; Leslie would stand up to anyone. Within two years she had emerged from her husband's shadow, obtained a tenure-track appointment, and begun collecting six-figure grants of her own. Having cut her russet hair short and exchanged her proletarian glasses for natty, electric-blue frames, she became half of a power couple. She and her husband lived on planes. He would reschedule his lectures, spend the first four days of the week in Ghana or Pakistan, return late Thursday night, teach all day on Friday, and on Sunday they would leave for other continents. She went to Latin America, he went to Africa and South Asia; they caught the same flights to conferences in England and the United States, and consulting contracts in the Caribbean. When I got together with my partner, Leslie and her husband invited us to their New Year's party. We danced all night between the living room's twin CD towers: hers with norteños, salsa, Lila Downs, Silvio Rodríguez, and Peruvian panpipes; his with Miriam Makeba, semba, kizomba, zouk, Cape jazz, and Youssou N'Dour. I had never seen my partner, a nose-to-the-grindstone post-doc who had clawed her way up out of poverty and parental abandonment and was wary of anyone who had been born with privileges, let down her guard as she did with them.

"Tell me how you dodged the bullet," I said to Leslie, looking out at the cobblestoned street.

Her exchange program had lodged her with a family in a lower-middle-class district of Guatemala City's Zone Three. She took classes at San Carlos, the public university where proletarian kids analyzed their oppression, the university from which a trickle of students fled into the mountains to become guerrillas; the campus whose every progressive professor of the 1970s and 1980s had been taken away by the army at four in the morning and found naked in a garbage dump, missing his fingernails, with a dozen bullets in his body and his testicles sewn into his mouth.

The civil war was winding down when Leslie arrived at San Carlos, but marches continued. At her first march, Leslie found a boyfriend. Her description of his heavy chest, brown eyes, and wavy black hair made me realize that this had been a more passionate relationship than her fling with a fellow aid worker in Nicaragua. Perhaps the purpose of this description was to set the scene; perhaps it was to impress upon me the relationship's seriousness. Her husband, who was sitting next to her, didn't blink; to live with Leslie was to assume brutal frankness as a norm.

The government was threatening to militarize the campus. The students were demanding freedom of expression, freedom to unionize. Their placards were spangled with hammers and sickles, and acronyms of guerrilla organizations; indigenous rights protesters mingled with the students. They gathered beneath the barrack-like three-storey modern buildings of the downtown Guatemala City campus and marched past walls blurred red with militant murals. Singing and pounding their feet, they stamped up to the short soldiers in their helmets and their green uniforms who cradled their Galils at their waists. Leslie grew breathless in the thin, pollution-laden air of the highland capital. Her throat constricted, yet as long as she kept moving, she knew she would be all right.

The soldiers were boys from villages who had been press-ganged into the army. They despised the big-city students for their running shoes and their watches, disdained the girls for their emancipation and envied the boys their girlfriends. They were intimidated by the slogans, confused that people who had better lives than theirs could side with the *subversivos*. Fifteen years later, Leslie was still struggling to understand where the hatred in the boys' eyes came from. The students shouted at the military to leave the campus. The soldiers remained rigid, did not budge, then from beneath his helmet one of them said, "Fuck off, you fucking Communist. Go to Russia with your whore of a mother." The students howled, arms beat against the air. Was a rock thrown or did the soldiers charge first? After they charged, students at the back began throwing stones and Gallo beer bottles. A bottle shattered on a soldier's helmet. Breaking formation, the soldiers ran in all directions across the square, chasing down students, grabbing them and beating them over the head with their truncheons. Three students lined up with an arsenal of Gallo bottles and unleashed a wave of glass at four soldiers who were slugging a girl's shoulders and head as they dragged her to the ground. One of the soldiers looked up, received a bottle in the face and keeled over backwards, his helmeted head clanging against the concrete. Faster than she could have believed possible, Leslie saw two of the fallen soldier's accomplices slide their truncheons into their belts, pivot in their boots and swing their compact Galil carbines to their shoulders. A bottle smashed into a black barrel.

The soldiers opened fire.

Leslie was retreating across the square with her boyfriend, resisting breaking into a run because she didn't want to abandon the girl on the ground. After the first two soldiers opened fire, spraying bullets in the direction of the university buildings, others lifted their Galils. A soldier she hadn't noticed, off to her side, swung around and glared at her over the short black barrel of his gun. Her boyfriend uttered a jeer.

The soldier squeezed the trigger.

Already shuffling sideways, beginning to run along the wall of the building, Leslie saw the bullet coming.

"You can't see a bullet," I said.

"I saw the line, the trajectory ..."

Running too fast to stop, she writhed into a shoulder-ducking turn that lashed her ponytail across her neck. She threw herself against the wall at the corner of the building. The bullet seared the shoulder of her blouse and hummed away into space as though pursuing a trajectory that would follow her for eternity. If she hadn't put on the brakes, if she hadn't twisted her shoulder, she would have been hit. Her boyfriend grabbed her wrist. They rushed around the end of the building and kept running until they were far from the campus.

"Later, when I realized I had dodged a bullet, I knew that I would be safe as long as I kept running." She laughed. "As long as that bullet never catches up with me."

"What happened to the boyfriend?" I asked, deciding to make her feel as uncomfortable as she had made me.

"That was hard. We were very young, but it was a real relationship. I thought about bringing him to B.C., but as soon as I got back there, I realized it was impossible. All I could do was get him out my system. Fortunately, my sister had a boyfriend."

She gave me one of her challenging smiles, revelling in withholding the story, and forgetting that I already knew it. At the New Year's party, Leslie had asked my partner whether she kept a diary. My partner shook her head. Leslie told her she was smart because when she was young she had left her diary on her bedside table. Her sister had picked it up and found out that Leslie had slept with her boyfriend.

"Do you know what he's doing now?" I said.

"He's a union organizer. He's a good guy."

"We should move along," her husband said, "if you want to reserve tickets to Lake Atitlán."

The husband was the culmination of the blur of speed that had enveloped her on the day that she dodged the bullet. How had she crammed in so much living prior to academia? Her return to B.C. after Guatemala had been brief. Unable to resist Latin America, she was soon in southern Mexico. At the next New Year's party, where everyone drank too much, she confessed that she had lived in Puebla for six years.

"Six years! What were you doing there?"

"I was married."

That was all she would say, even after a few drinks. Leslie spoke for hours about Mexican painting and pottery and warm, welcoming families and Zapotec religion and the role of Mexican mothers in offsetting *machismo* and the structures of Mexican trade unions and the pleasures of eating *picadillos* and *garnachas* and the Náhuat words that had crept into Mexican Spanish, making a turkey — *pavo*, in regular Spanish — into a *guajolote*. Her living room was draped in weaving from the markets of Oaxaca and Chiapas. Stumbling to the bathroom at one of the New Year's parties, I came face to face with a round-headed Olmec statue dominating an upstairs hall like a Buddha of the Americas. Leslie's Mexican husband was the black hole at the core of this universe. Had she really been married for six years? Hadn't she completed a B.A. and M.A. in Vancouver? Everyone has a core contradiction where the most intimate features of their personality misfire. Leslie's first husband was the subject that quelled her frankness, making her cautious and reticent. When the marriage had ended, she had fled to an unknown continent, becoming a doctoral student in sociology at a red-brick university in the English Midlands. The man we knew as her husband was a young British academic with an effortless gift for accumulating research trips, grants, and publications. A colleague had told him of the arrival of an impressive Canadian doctoral candidate. He had knocked on her office door assuming that "Leslie" was a young man. She cooked him *garnachas* drenched in pork grease, which he ate with her on two consecutive weekends before confessing that he was a vegetarian; he introduced her to hot cross buns thickly spread with marmite. Like many Englishmen educated at boarding schools, he seemed uncertain what to do about the fact that she was a woman. He kept returning for conversations about Africa and Latin America. He was tall and dramatic and sometimes scornful. One Saturday she said to him, "The problem with your analyses is that you miss the gender dimension." When he asked, in an outraged voice, what gender dimension she was referring to, she replied, "This, for example," and stepped towards him to seal their relationship.

When she asked him to look for jobs in her home country, our university made the best offer; she resigned herself to not returning to British Columbia. Once she became tenure-track, our boon years began. Every Friday night, the development profs and grad students met at a long table at the East African Asian restaurant in the nineteenth-century limestone downtown. Naive paintings of African families hung on the walls; the menu was curries accompanied by *mshikaki* and *ugali*. There was money in the university system for grants and new hires, and optimism that graduate students would get good jobs. Leslie's husband would talk about dockers he had visited in India, or an agricultural cooperative that had welcomed him to Burundi. There was a tall, burly man who worked in Vietnam who was married to a tall, thin woman who worked in Colombia. I didn't always join them. Sometimes I was too busy or too depressed, or was away on trips of my own. But when I felt uncomfortable walking alone downtown on a Friday night, as my students tripped past in drunken packs, yelling, "Hey, I'm in your class!" I had somewhere to go. Even after I got together with my partner, I was often alone as she put in long nights at the lab. Later, she began consulting in Japan. She never did find a free week to visit me during my five months in Guatemala.

One Friday afternoon, Leslie phoned to ask me to accompany her to one of the towns on the Lake Erie shore. Her husband was in Tanzania and she couldn't go alone. We drove south past fields of tobacco and ginseng, stopping in a small Scottish-Canadian hamlet of red-brick houses where the deserted main street was dominated by the United Church of Canada and a statue of a Loyalist; in the glimmering sunlight nothing moved until the stroke of five p.m., when a torrent of dark-skinned young men who brought their paycheques in from the fields poured down the main street. In a second we were out of the car. Leslie was working the crowd, not interviewing men so much as befriending them, her friendliness socially acceptable since she had a male escort. I nodded, shook hands and murmured formal greetings in Spanish as Leslie wrote down names and states of origin in southern Mexico. We followed the crowd to a bar on the edge of town that served Corona and Dos Equis to snare the migrant labour trade, discussing how many workers shared each toilet in their dormitories, whether Mexican food was available in the village, how many children back in Mexico each man was supporting, how they had been recruited for the temporary workers' visa program. The workers were courteous, reticent men. A tobacco smell came off their hands: not the rank stench of cigarettes, but a more resinous, alluring fragrance. I watched Leslie darting from one man to the next, collecting contact details and lining up interviews, zigzagging across the bar as though bullets were stitching through the gloom. Sometimes she would pause, and enter into a long, murmured conversation about the characteristics of a village or a region, or the difficulty of being away from a wife. We returned to town just in time for dinner with the tall couple and their graduate students.

The drive back from Lake Erie was smooth. After that, the bumps began. Money drained out of the system: colleagues who retired weren't replaced, class sizes ballooned, my department was cut, semesters in developing countries were vetoed by administrators uttering nervous palaver about liability, students who graduated with doctorates were relegated to teaching English in South Korea. Leslie and her husband, like the tall couple, kept their grants, but the mood was less ebullient, travel less freewheeling. Narco violence made swaths of Mexico and Central America too dangerous for research; religious violence put the Middle East off limits. One afternoon my partner came home after weeks in Japan and pushed me into the bedroom of my condo to make love in her concentrated, quality-time way that exalted me yet left me feeling that I wanted something that I could not have. We got up in the cool of the evening. Holding hands, we meandered downtown to the East African Asian restaurant. We didn't sit down, signalling that we had our own plans for the evening and were simply stopping by to say hello. My partner leaned over Leslie's chair and said, "Hey, what's that bump?"

I hadn't told her the news. Leslie smiled. "A few weeks ago, I said, 'Dear, there are only two of us here and we have a five-bedroom house. Why don't you step over here?'"

In a few months the bump became a little girl; eighteen months later a little boy followed. Leslie and her husband withdrew from evenings at the restaurant. One evening the next summer, I arrived on a Friday to find the man who did research in Vietnam standing in the doorway, looking around, as I was, for a group of people who weren't there. We sat down at a table for two and ate dinner together as awkwardly as a couple paired up by a dating agency. As we each kept an eye out for late arrivals, he told me about Vietnamese government policy towards bees. A few weeks later images of hovering, yellow-jacketed orbs circled in my brain when I heard that he had found a small bump in his stomach, like a bullet stitched under the skin. His doctor had dismissed the irregularity as trapped fluids that would disperse spontaneously. Yet, the bump grew bigger. By the time he found a doctor who took the protrusion seriously, it was inoperable; they would have to do chemotherapy to shrink it before it could be removed.

Our dinner together was the last time I saw him. Five months later he was dead.

After that, there were no more Friday nights eating curry and *mshikaki*. The roads we rushed over grew rougher, as though intimating to us that beyond the highways of far-off continents, a lethal bump lay in wait for each of us. After her partner's death, the woman who did research in Colombia abandoned a country that was overcoming civil strife and dived into others where violence was at its peak, spending weeks among the buzzing bullets of Honduras and Venezuela. The grad students spent less time with us now that we had lost our power to get them jobs. My partner stayed away for so long that, without consulting Leslie, I took the advice she had given me in Guatemala and went out with a Latin American woman. If infidelity was my way of extricating myself from my relationship, it didn't work. My partner did not dump me, did not even get angry. She sat down at my kitchen table and said, "I think it's time for us to move in together so stuff like this doesn't happen."

Our lives were stumbling improvisation. Only Leslie and her family lived according to plan. Younger than the rest of us, they gleamed with energy. Flush with the benefits of two full-professor salaries, bolstered by consulting fees, their travel covered by inexhaustible grants, they were everywhere: in Nairobi on contract to the Kenyan government; in Alberta and British Columbia interviewing the latest wave of temporary-visa workers; in Ottawa, testifying to a parliamentary committee; in Washington to give a seminar for Members of Congress; in Chile with their children on vacation;

squeezing visits to both Vancouver and the English Midlands into every school break so that their children would know both sets of grandparents; on all the important committees at the university; and in the park with their children each time I went out for a jog from the downtown limestone bungalow my partner and I had bought. Pushing her son in his stroller, with her daughter ambling beside her, Leslie said, "Next summer I want to make a long, slow trip from Mexico City to Guatemala City and visit all my favourite places along the way. You should meet up with us."

Breathless, I shouted over my shoulder: "I'll meet you in northern Guatemala!"

Her smile was a challenge, defying me to keep my word.

The next bump must have been there that day, undetected in the spring air. Leslie and her husband dropped out of sight. Leslie was off for the semester. News filtered back from the tall woman: yes, it was cancer, but not the worst kind. Cancer of the soft cells; in other words, of the bum.

"Cancer!" I said. "But Leslie's the healthiest, most vegetarian ..."

"Too much sitting on her bum in planes," my partner decreed.

"Lots of people sit on their bums in planes," I said. "I can think of someone who keeps going to Japan."

It was a cancer that was treatable. Where other women contracted ovarian cancer or breast cancer, and died of it, Leslie's cancer, like a wayward projectile, had struck her in a ridiculous, anodyne part of her body. She had dodged the bullet.

Yet, cancer was cancer, even when it wasn't the most serious type. To show her disrespect for the disease, Leslie went in for chemotherapy dressed in the suit in which she had presented to the U.S. Congress, wearing lipstick and high heels, with her hair freshly coiffed. The depressed people in the waiting room, lounging in their baggy sweats, stared at her. The first round of chemotherapy gave her pneumonia. She was hospitalized for eighteen days. Her husband continued to teach a full course load. He spent hours at her bedside, yet each lecture was letter perfect and two new articles appeared. It was all too much for me. I wanted to get in touch, but was afraid they didn't want to hear from me; I felt too inadequate — emotionally, academically, in my understanding of serious illness — to be relevant to them. I was mired in list-lessness, stuck in a provincial university that no longer attracted good students or gave me intellectual stimulation. Leslie and her husband had granted me vicarious membership in an Olympian inner circle to which the half-a-dozen respectable, but unoriginal, research articles that had got me tenure more than a decade earlier had not earned me inclusion. What could I offer my friends in their time of need? I kept to myself — on campus, in town, and in the bungalow.

"You could pay me a little more attention," my partner said. "We have a spare bedroom. We could have a child."

"You know who else said that? You're imitating her, aren't you?"

"I figure it might get us out of this rut."

"But what if we get ill? Leslie thought she had decades left to give her children …"

"She'll be fine. Everything always turns out fine for those people."

"They're not your enemies," I said.

Two months later, in the organic grocery store in the little plaza downtown where professors shopped, I met Leslie's husband. "Have you heard?" he asked, his eyes opening wide behind his glasses, his hands milling as though resisting the temptation to tug at the new shoots of grey at his temples. "Leslie's better. Her last examina-tion … they declared her completely free of cancer. It's a miracle!"

She had dodged the bullet.

I burbled inadequate words. I half-expected our boon years to return, but Leslie had returned from a region as alien and terri-fying as the Aztec underworld. Before, we had all known similar things about different countries, or sometimes the same countries; now Leslie knew things the rest of us did not know. It made her impatient. Rather than challenging me, she dismissed me as an irritating lightweight; less a gadfly than a mosquito.

I ran into them at a fall country fair to which they had brought their children. Leslie looked pallid in the September sunlight. Her hair was no longer russet, but bright blonde, and so stiff that I wondered whether it was a wig. The children were running in circles with other children. "Do you have any travel plans?"

"We're going to Cancún in a couple of weeks."

"Cancún? What happened to the trip from Mexico City to Guatemala City?"

"It's been a hard summer." She looked me in the eyes.

"I can imagine."

"No, you can't. You really can't imagine it at all."

The children returned in a rush. Neither the Friday evenings at the restaurant nor the New Year's parties returned. My intuition warned me that if I invited them to my house, it wouldn't work out. They might not refuse, but, harried yuppies all, we would never settle on a date that suited everyone. The cancer was gone, but the bumps remained. Feeling time grow short, I stayed home and worked on the book about Nicaragua that I had been promising to finish since the university had hired me. When the book came out, I gave a talk for graduate students in a downtown café. Halfway through, I stared into the shadow, where the lights had been dimmed so that my power point would show up on the screen, and saw two figures appear at the back of the room. When I finished answering questions, I threaded my way through the crowd, reaching Leslie and her husband just as they were leaving.

"I was in Nicaragua during the Sandinista Revolution," Leslie said. "I bet I never told you that."

I looked at her. "I remember."

That fall my partner had started a full-time job at the university: a job that might, if her research generated grant money, convert into one of the few remaining tenure-track jobs. Having curtailed her trips to Japan, she spent longer nights in the lab. When I told her that the fall development party was taking place at a young prof's monster home in a far-flung suburb, she said, "You go. You can take the bus out there, I'll knock off early at the lab and come and pick you up. That way I can say hi to everyone."

I went to the party. I greeted new graduate students and gossiped with colleagues about ignorant deans and corrupt vice-presidents. I drank punch. Listening to the insipid music, I longed for the resources of Leslie and her husband's twin CD towers. At a quarter past ten a text from my partner appeared on my cellphone: *Need more time. U take bus home?*

The tall woman, who had returned to working in Colombia, was edging towards the door. I asked her for a lift downtown. We left the house and climbed into her compact car. "It's too bad Leslie and her husband didn't make it," I said, as we wound along crescents of model-kit houses, each identical to its neighbour.

She was silent.

"How's she doing?" I asked.

"Her cancer's come back." I could hear her holding her voice level. "It's gone to her lungs and metastasized."

"No!" I said. "I can't — Leslie's the healthiest — It's not possible."

"The best she can hope for is to see one or two more years of her children's lives."

"No!"

"That's the way it's going to be. There's nothing you can do about it. That's what I learned when it happened to my partner."

I thought of her powerfully built husband who delighted in camping out for weeks in the Southeast Asian countryside. All the way home I focused on my memories of him to avoid thinking about Leslie.

"You should feel honoured she came to your talk," my colleague said as she dropped me in front of my dark bungalow. "She barely goes out now."

I went into the house and closed the door. I texted my partner to tell her I was going to sleep in the spare room so that she wouldn't wake me up when she came in. I felt a tremendous need to help Leslie and her husband, but I knew that any approach I made would be irritating rather than useful, more about me than about them. Only the tall woman, having been through this before, knew what to do. She spent time with them; I kept my distance. I avoided the do-gooders who made pious references to "Leslie's cancer journey," equating dying from a hideous disease with the trips full of discoveries that had nourished Leslie's twenties and thirties. I overlooked the fact that Leslie's parents had moved to Ontario, that the tall woman had lent them a house she had inherited from her husband to live in for as long as they needed it. I turned away from a colleague in the faculty club who murmured that Leslie's children were in counselling, that they were being encouraged to assemble "memory boxes" about their mother. Months later, when there was talk of the abandonment of chemotherapy, of a blood clot that required a rush to the hospital in an ambulance, of anti-coagulants that dissolved the clot at the cost of opening the lesions on the insides of Leslie's lungs, I walked away from the conversation. To pursue this infinity of ghastly details was pornography. I closed my eyes and tried to focus on the bullet, like people who claimed to dissolve their cancers by visualizing them. Leslie had misread the message from the protest march. She had thought that as long as she kept running she would be safe. Yet the bullet had missed her because she had put on the brakes; not because she had run, but because she had stopped.

Would cutting back on work and trips have saved her? This didn't make sense, either. No explanation made sense because there was no explanation. I tried to learn as little as I could. But Leslie herself insisted that I learn more.

One day I glanced up at my computer screen and there was her name at the top of my email. Her doctor had given her drugs that would make her feel full of energy for a week. Not realizing with whom she was dealing, the doctor had suggested that Leslie treat herself by doing something "a little adventurous."

Leslie got on a plane to Guatemala. By herself.

She had a research pretext: visiting a village that was the place

of origin of Guatemalan workers who were being mistreated in
southern B.C., in a case that she was writing about. But I knew
that wasn't why she was there. *You're dodging the bullet!* I wrote
back. A part of her knew that if she returned to Guatemala and
kept running, she could come to no harm. Though the signature
below her messages confirmed that she was writing from a mobile
device, two hours passed before she replied. I regretted my blunt-
ness, fearing that I had offended her by presuming an intimacy
that no longer existed between us, if it ever had. At last she wrote:
*I saw my host family and my old boyfriend. I went to the village
and now I'm in Antigua and I'm ill. Can you recommend a good
doctor?* I made a few suggestions. Two days later I received an email
from her husband: *All sorted. Leslie's on a flight home.*

Her memorial service was a "celebration of life." Wasn't dying
at forty-four bad enough; did a direct, forthright person also need
to be smothered in insincerity? The crushed-looking professors and
impatient deans and vice-presidents in the crowd were outnum-
bered by representatives of farm workers' unions and mute, sombre
Mexican and Guatemalan families. A Mexican altar had been
placed in the Lutheran church. The workers brought offerings for the
altar, paid their respects in silence, listened to hymns in a language
they barely understood, then rode trucks back to their makeshift
housing in the fields while the academic administrators went downstairs to eat the catered food. The farm workers' anonymity is the
reason that, now that I'm writing this down, I've called no one but
Leslie Engel by name.

I expected Leslie's husband to go back to England after her
death, but he had promised to raise their children in Canada. Now
that we're both alone — he a widower, I separated — I sometimes glimpse him stooped over his laptop in downtown cafés. His
aquiline features have softened, bringing out the face of a middle-
aged Englishman. One day he nodded, inviting me to his table.
In an offhand tone, he told me of Leslie's final moments. Their
daughter woke at dawn and climbed into bed with her mother.

They thought she had a few days left. As he reached out to take Leslie's hand, her body gave a start. She murmured in Spanish and died. He understood that the bullet she had dodged in another time and country had found her at last.

7

WHERE ARE YOU IN AMERICA?

MR. BOOM'S TAXI WAS parked at the curb when Doreen got out of the car from Kingston. His slack-bellied profile hadn't changed; he hollered his destination into the market crowd. His calls enticed a disused way of talking up into Doreen's throat like a custardy sweet sop, but when she told him where she was going and asked when he would be leaving, her patois sweetness came out stiffened by tight-jawed Toronto English. His slow face wrinkled as he mumbled his reply.

She stowed her backpack in the taxi's boot and sat in the front seat next to Mr. Boom. On the drive up from Kingston she had pressed her face against the window, watching the trees that were spotted with red akee fruit towering over the shorter palms and reedy grasses. It reassured her to see tropical and temperate plants tangled up in their haphazard knitting together of climate zones. The driver had overtaken slower cars on curves, flouting the billboards that said: *Undertakers Love Overtakers*. He had pressed down on his silver-studded accelerator until the speedometer needle swung up to 140 kilometres an hour.

Mr. Boom drove at a more sedate pace, making her remember trips into town in Boom's taxi when she was a girl. Four or five people would squeeze into the back seat. She had sat on Mam's knee, cradling the green guava from Auntie Jane's orchard that Mam would dole out as a gift when Doreen complained about travelling into town. She wasn't allowed to eat her guava until they had stepped out of the taxi in the market.

Three women too young for her to have known them as children now slid into the back seat. The driver's seat sighed beneath Mr. Boom's weight. When he turned the key in the ignition the radio came on. Doreen watched the houses growing smaller and poorer as they passed the edge of town, aware that where she used to be able to name the families who lived here, now she saw only their poverty. The BBC World Service announcer summarized a debate in the British Parliament. At a curve in the road a woman as broad as a hillside stood resplendent in a shimmering blue dress.

"Auntie Jane!" Mr. Boom called out the window. "How far you goin', Auntie Jane?"

Not here, Doreen thought. But Auntie Jane did not hesitate. She opened the front door on the passenger side and would have sat down on top of her had Doreen not shimmied up onto the coffee-cup holder dividing the front seats. She sat perched between the driver and Auntie Jane, her gifts scrunched in her lap, her head pushed against the shag ceiling, and her knee braced against the dashboard. Mr. Boom and Auntie Jane spoke to each other in swift patois, their conversation skimming over her thighs. It was hard to believe that this woman with the smeared skin of mixed African and Indian ancestors, who had grown even larger than the place she occupied in Doreen's memory, was pressing against her leg. She looked up at Doreen. "Where you from, Miss?"

Suppressing the urge to identify herself, Doreen said, "I was born here!"

"Lots of people was born here."

The voice of the BBC announcer was rising out the window as the car wound down into the long gully. Auntie Jane and the three girls in the back got out at a tiny zinc-roofed shop halfway down the gully. Mr. Boom drove in silence to the end of the road. As he opened the boot for her, she paid him what she hoped was the right amount. She had sworn never to pay foreigners' prices.

He accepted her Jamaican dollars. She shouldered her backpack, grabbed her gifts, and headed up the dirt track. Deep ruts scarred this road where cars could no longer pass. Bougainvillea and hibiscus blossomed above her head with violent brightness. Ants scurried up the tree trunks in currents as thick as sludge. The shrieking of crickets, rising in a deafening wave, made her feel under attack. When the shrilling subsided, she caught her breath and shook her gift-laden arms in a futile attempt to toss off the mosquitoes. The mosquito bites she received here swelled up to twice the size of the bites she got in Toronto. Yet this was her place. She peered ahead past the broad leaves. Four years ago, the last time she had walked this road, people had come out to greet her, making her ashamed to have forgotten their names. This time, it seemed, her sister had not warned the neighbours of her arrival. The heat and the steep hill made her stop and dig out her water bottle. She could hear men working in the riverbed below, piling up stones. Four years ago they had been amassing stones to buttress the embankment where the road had washed away, in the hope of making the district once again accessible by car. Startled by how little progress they had made, she thought of the new towers that had sprung up during the same period to wreck the view of Lake Ontario from her twelfth-storey condo. She climbed the slope with small steps, her mind treading water in the hot humid air.

"Hey, Miss!" a voice called from the riverbed.

She started away up the hill. Her right heel caught on a rut, hurling her to the ground. She just managed to fling out her palms to break the fall. When she got up, winded, her knees feeling bruised, the bags of gifts lay in the ruts in front of her. A mosquito settled on her shoulder. Tears rose to her eyes as she swatted it away.

"Hey, Miss!"

She pulled herself upright, feeling the backpack tug at her more heavily than before, gathered her gifts and continued up the hill until she reached the narrow path that forked off through the trees. Shade enclosing her, she climbed over the succession of rocks that formed a natural staircase. The sludge of ants on the tree trunks thickened. The Ethiopian apple trees were close enough that she could see the apples' scarlet skins and taste their white flesh, lighter and less dense than the flesh of the apples sold in Canadian supermarkets. The longing for the taste of guava struck her like a pang. It lodged in her stomach as she reached the top of the stone staircase and crossed the yard towards the blue and white house hidden in the trees.

Rachel's television was broadcasting a reality-TV show Doreen sometimes watched at home. Through the open doorway she could see the stacked TV and stereo components and pick out the new DVD player Rachel had boasted about on the phone. She went in the door and turned the corner to find Rachel sitting in the armchair. Rachel pointed towards the screen. "Me no like that brother. He two-faced."

"You see what he do last week?" Doreen said, shrugging off her backpack and sitting down on the sofa.

"Don't blame him for it all. That girl she a slut. She a slut with a big bottom!"

"That's true," Doreen said. "She has the big bottom."

She imagined how astounded Philip would be by this scene. His Anglo-Scottish family hugged like wrestlers each time they got together for a holiday. If he were here she would be scrambling to offer him explanations for Rachel's diffidence, for her own comfort with this way of being welcomed after four years of separation. She could tell him it was the fault of his English fore-bears, who had colonized Jamaica with a culture of cool irony and beaten stoicism into her ancestors through slavery until families grew accustomed to living apart. She could say that their lives had been too hard for the luxury of exposed feelings. The thought of having to say things like this irritated her. She was glad that Philip was not here. The fact of her relief at his absence brought him back; his imagined presence cancelled out the advantages of making this trip while he was away.

Rachel gave her a look. "Mam says you got a new man about the place. He not come with you?"

"Philip's in international development. He's working in El Salvador." She paused for a moment, wondering whether Rachel had heard of El Salvador. "In Central America," she said. "Not far from here."

She watched Rachel's stolid chin nod, noting the lack of resemblance to her own sleek lines. As with her other siblings, what she and Rachel shared was Mam; they all had different fathers. She supposed she must have more siblings through her father, but not having met them, or even knowing where they might live, she did not consider them family. People were family because they were related to Mam.

"We have a sermon on El Salvador in church," Rachel said. "Dem like war."

"Not anymore. That's over."

They watched the television. In a few hours Rachel's children would trail home from school in their ironed white-and-navy-blue uniforms, and Rachel would cook supper for them, and throw the slops onto the garbage pile at the side of the house, just as Mam used to do when Doreen was growing up here. The children, who were teenagers now, would do their chores and their homework.

The wind soughed through the trees and flowed in the open windows, and a new barrage of cricket chirping, more deafening than the last one, dinned out the sound of the television. The boards creaked, reminding Doreen of the flimsiness of the partitions dividing the back of the house into rooms, the every-second-day water supply, the intermittent power cuts. She glanced up at the ceiling, whose slow caving-in had advanced since her last visit. Floods had left wide holes, edged with blackened rot, through which she could see the underside of the corrugated zinc roof. Two years ago Doreen had sent money to help repair the ceiling, but the money had been misspent by a brother with too many girlfriends and the rot's progress continued. Mam was supposed to send money from Miami the next time she got paid, but Doreen doubted it would be sufficient or get into the hands of anyone reliable enough to do the work.

Rachel kicked the plastic bags that Doreen had set on the floor. "Me wan' see dem gifts."

Doreen opened the bags, displaying one by one the shoes, shirts, and blouses she had bought for Rachel and her children. There were jotters for school, packs of pens and pencils, and a bag of Mars bars that Rachel put in the refrigerator to harden. She examined the clothes and shoes, asking the price of each item in Canadian dollars. She converted the prices to U.S. dollars, then to Jamaican dollars. "Satty, this blouse too small for me daughter. She big now, she a big girl with a chest. You give me money, me buy another blouse."

They haggled until Doreen pulled sixty Canadian dollars out of her wallet to replace the gifts that would not fit. She never stopped paying for having left this house. Yet, unlike Mam, she had not run away. At the age of seven she had been put on a plane and sent to live with relatives in Toronto, told that there she would have opportunities. She followed instructions, grasped the opportunities she found, went to university, worked for a high tech firm, bought a condo. By the time she reached university Mam had left for Miami to clean rich people's houses in order to maintain the house. Her departure wiped out Doreen's fading thoughts of moving back.

Her sister was silent. After a few hours in front of the television, they would start to laugh at the exasperating behaviour of fellow siblings or the childishness of men, their conversation dipping and rising as it swung from English to patois. Rachel mocked Doreen's patois incompetence and called her by her patois name, Satty, or meditator, a reference to bouts of childhood dreaminess that she had long ago put behind her.

"Your new boyfriend," Rachel said. "He as tall as the last one?"

Doreen got to her feet. "I'm going for a walk. Me wan' see the township."

Rachel shook her head at Doreen's poor patois. As Doreen stepped out of the house the breeze that moved the branches in their perpetual slow thrashing dispersed a hellfire sermon broadcast by a loudspeaker car at the bottom of the valley. She walked down the stone staircase. When she reached the track she remembered the way. She followed one path to the next path, the paths strewn with long brown leaves dragged at by the wind. The houses tilted in the humid glare; people whose names she should have remembered spied on her from inside.

Auntie Jane's house was the biggest one in the district. Her Hindu father had poured the savings from his two shops into this stout wooden building with a wide front porch overlooking hillside orchards. Doreen climbed the swept stone staircase to the front door, her gaze lingering on the guava trees. When she knocked, Auntie Jane came to the door with the top of her dress undone, exposing her mountainous breasts down to the tops of her nipples.

"Good evening, Auntie Jane." The afternoon greeting flowed from her throat as smoothly as rum.

"Good evening. You the girl from Boom's car. What you want?"

"I want guavas."

"They no good. They not ready." The door started to close.

"I used to come here with my mother. I'm Rachel's sister."

Auntie Jane studied her, one hand holding the door open while the other buttoned her dress. "Which one?"

"Satty."

"I remember you. Where are you in America?"

"In Canada."

Auntie Jane turned towards the interior of the house and shouted in patois to her grown daughters to bring a bag of guavas from the orchard. "You come back here and you want something, don't you? You all bring the gifts when you come but the gifts don't do nothing. What you want?"

"I don't know," Doreen said. She sat down on a wooden bench on the porch, the wind in her face making her breathless. Vivid green hills flowed as far as she could see. "I want to eat guavas sitting up here with this view. When I was a little girl Mam make me wait until we get to town to eat the guavas. I've never eaten guavas here on your porch."

"You don't want to eat them at your house?"

Doreen leaned back on the bench. Custardy sweet sop gummed up her voice. She listened to the sound of the girls in the orchard, hoping she would recognize the taste of guava. "No," she said, "I was never happy there."

8

LA SANTIAGUERA

OPPRESSED BY THE DRAB immobility of Lake Ontario far below
the window of her twelfth-storey condominium, Doreen pined for
the island where she had been born. But Jamaica, thick with memories, weighed her down with family duties. In the past, twice on
her own and once with a man, she had substituted obligation-heavy
treks home with short vacations in Cuba.

"I'm not going to some resort," Philip said. He had been restless
since his contract in El Salvador ended. As the colour faded from
his cheeks, his face grew inert. He sat in an office in Markham
writing grant proposals in the hope of making a well-funded
return to Latin America. A box of Timbits open on his desk, he
fled screens clogged with his own administrative prose by flicking
over to his email and tapping out messages under glass — messages
in flat bottles, he told her — to acquaintances in Ottawa who
worked for NGOs that had more money or better access to government tipoffs than his pitiful outfit. The rare replies he received
made him moody. Hoping not to be in Canada for long, he had
rented a studio apartment opposite a shopping mall in Markham.

Now, restless at being stranded far from downtown Toronto, he spent nights at Doreen's condo more often than she had expected after their long separation. She saw him growing proprietorial, loitering in the kitchen. "Poor you," he said, when she came home from her job at MicroTransitions North in Mississauga at eight p.m. How to make him understand that she *wanted* to work late? Philip might be spinning his wheels, but her career was gathering momentum. She would sell her next generation of software to the world.

She listened, heating her jerk pork in the microwave, as Philip expanded on his dislike of resorts. How did she expect him to endure artificiality when his experience of Latin America was threadbare highland villages, back-country buses teetering over bottomless ravines, remote plateaux demanding the sowing of experimental crops, debates about latrinization, long days spent recording the shy discussions of peasant women's cooperatives? Refusing to reply, she sat down at the kitchen table and looked him in the eyes. "I was in Havana for a conference once," he murmured. In a weak voice, he added: "I'm *not* going to Varadero."

Two evenings later, after a session on Doreen's laptop, they settled on a resort near Santiago. "We're not even going to be close to Varadero," Doreen said, as she clicked after typing in her credit card number. "Are you happy?"

"Santiago's where the Afro-Cuban culture's really strong. There's this Cuban sociologist named Ortiz I read in grad school ..." She watched him realize that he was treading dangerous ground by presuming to define black people; he beat a retreat into domestic gruffness. I know him so well, she thought, as she heard him say, "As long as I don't have to spend all my time in some mindless resort. As long as I can get into the city."

⁓

STANDING NEAR THE FRONT of the crowd, waiting to be called to board the delayed flight, Philip observed a pudgy man, whose gleaming shaven head had demoted his body to slump-bellied cargo, approach the information counter. The man wore a white sweater with a scarlet maple leaf on the chest; a Toronto Blue Jays logo decorated his vinyl carry-on bag.

Philip cradled Doreen in the curve of his arm. "Spot the American," he whispered in her ear.

"Don't go hassling him," Doreen said. "He just likes the Blue Jays."

"Uh-uh. He's trying way too hard."

As they watched, the man responded to a question from the attendant by producing his passport. To Philip's satisfaction, the martial eagle, its left talon clutching a sheaf of arrows, snapped into sight on the blue cover.

"I told you so."

"Don't pick on him."

"Americans always try to pretend they're Canadians when they sneak into Cuba," Philip said. "You should've seen this guy I met in Havana. Crewcut, loud suit, loud voice. You only had to listen to him — 'Howdy! How you-all doin'? Ahm from *Ca*-nada.' So I ask him where he's from, like what part of Canada? 'You know, *Ca*-nada! Up north!'"

"Don't be rude," Doreen said. "They can't help it if their government makes them tell fibs. Anyway, I like going to a place where Americans have to act ashamed."

"Personally," Philip said, "I was hoping we were going to a place where there wouldn't be any Americans."

AT CUBAN CUSTOMS AND Immigration in the hot Santiago night, the name of Antonio Maceo, the partly black general from Cuba's war of independence against Spain, lodged in Philip's mind. The airport was named after Maceo. Immigration took hours as the young women in their faded uniform tunics asked the same questions again and again in halting classroom English until they believed they had understood the tourists' replies. Philip speeded up the process by switching to his fluent Spanish. The young woman questioning him filled in the form in front of her with swift squiggles. She assessed him from beneath a curved eyebrow. "Are you here alone?"

Oh no. She thought he was a sex tourist. In a rushed voice, he assured her that he was here with his girlfriend, his *novia*, his *compañera*. "She's right over there, being interviewed by your colleague."

"¡*Qué lástima*!" the young official said. "What a pity!"

She handed him his passport, the tourist visa folded inside, and turned to the next tourist.

His passport was opened again at Customs, where the official gazed at Philip's collection of Central American immigration stamps: his one-year Salvadoran visa, the pages of stamps chronicling his various exits from El Salvador, his entries into Guatemala, Honduras, Nicaragua or Costa Rica for business or pleasure, his exits from those countries and the re-entry stamps collected upon his return to El Salvador. The official, a compact mahogany-brown man with a shiny, clean-shaven face, ringed the margins of the form he was completing with jotted explanations of Philip's trips. "Costa Rica? Was that business or pleasure?"

"Business. A conference."

"A conference on what?"

"Latrines. Latrinization in Central America."

Philip watched the official clench his pen as he tried to squeeze the words *congreso sobre letrinización* into a corner of the form. The man shook a cramp out of his fingers. "You have crossed too many borders."

Doreen, her formalities completed, arrived at his side. The official regarded her with surprise. "What do you want?" he asked her in Spanish.

"This is my *compañera*," Philip explained. "She doesn't speak Spanish."

"*Parece santiaguera*," the official said. "She looks like a woman from Santiago."

"She was born in Jamaica," Philip said, "but she lives in Toronto."
The official wrote this information on Philip's form.

Feeling compelled to produce an explanation, Philip said, "We're like the parents of Antonio Maceo." He felt himself slipping into a man-to-man Hispanic jocularity that he wouldn't dare try to replicate in English. "Perhaps our son will be a general."

The official concentrated an anxious look on the form, limp with the quantity of ink he had pressed into its poor stock.

"What was his problem?" Doreen asked, once the official had dismissed them. They walked out of the terminal and joined the lineup for the bus that would take them to the resort. As the line-up stagnated, Philip described his interrogation. Doreen gave the handle of her suitcase an impatient tug. "Why did you have to tell him *my* life story?"

DOREEN RESTED HER HEAD on the pillow, enjoying the cushion of the short dreadlocks into which her friend Debbie had twisted her hair prior to their departure. Philip was snoring in the next bed. Mam would be furious if she saw Doreen flaunting a hairstyle she considered appropriate for girls who took drugs and didn't respect themselves, But Mam was far away in Florida, cleaning rich people's houses — except that here Florida was close. Doreen didn't see Mam often enough to waste her visits showing off vacation photos. Before she went back to work she would buy hair extensions and have her hair braided with twists of brassy red, in a style Mam liked, to compensate for having secretly defied her here in Cuba. Once, when he came back to visit her from El Salvador, Philip had stroked her shoulder in bed and let his hand curl around the back of her neck until it touched the place where her hair began. She had just switched, at that point, from straightened hair to braids. "So what's your hair *really* like? I mean, what would it look like if you didn't do anything to it?"

"Mind your own business," she replied. As she listened to his industrious snoring, the memory made her laugh. Yet the laugh, she recognized, was rocky with irritation. Why did he have to be like that? Always asking nosey questions? She had expected a blond guy from Kingston, Ontario, whose family history in Canada went back as far as those old limestone buildings, to show more respect. His questions about her upbringing with her relatives in Toronto never stopped jabbing at her, asking how it had been, whether she had experienced any problems, any tensions; asking, without stating it, what it had been like growing up *black*. This was the last subject Doreen wanted to think about; she preferred to discuss the evening's top stories on CBC *Newsworld*. She should have realized that a guy who wanted to save the Third World would bring his do-gooding habits home to his relationship. After she got to know Kingston — *his* Kingston — just an old town full of white people, she understood better his curiosity about her Toronto childhood. But really, there was nothing to it; sometimes somebody gave you a bit of attitude, but mainly the different groups all went about their own business and, unlike Philip, knew better than to be nosey. It was like in Jamaica: "From many, one nation," they said. And that was what she liked about Cuba, too: black, brown, white, all mixed up together, it didn't seem to be a big deal.

She fell asleep and woke and fell asleep again, and each time she woke Philip was snoring like a billy goat. In the morning he got up, opened the curtains, and gaped at the palm trees and the beach below the window of their second-storey room. The long, low hotel covered a shelf of rock between high, igneous-looking cliffs and the ocean. Jamaica was out there, she thought, less than eighty kilometres south of Philip's hip; she could feel the shoreline pressing against the rim of the horizon.

"Wow, that's amazing!" he said.

"You see, you like resorts."

"I like the Caribbean ..."

Over breakfast they met paunchy, middle-aged Brad who wore baggy shorts and was staying at the resort with his Cuban wife,

Lucila. Having married a year ago, they had not yet cohabited long enough for the government to grant Lucila an exit visa. Brad flew down whenever he could to log time with Lucila; the hotel kept a record of the weeks they spent together. To Doreen's surprise, Lucila was only about fifteen years younger than Brad; a woman in her late thirties, with medium-brown skin and straight black hair, nice enough looking but too heavy in the thighs to pass for a sexy young chick. Doreen was ready to be impressed until Brad opened his mouth. Why, she wondered, were the Canadian guys who came down here looking for women, always so negative about the Revolution? "I've got inside information," Brad said, "Fidel's gonna be taking off for Switzerland any day now —"

"That's not true," Philip said, gulping down his second fried egg. "Whatever you think of Castro's human rights record, he hasn't enriched himself and he is totally committed to Cuba." He turned to Lucila and asked her a challenging-sounding question in Spanish. Lucila looked terrified, glancing first at Brad, who didn't seem to speak Spanish, and then at the white-garbed waiters who were passing between the tables to collect plates and cutlery. Doreen wished they were at the next table, where two York University professors were talking about the mayor of Toronto, or even with the boisterous Italian family from Hamilton (the women's garish, big-hair perms and plastic handbags alone told her they were from Hamilton), who had got up early to nab the table closest to the water. When Lucila failed to reply, Philip told Brad, "You need to rely on better information."

Brad rolled his eyeballs. Doreen laid her hand on Philip's shoulder, saying, "It's almost time for the meeting, sweetie." She guided him away from the dining area, where the late risers were lining up for their first breakfast of the vacation, the men slapping three fried eggs onto their plates, the women prodding the fish with their forks and casting suspicious looks at the guavas and mangos: fruit they didn't recognize — poor them! Two large blond families were speaking Ukrainian or maybe Polish. It must be Polish; you'd have to be Catholic to have that many kids. Doreen had figured people from those countries wouldn't come to Cuba. Jerzy, the old Polish security guard at work, hated communism so fanatically that he had torn down the head software developer's Che Guevara poster. But, these days, who cared?

She located the stage and the metal chairs behind the swimming pool. "See, hon, this is where they have the shows at night."

"What? They have shows at the resort? Look, there's great music in Santiago. We can go in there —"

"Try it," she said. "Maybe you'll like it."

He sat down on a chair in a huff. The sun's heat exceeded her expectations. As the other tourists filed in from breakfast and Cubans wearing orange shirts bearing the tour company's logo assembled on the stage, Philip became mutinous. "I'm not sticking around for this," he said, as the shaven-headed, slump-bellied American ambled up wearing Nike runners with extra-thick soles, acrylic shorts boasting a red stripe down the side, and a T-shirt of the CN Tower. The sun beat down. The tour company employees, who spoke English much better than the Immigration officials — some of them even repeated their instructions in confident French or Italian — took turns explaining how meals, shows, and excursions worked. Philip swung his head in misery. "I *work* in the Third World, I'm not going to be treated like some tourist."

She pressed her finger to his lips. Seeing that she was going to have to give up her first morning by the pool, she said, "After this is over we can go into Santiago."

SITTING IN THE FRONT seat of the Renault taxi, Philip watched the light cook the green bulges of the Sierra Maestra. Cool-looking shadows unravelled down the troughs between the ridges. The window was open and the wind rushed into his face. Doreen sat in the back with Dave, the Indigenous social worker from the Six Nations Reservation, who they had recruited to share the taxi with them. Philip's opening round of banter with the driver having lapsed into silence, he was free to observe the shapes of the mountain range where Fidel Castro had launched his uprising in the 1950s. The Québécois guy they had met in the lobby had ridden up there on the portable bicycle he had brought down from Montreal. As he enthused about the friendly little villages he had ridden through, Philip thought: I might do that, too, if I were here on my own. Doreen's prissiness had come as a surprise; it was the last thing he had expected from someone who had been born in a Third World village. She had refused to visit him in his project in El Salvador because he was living in a hut. Or that, at least, was the reason she had given him.

The taxi swept past the agricultural cooperative: sloping fields where men herded big-horned cebu cattle with long Asiatic snouts. The cooperative's housing consisted of two-storey blocks of white-washed adobe flats, the wooden slats of the shutters pulled down against the heat. Children in uniforms of bright red shorts and white T-shirts, shod in running shoes, were drifting home from school for lunch. Lanky boys, their books folded against their hips, took turns drilling a soccer ball against a wall. It was a simple sight, but it stunned him. In Central America flats like that would belong to well-off city people, not farm workers, and half these rural kids would be barefoot and out of school. He imagined himself showing this sight to his Salvadoran latrine-builders and realized that the decent housing and indoor toilets would sur-prise brown-skinned Salvadoran peasants far less than the sight of black children wearing uniforms learning to read and write. That, they would maintain, was impossible. Racial prejudice was always more ingrained than any ideological bias. Each time this sort of perception entered Philip's mind, he crunched down hard on his emerging sense of self-congratulation, conscious of all the residual racist crud polluting his own reactions like knots of sticky garbage he hadn't yet found the broom to sweep away. When the social worker asked what the "CDR" painted below the portrait of

Che Guevara on the building closest to the road stood for, Philip heard himself supplying the words, "Committee for the Defence of the Revolution. They run the building."

"Oh yeah, kind of like a First Nations housing co-op."

The taxi turned onto the rough blacktop road that led into Santiago. The Sierra Maestra was on their right, the sharp chasms between successive summits cloud-grazed now and more ethereal in their remoteness. Dave said that his biggest worry about coming to Cuba — it was his fifth trip, he was putting his vacation money behind a system that housed and educated the poor — was that Cubans couldn't travel. "I come see them, they can't come see me." Philip pointed out the insurmountable obstacles to travel confronted by people in other Latin American countries: corrupt officials who demanded a bribe of ten years' salary before a rural schoolteacher, let alone a peasant, could receive a passport; the impossibility of obtaining a visa to the U.S. or Canada. He cut himself short, knowing that he was embarrassing Doreen. The sight of the city's outskirts dealt another blow to his Central America–trained senses, astonishing him with the absence of shanty-town sprawl, the "belt of misery," as Latin Americans called it. Havana and Santiago must be the only two cities in Latin America not to be ringed by this hellish seething growth. Here, where the countryside supplied jobs, clinics, schools — and Committees for the Defence of the Revolution — the exodus to the cardboard shacks had been stemmed.

His lofty thoughts left him unprepared for the smack of the sun-guttered city against his senses. He rolled up the window as a truck spouting blue fumes settled in front of the taxi. A grey haze bathed the lines of people waiting for buses on the sidewalks as motorcycles hacked past, concrete socialist apartment towers jutted up behind the close-set adobe buildings and generous squares where the statues glittered behind colliding molecules of sunlight and exhaust. The driver turned down a side street where the adobe was whitewashed; mahogany-coloured balconies were strung with a profusion of electrical wiring. In the back seat, Dave and Doreen's banter about the buildings' crumbling glory ceased. The taxi stopped at the corner. They paid, got out, and found themselves on the central square, the white Moorish arches of City Hall facing the cathedral on its hill across a patchwork of red tiles, bushes and benches; the two remaining sides of the square were dominated by ancient grey columns and taut crenellations reflecting conquistadors' sombre dreams of grandeur.

Philip laid his hand on Doreen's arm and guided her across the street. Two Cuban men cut across their path. "*Jin-e-te-ra!*" one of them rhymed out at Doreen.

"What his problem?" she asked.

"He thinks you're a prostitute."

She pushed her face close to his, lifting her sunglasses. "Don't you think about me like no prostitute."

"I didn't say — I just said —"

"You behave yourself."

Dave, having made himself scarce, returned to suggest that they visit the colonial buildings. In one building, two old men were selling naive landscape paintings. At the sight of Doreen one of them got to his feet and offered to show her friends the upstairs rooms. Doreen responded with a blank look and a glance in Philip's direction. "We'd like to see the upstairs rooms," Philip said in Spanish. As the old man, who looked like Sancho Panza, shot a mystified glance in Doreen's direction, Philip said, "She doesn't speak Spanish."

The man shook his head. "*Parece santiaguera.*"

"He says you look like a woman from Santiago."

"I got it," Doreen said. They climbed broad marble stairs fit, if not for a king, then at least for a colonial governor.

The man opened a vast swinging door and led them into a dusty room of plush scarlet cushions, drooping brocade and inlaid mahogany panels. The grandiose surroundings made him look as though he had roped up his mule on the street below. He pulled back a curtain, led them onto a balcony, and waved his arm towards the red roof-tiles of the white City Hall. "This is one of the few places where a man like me can look down on those who govern us."

They left the room and stepped onto the vast red-tiled second-floor landing. Philip offered the man a peso for his trouble. The man pocketed the bill. He continued to hold Philip's gaze. In a strangled formal voice, he said, "I would like to give a kiss to *la santiaguera*."

"He wants to give you a ki —"

Before Philip could finish translating, the man hugged Doreen and kissed her cheek. To Philip's surprise, Doreen acquiesced to the embrace. The man released Doreen and turned away across the landing. They walked down the viceregal staircase in silence. Dave moved ahead of them. Philip wished he could think of something to say to Doreen. The space between them felt enormous. It was a relief to step back out into the square and share the bath of the sticky sunlight.

They brushed off men who wanted to sell them cigars. "Let's head down to the harbour," Dave said. "I want to check out the clubs down there."

~

DOREEN WATCHED THE PROSTITUTES dancing with the tourists. They weren't really prostitutes, she thought, just girls out for a good time and some hard cash. The club was an old house whose adjoining front rooms had been filled with tables. The singers in the band, two middle-aged ladies with brown skin and dyed-blonde hair, looked as though they'd had a couple of kids; flanking them were the skinny, incredibly old guys playing steel guitar and some kind of horn that even Cubans seemed to expect in their clubs ever since that *Buena Vista Social Club* movie. The moment they sat down a big black guy bounced up to her and said, "*Vamos a bailar* ..." followed by a lot of stuff she didn't understand. Philip had already explained three times that she didn't speak Spanish.

"I've never had this happen before," she said. "It must be Santiago."

"Maybe it's because you're with me."

What kind of attitude was that? He knew she had been to Cuba before with a white boyfriend. He should just leave her alone. She was supposed to be on vacation and she wasn't getting any peace. The shows at the resort had turned out to be crap, giving her little choice but to agree to Philip's requests to go into Santiago in the evenings. Returning to the hotel late, they got to the beach late in the morning, when most of the deck chairs were taken. Philip insisted this didn't matter since they could still go swimming. "You don't understand," she said. "I don't want to swim. I want to lie on the beach."

"But you don't even lie in the sun!"

"That's how I take my vacation. I lie on the beach, but not in the sun."

Everybody was giving her attitude. It had been the same that first day, when they had walked down the hill towards the harbour. On the way out of the square, they had seen a young Canadian guy sitting on a park bench with his arm around a local girl. When Philip made a remark about sex tourism, Dave said, "I ain't gonna condemn what two consenting adults decide to do. These girls don't have pimps. They're freelance." They had passed a statue of José Martí occupying a square. Doreen remembered Martí's moustache from earlier trips to Cuba; he was Cuba's national hero, his picture was everywhere. It was funny how everybody thought of Cuba as being Fidel, yet when you were in Cuba you hardly saw Fidel's picture; it was just Martí and Che Guevara. She was turning this over in her mind and wondering where the heck Dave and Philip thought they were taking her in this heat, still arguing about the prostitutes, when a door opened in the long wall of adobe houses and she felt a bottomless terror pull her heart down into her guts.

"Hey, Doreen," Philip said. "Look at this. *Santería*."

She knew what it was. She didn't even have to look. The spirit of what the men behind the door were doing froze her soul before Philip and Dave could crane their heads towards the darkened room. A big-bellied idol leaned back against the wall with herbs and grasses at her feet. She had come all the way from Africa; Doreen could feel her origins in the way the sunlight grew dark before her eyes. The two men inside were grinning. She sensed, without hearing or feeling it, the chicken squirming in a man's grasp farther back in the darkness. The men were inviting Philip and Dave into the room. When they caught sight of Doreen, they uttered words of recognition. It wasn't that phrase she kept hearing — "*Par ici santiaguera*," or whatever — but some other words, maybe not even Spanish. Recognizing the words without knowing them, she backed off fast.

"Come on!" Philip said.

"I ain't goin' in there," Doreen said. "You go yourself if you want but I'm not sleeping in the same room as you tonight if you do."

Philip, his expression changing, shrugged his apologies to the men inside. He and Dave came up on either side of her and they continued down the street.

"That stuff freaks me out," she said, shuddering at the cooling of the sweat beneath the shoulder straps of her tank top. "People can get hurt that way."

"There's stuff like that in my culture, too," Dave said, "but I'm too far away from it. I don't feel it anymore."

"I feel it," Doreen said. "It scares the shit out of me."

They walked down to the harbour where portraits interspersed with slogans showed off dramatic black-on-white murals of heroes of Cuban independence. There was Martí again, and Ché Guevara and, unusually, Fidel, one more face in a row of faces. Philip curled his arm around her shoulder as, in a way that made her feel uneasy, but, at the same time, as though he really liked her and was really trying, he told her that the darker man with the moustache was the part-black general from Cuba's war of independence.

"I'd like it better if it had more pictures of women," she said.

"You have to admit the slogans are cool," Philip said. "*Rencor eterno a quien nos ataca.* 'Eternal hostility to people who attack us.' *La libertad es un premio que la justicia da al trabajo.* 'Freedom is a prize that justice rewards to work.' Why can't we say stuff like that in Canada?"

"That's the whole goddamn problem with Canada," Dave said. "We repress all that stuff to keep the neighbours happy and the only way we can let it out is by taking goddamn vacations in Cuba."

⁓

THE WOMEN WITH THE dyed-blonde hair were getting ready to start another set. They had found this club on their walk with Dave the first afternoon and arranged to come back here together. Dave had invited Muriel, a divorced social worker from Brampton; the four of them had shared a taxi into the city. Yesterday Philip had managed to grab an afternoon in town by himself. He had nosed around the area where Doreen had made him turn his back on the two *santería* guys — *santería, santiaguera,* he thought, it was a shame the *santiaguera* didn't like *santería* — only to discover that the Afro-Cuban festival inspiring the ceremony to which they had been invited had ended the day before. He wandered up the packed side streets off the square, enjoying the anonymity lent to him by the rowdy crowds and the dark shadow. Wearing an old baseball cap pulled down over his forehead, he felt, irrationally, that his white skin stood out less obtrusively than usual. Small bakeries and cafés attracted long lineups. Philip stepped into a half-abandoned second-hand bookstore. The stiff, yellowed books lay rigid on the display tables in generational rows. Closest to the back were books in Eastern European languages: Russian, Czech ... was that Romanian? Then came rows of untouched volumes of the works of Lenin in Spanish. At the front of the long table, a book of essays by Northrop Frye and a novel by Margaret Atwood attested to the arrival of Canadian tourists as the latest wave of *internacionalistas* to prop up the Revolution. Were their multi-coloured dollars supporting Cuba's independence, or were they simply laying the groundwork for the arrival of the Americans, whose ultimate dominance everywhere was inevitable? The question throbbed in Philip's head as he moved on to a new bookstore on the main square, where he noticed that some of the older dissident writers were back in print, Lezama Lima and Severo Sarduy displayed in shiny new editions. He stepped out into the sunlight at the base of the cathedral and spotted a shiny bald head and a loose-fitting Montreal Canadiens T-shirt disappearing around the corner with a puffing stride. He hurried forward, but the American, if that was who it had been, had disappeared. A steep side street cut downhill and out of sight, children in red uniform shorts and women gripping plastic bags hurried past him on their way home, a tall guy ambled up and asked him if he wanted a taxi. He had not got around to telling Doreen about this moment.

She took his arm as the music whirled up in its jangling clatter of steel and strings. The two women began to sing a song from the point of view of a man praising his *mulata* lover. Listening to the women taking over another point of view — almost his point of view — Philip felt light-headed. He pulled Doreen close and chanted the chorus into her ear. "Hey," she said, "why don't you say, '*Te quiero?*' Isn't that what you're supposed to say? Doesn't that mean I love you?"

"Do you want to dance?"

"Not if everybody's going to think I'm some prostitute."

Sitting side by side in the front row of seats in the smaller of the two front rooms, they watched the madcap dancing in the larger room. A blonde woman in her late fifties was hopping up and down in front of a tall Rastafarian. An older white man was gripping the ass of a brown-skinned teenage girl as they rocked in a see-sawing embrace. Two aging German hippies, a man and a woman, danced with Cubans of the opposite sex. It was hard to spot a couple where the two dancers were from the same country. Of course, people would think the same of Doreen and him ... He glanced across at Dave and Muriel, who were bargaining with a man selling watercolours of Fidel smoking a cigar. A petite girl with dark eyes and light skin slipped into a seat in front of the dancers. Turning around in her chair, she scanned the room with a narrow-eyed gaze of ruthless assessment. He watched her observe his hand resting on Doreen's forearm. A skinny young guy in a white T-shirt sidled over to the girl and began to talk to her; her shoulders stiffening, she looked away.

"Did you see that!" Doreen said. "Did you see the look in her eyes? She wasn't even going to talk to a Cuban guy."

Philip nodded his head, staring at the petite girl, with her neat handbag and her dark hair pulled back in an efficient little ponytail. Afraid that Doreen would be upset by his scrutiny, he looked in the direction of the door as two buxom women pranced in.

"Here come the drag queens," Doreen said.

"You think so?"

She laughed, sounding more relaxed than at any point in their vacation. "Actually, it's kind of hard to tell."

The two women were wearing dark high-heeled pumps and dresses that fell to their knees. Their smooth ankles gleamed in the reflections of the band's brass instruments. They sashayed forward and sashayed back, their elbows digging the air. Their necks and ears were laden with Caribbean treasure troves of gold. Their lips were an extravagant pink, their cheeks lavishly rouged. The familiar hardness that firmed up the features of the woman in the burgundy dress made Philip think that Doreen might be right that these were men in drag, or at least that this one was. The big woman's dancing partner, whose dress was a dashing aquamarine shade, was lighter on her feet; her breasts and shoulders trembled as she vibrated to the music. The woman with the face of familiar-looking hardness squirmed her thighs, struggling to keep up with her partner. He noticed the German hippies, the ancient bass player, the Rastafarian — almost everyone except the old guy who was squeezing the young girl's ass — rubbernecking at this large, curious couple who were taking over the dance floor. Dave caught Philip's attention and raised his eyebrow in a gesture of shared laughter that pried Philip to his feet. He found himself walking across the floor. Bending over, he asked the petite girl with the dark hair to dance. Her dark eyes barely registered his presence as she hopped to her feet and took his hand.

⁓

NO WAY WAS SHE putting up with this shit. What did Philip think he was doing? She could feel Dave and Muriel staring at her. To her bitter satisfaction, the moment Philip left his chair the big black guy came back and said, "*Vamos a bailar ...*" Not understanding the rest of what he said, she told him, "I only speak English."

He shook his head. "*Pareces santiaguera.*"

She elbowed her way into the crowded front room. The German hippies and the Cubans they were dancing with had been elbowed up against the microphones. There was Philip hopping around like a fool with that little white whore. He was avoiding her eyes; he knew he was going to get it.

She would show him how to dance. Unlike Philip, she could hear the music, bob on its peaks and sidle down its troughs. The big guy knew how to dance, too. Soon they were trotting up a storm. Some drunk yelled encouragement in Spanish. She started moving faster. She could feel the clack of the high heels of the big gals at her side trying to keep up with her. The swish of that hair, it had to be a wig. She saw the posters of cherry-red 1950s high-finned cars on the back wall; she was looking everywhere except at Philip. If he did this right in front of her, how was she supposed to trust him in El Salvador? She let the big guy take her hand and spin her around even though the space was too narrow. She heard a whoop and the big guy spun her again, she was laughing and dizzy, she didn't usually dance in clutzy old running shoes, the treads caught on the creaking boards. Staggering to keep her balance, she watched Philip step past her and run straight into the big gal in the burgundy dress. What was going on? Philip was a terrible dancer, but she had never seen him do anything this clumsy.

Philip's gym shoes landed between the big woman's pumps, their ankles became entangled and they toppled together, then fell towards the floor. The big woman yielded a deep-voiced moan. Her dancing partner reached out in vain to catch her, the crowd separated, the lead singer missed a beat. Doreen stopped dancing as the big woman, sitting on the floor with her log-like legs motionless in front of her and her wig-thick hair falling askew across her right eye, yelled, "Jesus Christ!"

Philip hopped to his feet, buoyant with his bright childish look that charmed and alarmed her. "D'you not see, Doreen? It's the American. The guy from our resort." Turning to the staring Cubans, he said something in Spanish.

The gal on the floor, who was getting to his feet with heavy-footed assertion, had understood. "Don't you go tellin' them I'm an American, you hear? I don't care if they know I'm in drag, but don't you go tellin' them where I'm from."

The music had ceased. Doreen saw the petite girl, thwarted fury compressing her dark eyes, give the situation a quick once-over and then slip away to the bar. The triumph she felt on observing the girl's frustration almost wiped out her anger with Philip. She swore to keep her rage fresh until she had a chance to tell him exactly what she thought of him. Behind the girl she saw the German hippies give their dancing partners a farewell handshake and a bow, and retreat together out the door. Doreen watched them go with combined relief and dismay. She was glad they weren't sex tourists, but she knew that Philip was going to say that if another couple could dance with Cubans for the evening and then go home together, why couldn't they? Because they hadn't talked about it, that was why. Staring at Philip standing with a defiant look on his face as the big guy-gal lumbered towards him with whining rage, she thought: maybe I don't know him that well.

THE AMERICAN PUSHED HIS jaw close to Philip's face as the lead singer announced that the band was taking a ten-minute break. The rouge on his cheeks had been smeared; horsehair wig-strands were mired in the smears. He wheezed for breath. "What'd you think you're doing?"

"I recognized you," Philip said. "What are you doing here anyway?"

"This is the one place where I can dress like this and nobody in my hometown is ever gonna know. I can let it all hang out. Is it any skin off your ass? You think Cuba's just for you?"

Before he could reply, Philip felt a touch on his arm. "Come on, sweetie. I don't think they want us here anymore."

Two big guys in white T-shirts moved up behind Doreen. The police, who had been standing guard on the street outside when they arrived, had settled into the doorway. He glanced at the American trying to swallow his despair. The American's dancing partner stood behind him, a hand lingering close to his shoulder.

Philip turned towards the door. Doreen, Dave, and Muriel followed him. He glimpsed the bouncers closing in on the American and his dancing partner. They rode a taxi back to the resort in silence. When they got to the room, Doreen went to bed. Philip leaned over her in the dark, stroking her cheeks and murmuring: "*Te quiero…*"

"Stop hassling me." She rolled over and pulled the covers over her head.

He padded barefoot to the window and peeped between the curtains at the short beach and the sluggish black tide making curtailed slapping sounds as it receded across the sand. Too alert to sleep, he turned on his Walkman and spun the radio dial until he heard a voice with a strong Cuban accent say, "*The great president George W. Bush has brought freedom to Iraq and soon he will bring freedom to Cuba!*" Where was he? What had happened? He felt borders sliding beneath the soles of his bare feet. As the announcer continued, he realized he was picking up the Cuban exile station from Miami.

He put the Walkman away, went to bed, and tried to sleep. In the morning the American came down late for breakfast, dressed in a plain white T-shirt. He sat by himself at a table overlooking the gleaming water. Turning away, Philip carried his tray to an unoccupied table. As he and Doreen sat down, Brad and Lucila joined them. "Did you hear the news?" Brad said. "Fidel bought a condo in Zurich!"

Over his scrambled eggs, Philip caught Doreen's eye and received the gift of the rough edge of her smile.

9

AFTER THE HURRICANE

FOR THIRTEEN HOURS, FROM the time the plane lifted off from
London, crossed the Atlantic, landed at St. John's, Antigua,
then travelled the final hour over the Lesser Antilles — visible out
the window as a trail of dark green blood spots flowering on the
translucent pale-blue slab of the sea — up to the instant they
landed at the little Cuban-built airport with a bump that woke
the passengers who had lapsed into an alcoholic stupor, Philip
waited for Doreen to speak. She had uttered her last words in the
departure lounge. When a flight attendant brought in the barrell
kids — small children going home to visit their families, their names
written on bibs that hung across the fronts of their pink pinafores
and white dress shirts — Doreen exclaimed, "That was me! I grew
up travelling like that. Except, for me it was between Toronto
and Jamaica."

She remained silent as they picked up their luggage from the
carousel and found their way outside where a beaming German
couple held up a sign that said *Philip & Doreen*. "Mitzi," said the
attractive wife, who looked older than her wiry husband. "This is

Fred." She smiled. "When people book online, you never know what to expect."

Doreen met his eyes. They knew this reaction: the exuberance that camouflaged nervousness when people were uncertain how to respond to an interracial couple. As they climbed into the back seat of Fred and Mitzi's Jeep, Philip sensed Doreen's disappointment.

The vacation had been her idea. She had persuaded him months ago, when they had realized that their business trips to England would overlap, that they should take advantage of the cheap deals available from London. She had overcome his resistance to package vacations by finding an online offer for a remote lodge: three holiday cabins on an isolated point overlooking a tiny bay on the island's southeast shore. With the bright-eyed girlishness she revved up whenever she was openly trying to twist his arm, Doreen enumerated the advantages: the private beach; the outside world accessible only via a forty-five-minute vertical hike up the coastal mountains to the highway; a stash of tinned food strongly recommended; free airport pickup; a low price for a week's accommodation on the condition that they tell their friends about the place when they got home.

He dozed against the door as warm air flooded the Jeep. Fred was driving through deep gulleys where a dozen shades of green vied for the sunlight. Tall, droop-leafed coffee plants grew close to the road. As they climbed, houses on stilts bobbed up above the vegetation at the tops of the ridges like gravity-defying cubicles rising towards heaven. Fred braked to ease around a construction crew that was repairing the guard rail. "Two years ago," he said, "there was the hurricane. It will take years to repair the damage."

On a cliff-face cleared of undergrowth, red spray paint announced: *Cuba and Grenada. Friends forever.*

"After the hurricane, they couldn't rescue people because the roads were blocked with fallen trees. The Cubans came and cleared the roads."

"Some of the same Cubans who were here under socialism in

the 1980s came back," Mitzi said. "People welcomed them like they'd returned from the dead. When the international aid organizations arrived their job was easy because the roads were clear."

"I work in international aid," Philip said.

"Mitzi," Fred said, "we shouldn't talk about politics with our guests."

"It's all right." Philip repeated the formula he had been obliged to utter a dozen times during his days in London, "We're not American, we're Canadian ... we took our vacation in Cuba last year."

Doreen, looking out the window at the construction workers in their white T-shirts and black hard hats, nodded.

Clinging like a contour line to the flank of the mountains, the two-lane blacktop road hurtled them past abundant greenery speckled with little white houses. Here and there, a village clustered around a greystone church that looked as though it had been airlifted from a meadow in rural England; vendors cooked snacks on Primus stoves at the edge of the road. Fred turned off the blacktop and geared down. The jeep crawled over huge ruts. By the time they emerged onto the point, darkness was falling and they caught only a glimpse of Fred and Mitzi's white stucco house looking out over the dull sea and the three wooden cabins facing the bay. Fred crossed the yard and disappeared into a shed. A generator came on. The roar of the sea in Philip's ears and the air's moisture made the glow of the lamps strung from wires around the yard feel as fragile as life itself.

He hugged Doreen. "You're not regretting this?" he murmured. "You don't think we should have cancelled?"

"I couldn't be doing nothin' else now," she said.

"You are the only guests," Mitzi announced, leading them towards the cabin closest to the stucco house. She offered to cook them supper. Philip said that they were tired and would go to bed. In the cabin, where the bed was enclosed in a tent-shaped mosquito net, they hung their plastic bags full of crackers, tinned sardines and tuna from wooden pegs in the bathroom and tied themselves up in the net. The surf smashed on the beach. He opened his mouth to ask Doreen whether she was going to be able to sleep. Then he was awake and it was bright daylight. The room felt like a box vaulted up into the sky and shot through with light. It was barely five-thirty in the morning, but there were no curtains on the broad windows overlooking the sea and the sunlight was warming their bed; the roar of the waves sounded louder. When he slipped out from under the mosquito net, the whiteness of the surf hurt his eyes. Doreen got up, the strap of her rumpled nightgown twisted on her shoulder. Her hair was a mess. Not Afro enough to remain short and tight, yet too Afro to fall into an elegant shape as it grew out, Doreen's hair was her constant preoccupation. Seeing it clustered into two beehive-like bunches, one halfway down the back of each side of her head, made him feel a horrible sadness. He hugged and kissed her.

"If you think we're gonna get up to any monkey business with these windows you can forget it." She sidestepped him and scanned the beach. "Look! A fishing boat come in!"

Before he could move, she had opened her suitcase and begun to dress. She raked her hair into shape in front of a mirror and was out the door and hurrying down the path to the beach, Fred and Mitzi's dog bounding at her heels. On the sand, a man was lifting plastic buckets out of a small boat. Two large women were walking towards him. By the time Philip dressed and got to the beach, the women were bargaining with the fisherman for his catch.

"You want one that's skinny like me," he said, "or one that's fat like you?"

"Fat like me!" a woman said. Their voices were as rhythmic as the waves, but they spoke standard English, a relief to Philip, who struggled to understand the Jamaican patois of Doreen's sisters.

As soon as the fish changed hands, Doreen stepped forward to scrutinize the contents of the buckets. "That one!" she said, pointing.

"That one cost nine," the fisherman said.

"M'give you six," Doreen said, her patois surfacing.

"Eight and he's yours."

"Seven an' I don' go no higher."

"For a pretty woman I go to seven."

"Hon," Doreen said to Philip. "You got some money? What money it have here anyway?"

"Eastern Caribbean dollar," Philip said. He laughed. "I like the way you bargain when you don't even know what the money is."

He paid the fisherman, who looked Doreen up and down. "Where you come from?"

"Jamaica," Doreen said, supplying the answer she gave to black people who asked her this question. When white people asked, she said, "Toronto."

The fisherman's lean ribs pressed against his skin in the gap where his shirt hung open. "The Jamaican woman she have a nice shape."

As Doreen took the fish, Philip laid his arm around her shoulders.

"A Jamaican girl she live up the hill here," the fisherman said. "She marry a man from here. You go see her. She be wanting company from home."

As they climbed the path, the dog trotting in front of them and panting at the fish, Doreen whispered, "Man, the people here look like they just got off the boat from Africa! They're not mixed at all!"

He followed her, his feet slipping on the path. Doreen was as proud of her upturned Hindu eyes, long Arawak jawline, half-Scottish grandmother and one-quarter Chinese grandfather, as she was of her African heritage. She said she felt most comfortable in places like Jamaica and Cuba, where there was a language to talk about people like her, or cities like Toronto, where mixing was the daily business. Worried about how she felt here, he said, "At least they appreciate the Jamaican woman's nice shape."

"You sure put your arm around me fast! 'Nobody's touchin' *my* woman.' And you say you're not possessive!"

Daylight lent the point a ragged appearance. Long grass entwined with creepers was encroaching on the yard beneath the wires where

the lamps hung. Fred, dressed in a floppy-brimmed sun hat that
threw his face into shadow, was swinging a scythe at the undergrowth. They went around the corner of the house and found Mitzi
on the covered patio, clearing up the breakfast dishes. Through an
open doorway they saw a local woman sweeping the floor of an
industrial-sized kitchen. "This is Georgina," Mitzi said. "When we
have tour groups, Georgina and I cook for twelve!" She crossed
the tiles and wrested the fish from Doreen's hands. "You want me
to freeze it?"

"Thank you, Mitzi. I'll cook it the last night."

"Georgina, put this body in the freezer!" Mitzi said with a laugh.

Philip couldn't look at Doreen.

"Mitzi," he heard her say in a level voice, "do you know if I can
get a flight to Jamaica from here? I might have to go for family
business."

Mitzi frowned. "There are not many flights between islands....
You're not leaving?"

"If I go, it only for two, three, days. Philip stay here."

"You know there is a Jamaican girl who lives up the hill on the
other side of the beach?"

"The fisherman told us," Philip said.

"She cuts hair," Mitzi said. "She studied this in Jamaica."

"Until Macey come, there's no one around here who cuts hair,"
Georgina said from the kitchen.

Mitzi nodded. "This is such a small island that people don't have
the opportunity to learn a trade."

"That's why we came here," Philip said. "They said there was
nothing to do." He still couldn't look at Doreen. "I guess we'll go
back to our cabin now."

⁓

THEY WOKE AT FIVE-THIRTY to the sound of the waves. No matter
how hard they tried at night to kill the saboteur mosquitoes that
slipped inside the net, each morning they found fresh bites on their

shins. By the third day, in spite of the fact that his skin was so light and hers so dark, matching reddish scabs shielded the space between their ankles and their knees like the greaves of centurions who belonged to the same expeditionary force. They prepared their meals of crackers and tinned sardines on the balcony, sweeping the crumbs over the edge to discourage the ants which crossed the planks in tiny swarms that moved as fast as a tropical storm running in over the sea. Each day they had a morning swim and an afternoon swim. The water was warmer in the afternoon, but the weather was more turbulent. Big black clouds built up over the mountains. Between swims, they read paperbacks on the balcony and took walks uphill, where trees brought down by the hurricane blocked the clipped English lanes that ran through the tropical undergrowth. They skirted slack-bellied brown cattle that grazed in groups of two or three and tiny shepherd boys sleeping in the grass. Their customary non-stop banter about politics slowed. He struggled to convey to Doreen his sensation of being in a place where nothing more could happen. Fred and Mitzi talked about the revolutionary government; the Cubans; the American invasion; the next twenty years of slow decline; then the hurricane, which knocked over the nutmeg trees, the core of the island's economy, like men shot dead. They drove Philip and Doreen up the coast to see the empty nutmeg factory in Grenville, where a bitter foreman waved at the echoing factory floor where hundreds had worked. "They're all gone," he said. That evening, the conversation Philip had imagined them having about the island's problems failed to happen. As soon as night fell, Doreen undressed and went to bed. It surprised him that she, who under normal circumstances refused to kiss him if there were a finger's-width crack between two curtains in a hotel room, took off her clothes with unflinching confidence in this cabin where broad bare windows exposed them on two sides. Doreen was right, of course, that there was no one out there, that in the all-engulfing darkness of the rural night no one could see anyone else; yet, her abandon suggested a change in her mood, even a shift in her personality. He felt one step behind. He toiled to catch up to her in the hot fury of her beautiful slender black body. At each climax he felt gripped by the need to go deeper inside her. He wanted, with a rage that unnerved him, to give her a child, as though this fusion of their beings might break down her silence.

Fearing the mosquitoes, neither of them went to the bathroom after lovemaking. He eased off his condom, tied it around the neck and wrapped it in toilet paper. In the violent suddenness of the dawn, he woke to see the twisted nub of latex-bulged tissue paper glowing with the luminosity of a recently evolved life form.

On the fourth day they walked to the village at the top of the hill. The coastal highway ran through the centre of town. Soaked with sweat from the climb, they found a corner store where they could buy soft drinks. The woman behind the counter offered a computer where they could check email. Against their judgment, they agreed to break the spell of their removal from the world. The sight of dozens of work-related messages made Philip feel irritable. He logged out. Doreen studied her messages in silence, read a few of them, and offered no comment during the long downhill walk to the beach. Her reserve persisted into the next day. In the afternoon, as he watched her emerge from the water in a tan-coloured bikini, her unruly hair rolling on her shoulders in the wind, he handed her the towel she had draped across the trunk of a fallen palm tree. As she smiled into his face, he said, "You don't want to talk about it?"

"Nothing I can say's going to change anything."

"But, Doreen, isn't it better —?"

"I don't feel like talking."

On their fifth night, feeling penned in by the small bay, they splurged on a cooked dinner on Fred and Mitzi's balcony. That afternoon a group of young people had driven two jeeps down through the bush and set a bonfire in the short, goat-gnawed grass which began just above the brown sand. As Philip and Doreen watched from their balcony, two of the young men felled a tapered coconut tree. Doreen winced as the tree hit the ground. To the sound of gangsta rap, the young men stripped the tree of its coconuts and sat down with their girlfriends to drink rum, eat coconuts, and roast hot dogs. An hour later, when they drove away, they hurled jeers in the direction of the point and left their bonfire burning. The evening breeze skimmed in off the sea, driving the fire across the short grass in the direction of the bush.

Fred appeared, hurling curses at the empty beach. A bucket in his hand, he descended the path in jerky leaps. He opened a faucet at the end of a long, rickety pipe and filled the bucket with water. He emptied the bucket over the flames, returned to the faucet and filled the bucket a second time, then a third. By the fifth dousing, the fire was hissing into submission. Fred continued pouring water over the charred logs and scorched grass long after the fire had gone out.

That evening, as they ate their steaks and corn on the balcony, where the breeze had grown cool enough for Doreen to drape a long-sleeved shirt over her tank top, Fred was raging. "People here used to have a culture of living with their island! They climbed up the tree to get coconuts. Now every time they want a coconut they cut down a tree!"

"Young people think they can have everything lickety-split like on TV," Georgina said.

"That's what we came here to get away from!" Mitzi said. "Since the hurricane everything is worse." She looked at Doreen, whose loose-sprung curls were falling into her face. "Macey isn't like that. I think that in Jamaica they teach people to work."

"Lots of Jamaicans have two jobs," Doreen said, growing animated. "But it have lazy people like everywhere else."

"Tomorrow you must visit Macey," Mitzi said. "You won't have time on your last day because we must drive to the airport. I will give you directions!" she said, stepping into the kitchen for paper.

Next day, after their lunch of water biscuits and sardines, Philip said, "Do you want to visit the Jamaican girl?"

"I guess."

"Are you thinking about the trip to London?"

"I'm trying not to think about anything. Let's visit the Jamaican girl," she said, getting to her feet.

They walked the length of the beach and found the path described in Mitzi's directions: a bald zigzag that climbed through the undergrowth at an angle so steep that they had to grip the bushes and haul themselves up hand over hand. Sweating and gasping, they emerged onto a sloping headland and followed a broader path, worn wide by cattle and clipped by goats, past ruined one-room houses, the sheet metal torn from their roofs glinting in thickets of long grass. Turning around to catch their breath, they saw the point where they were staying projecting out into the sea like the tapered blade of a shovel laid on the dark blue water. They followed the path until it intersected with a steep single-lane black-top road.

When they got to the top of the hill, a long-legged young woman wearing a white T-shirt and short twisted dreadlocks came out to greet them. "How are you, Doreen? Finally, you reach! Every day, I ask m'self why that Doreen don' come visit me?"

"You knew I was here?"

"Girl," Macey said, lowering her voice, "on this island, everybody know everything. I can't say a word to your boyfriend here unless you keep right in the middle of the conversation. Oh, these small-island people are suspicious! Sometimes I wish I back in Kingston where nobody know my business."

She waved them towards her house. Grey roof tiles had been hammered to the front of the porch. The three of them sat down on the steps. Macey's skin was of a lighter brown than that of the Grenadians; her face was round, with a wide mouth and a strong chin. "I thought I miss my family here. Instead I miss my privacy."

"You can't forget your family," Doreen said.

"But I gotta say I like it here. It peaceful. In Kingston you got to watch your back." Looking at Doreen, she said, "Girl, you need a haircut. Why don' you come see me the day you reach?"

"I wasn't ready."

"You ready now?"

Doreen gripped Philip's arm. "I ready."

Macey got to her feet. "Why kind of haircut you want?"

"I want straightenin'," Doreen said, standing up.

"Straightenin' gonna cost you. I go into St. George's to get the solution. For straightening, I charge fifty EC dollar."

"Sweetie," Doreen said. "We got fifty EC dollar?"

"I think so." Astonished by Doreen's compliance, Philip wondered whether Macey's offer had contained a cultural signal, indiscernible to his eye, which ruled out bargaining. He found fifty EC dollars and handed them to Macey. The young woman took the money and disappeared into the house. "Straightening cost twice that much in Toronto," Doreen said in a whisper. Macey returned carrying a towel, a bucket and a container of straightening solution. She wore white gloves like a pathologist. She sat Doreen down on a plastic chair on the porch and wrapped the towel around her shoulders. As Macey set to work, Philip backed away. The scabs on his shins itched in the heat. At the side of Macey's house, the frame of a black chest of drawers, stripped of its innards, sat tumbled on its back among scattered pieces of lathe fanned out across red-brown earth.

"Why you come here?" Macey said. She doused and lathered Doreen's hair. She dragged Doreen to her feet and bent her forward. Doreen braced her elbows on the rail of the porch. She made Doreen lean over the rail until she was staring down at the hurricane wreckage. The wood and cardboard had half-sunk into the earth, becoming one with the soil in a coarse humus. "Why you come to Grenada?" Macey lathered and rubbed until she was hauling Doreen's head up and down. "Why don' you go to Jamaica to see your family?"

Doreen gasped. Suds ran across her cheeks. "I go to Jamaica next week for my brother funeral!" she shouted. She stood up and burst into tears. A man on the other side of the road stared at them. Doreen shook herself out of Macey's grip. Philip rushed up the steps and hugged her trembling body. Her hair crushed by lather, Doreen's head shone forth in its strong dark roundness as her lips nuzzled his shoulder.

She turned around and let Macey's hug receive her. "We book this vacation, then they murder my brother in Kingston. They going to do an autopsy so they put him on ice so I decide to go on vacation anyway. I think maybe being around West Indian people do me good."

The two women rocked together like coconut trees whose suppleness belied the force of the wind. "It be all right, Doreen," Macey said. "I happy you come and see me."

Doreen gave Macey a squeeze, as though she were the one offering comfort. She stood up, strong and independent as she had always been and yet, Philip sensed, older. "Straighten my hair good, Macey! My hair gotta shine for my brother funeral. And try to do it quickly, please. Philip and me goin' to Fred and Mitzi's place. Tonight I'm cookin' a fish dinner."

10

WHO KILLED MARTIN COOMBS?

A MAN WITH A gun. In a West Kingston bar. Martin stood tall in his bright red guayabera shirt, bought with money he'd made wiring a rich family's house in Constant Spring Gardens. The last time Doreen came back from Canada she'd told him, "You're forty-one, Martin. You got three daughters. Now Rachel go up to the States you has to look after her daughter, too. You goin' to be her uncle *and* her dad. And don't forget her son. You got to set him a example. You the only adult in the house. You got to stop spendin' nights in Kingston chasin' no-good girls."

There was no work in the parish, in the hills that surrounded the blue-and-white clapboard house Mam had left them when she'd gone to Miami to clean stucco mansions for rich Cubans. Martin went down to Kingston for work. Even when there wasn't work, he went to Kingston to eat with his cousins at Juice Patties. Cousin John, the cop, sat with his back against the wall. "I'm on the street," he said. "I don' show my back to nobody."

Last year the construction business had picked up and Martin put in eight months wiring new apartments. He gave money to the mother of his two younger daughters, then he saved until he was able to buy a second-hand car. He was the proudest man in the parish. No more riding route taxis back up into the hills, no more staying overnight in Kingston even when there wasn't a girl he wanted to sleep with. He was his own man. The car was red, like his favourite shirts. He hung a miniature plastic soccer ball from the windshield and drove home in an hour, taking the curves so tightly that he could see past the sign that said: *Don't Teach Your Garbage How to Swim*. He glimpsed the foaming river at the bottom of the lush ravine. When he reached the dirt roads of the parish he slowed down, parked the car at the spot where the road had washed out and hiked up the hill to the stone steps, draped by the low branches of the Ethiopian apple trees, which led to the house. He showed off the car to his sister and nephew and niece. That night Old Man Austin and his sons drenched the car in gasoline and set it alight. The *whunk* of the explosion woke Martin up. "You no' goin' to have nothin' us don' have!" Old Man Austin said as Martin ran towards the flaming ruin. Mam said later that was when Martin died. It was those lazy envious no-goods that killed him. What she said at the time was, "Jamaica gone to the dogs. Martin even if he work they don' let him get ahead. When I got Rachel here in the States, I make sure Martin get the visa next."

MARTIN STOOD AT THE bar, a curl of chest hair visible through the keyhole-shaped neck of the guayabera. The girl was slinky, her hair straightened and gold-highlighted. She was alone. At least she was acting that way. In the corner rude boys were drinking Red Stripe. They didn't utter a squeak about Martin cozying up to the girl. Maybe he should have asked himself why a girl that fancy-looking was standing by herself. The gang boss came in and yelled at Martin to get away from his girl. Martin hit the street, figuring he was safe. The gang boss gave his girl a slap, then chased Martin down and shot him in the back of the head.

That was the story they heard from Gerard, Rachel's seventeen-year-old son, when he phoned his mother to say that Martin was in hospital in a coma. Rachel had been in the States for less than a month. Mam had moved into a two-bedroom apartment so they could live together. Rachel was working for the same agency which sent Mam out to clean houses. They were in debt for furniture and moving expenses. Minnie, the youngest sister and the fattest woman in the family, had come back from Brooklyn, where she'd gone to live with her no-good Haitian boyfriend until he took off with some skinny girl from Trinidad. She and her four-year-old daughter were sleeping on the couch. When the phone rang at three o'clock on Saturday afternoon Minnie grabbed it, angry at the interruption in her nap. Mam was in the kitchen cooking jerk pork and ackee and saltfish to put in the fridge for Minnie and the little girl to eat next week while she was at work. Gerard's low voice, trying to sound like a man even as he spoke too fast, overwhelmed Minnie, who squelched a sob just long enough to call out to Rachel that her son was on the phone. Rachel listened to Gerard explaining that he and Monique had thought Martin was in Kingston with a girl. Then this morning the police car had parked where the road had washed out. Rachel, imagining her children alone in the house, said, "You keep goin' to school! You get you A-levels, you have a future when you come live with me in America."

Minnie grabbed her shoulder. "You gonna tell Mam?" she whispered.

"I no' tell her." The first thought that came into her mind, Rachel told everybody later, was how Mam still cried if anybody mentioned the route taxi accident thirty-two years earlier that had killed her first baby-father, Martin and Rachel's dad. She felt tongue-tied and ignorant. Other people probably knew what to do when their brothers died; her first sob came from sheer helplessness.

"We have to tell Mam!" Minnie whispered, shaking her. "You do it, Rachel. You and Martin has the same dad. That why you both Coombs. Nobody else in this family called Coombs."

"I don' know how." Rachel said goodbye to Gerard and replaced the receiver. They heard Mam singing her Pentecostal gospel songs in the kitchen. She bit her lip. "I don't know what to do."

"Us gotta do somethin' ... ask Satty!" Minnie said. "She a doctor."

"Satty a snob," Rachel said. "She think she special because she live in Canada and have a rich-people job and some jake for a boyfriend."

"So you tell her." Minnie got to her feet. "Poor Martin!" She sat down on the couch and squeezed her daughter against her chest. "Rachel," she said, her voice swamped with tears as Mam's voice rose in the kitchen. "You gotta do somethin'!"

⁓

DOREEN, POSTED TO LONDON for three months, came back to the short-term efficiency flat off Russell Square, rented for her by Micro-Transitions North, longing for a shower after thirteen hours of meetings. At the sound of the phone, she cursed Philip. She'd thought it would be great for both of them to be over here for work at the same time, then go on vacation to Grenada together from London; but Philip, barely having set foot in the city, had fallen for the British vice of the cheap cellphone. He delighted in calling for no reason at all. His failure to understand that her work took up more hours in the day than his aggravated her; last night she'd come home to find four messages, strung out over a five-hour period, on the flat's answering service. The memory made her almost mad enough to refuse to get out of the shower. The first three weeks, when she had been here alone, had been less nerve-racking than the three days since Philip had arrived, supposedly to finalize the details of an international grant application for a project on violence in rural Colombia, but in fact, so far as Doreen could see, to spend afternoons in wine bars catching up with "old friends," which was what he called women he'd had flirtations with in far-away countries. The fact that these women were now married, or in long-term relationships, barely soothed her ire.

Anger drove her out of the shower. It was better to answer than to encourage him to spend the rest of the evening staring into the eyes of Nadia or Renata or Désirée. The whiff of emotional blackmail hung in the air of the flat, stuffy in a way unique to British flats with tiny proportions and hissing forced-air heating. She brushed past the towel draped over the lip of the sink. Her discarded pantsuit hung over the back of the couch like a substitute body gone limp. She answered the phone. Water, dripping off her hair and shoulders and breasts, dotted the tiles.

"Satty!"

The sound of her patois name struck her with a pang. She loved the way her mind raced when she was working; she was happy that Philip, in spite of his old friends, didn't actively betray her, but sometimes she forgot how much she missed West Indian people. They were the only people with whom she could relax; not so much her sisters and brother — who sometimes stared at her as though she were a space alien, even though, in the end, they were all Mam's children — but West Indian people met at random. She revelled in the way words and places from her childhood surged up in the mouths of strangers. She was disappointed not to have met West Indians in her work in London; the few engineers who weren't white English were Hong Kong Chinese, or else they came from India.

"Satty! That you?"

She let the name reverberate around the inside of her head. "That you, Rach?"

"Satty, you gotta talk to Mam. They shoot Martin. Minnie and me, us can't tell her. You gotta tell Mam. She in the kitchen —"

The flat's closeness tightened. "Shoot him where?"

"In the head. He in the hospital in Kingston. You got to tell her —"

As soon as Doreen heard the word "head," she knew he was going to die. The droplets of water on her skin sucked the heat out of her body. "I'm naked," she heard herself say, as she began to shiver.

"Don't cry, Satty! You got to tell Mam —"

"M' naked," she repeated, slipping into her Canadian girl's incompetent patois, which under normal circumstances reduced her sisters to giggles. "M' in the shower when you phone." She sat down on the couch, feeling it scratch her bum. "What I tell her? Tell me what happen ..."

Rachel told her the story that she'd heard from Gerard. "That all you know?" Doreen said. "Nobody ask Cousin John? He can check it out."

"Satty, you gotta tell Mam —"

Before Doreen could reply, Rachel put down the phone. A moment later she heard Mam's yawning voice reeling with courage and confusion. She adored her mother, helped her when she could, and was delighted that her mother was proud that one of her children had gone to university, was respected, and made good money; even though she felt exasperated by her mother's relentless humility. Doreen hated going down to the States, where black people lived in separate neighbourhoods from white people. But, being a faithful daughter, she made the trek to Miami once a year. Last year she'd invited Philip along and they had stayed in a hotel on Miami Beach. When she'd introduced Mam to Philip, Mam had looked at her sandals and said in her clearest, most correct English, "When I was young, we so poor I go to school barefoot." Doreen felt touched and terrified by her mother's need to confess the misery of her origins to a middle-class white Canadian. Or maybe it had been inverted boasting; Mam's way of telling Philip that even her rented apartment in Little Haiti was an achievement. The sight of Mam staring down at her sandals intruded on Doreen's mind as she tried not to think about Martin lying in the hospital. As always, Mam was worrying about others. "Satty? You in England? They treat you all right?"

"M'work go good, Mam. But Mam, we got terrible news. I don't know how to tell you this. You has to be brave. They shot Martin in Kingston. He in hospital with a bullet in his head."

"It not true! It not true! It not true!" The phone clunked down. She could hear Mam's voice hollering across the room in the Miami apartment. Doreen's shivers worsened; her body began to shake. She felt abandoned on the wrong side of the Atlantic. She wished Mam would come back to the phone. She wanted to be with her family. She wanted her mother. The sound of Mam's cries grew weaker. Doreen imagined Rachel and Minnie trying to comfort her, she heard Minnie's daughter shriek. Mam picked up the phone again. "Don' believe it, Satty. It all lies. Dem lazy people in that parish so jealous of Martin they say any old lie ...!"

Brisk practicality insulated her from Mam's pain. She remembered finding this strength in herself as an eight-year-old a few weeks after arriving in Toronto, when she realized she wasn't going to see her mother and siblings again, except during vacations, and that the important things in her life were becoming a normal Canadian and doing well in school. She stood up. Her practicality had toughened her to compete with the Chinese kids in math and science classes in high school, where guidance counsellors told West Indian girls with good marks to go to community college and advised white and Asian kids with the same marks to go to university; her brusqueness had spared her lingering breakups with boyfriends, freed her to abandon jobs in which she had been stagnating. She had never felt more grateful for this strength than she did now. "Rachel!" she shouted, until Rachel picked up the receiver. "I'm gettin' off this phone. Call me when you have news."

She hung up and went to get a towel.

MR. PATWARDHAN KILLED HIM.

That was what Rachel told Doreen after the funeral. Mr. Patwardhan, a fine-boned man who dressed in white shirts and wore his hair long to show off its straightness, owned the parish store. The store stood beneath two tall trees that held red akee fruit aloft. Mr. Patwardhan trimmed the hibiscus plants around the side of the building and threw his garbage behind, where he kept a pig on a tether. In the gloom beneath the shack's zinc roof, he listened to the BBC World Service. He had a scale for weighing rice and wooden shelves stacked with loaves of bread, canned meat, chocolate biscuits, and Coca-Cola. He lived with his wife and three children in a yellow clapboard house just below where the road had washed out; he drove a Chevrolet, which he kept in a padlocked garage. Mr. Patwardhan was proud that his wife's mother had come over from India; he ignored the fact that her father had been Mam's uncle and that his children looked as mixed as many others in the parish.

Mr. Patwardhan's store was also the post office. He sold stamps, received packages that arrived from relatives overseas, and changed American and Canadian dollars at the day's official exchange rates, of which he remained mysteriously informed even when the telephone lines were down. When Doreen was a little girl she went into his store to ask him the cost of a stamp for a postcard to Canada. Mr. Patwardhan must have been young then, in his twenties, although in her eyes he brimmed with adult authority. "How you know about the whole world, Mr. Patwardhan?" she asked.

"I a civilized person," he said.

Doreen remembered this when Rachel told her that Martin's visa had been mailed to Mr. Patwardhan's store. The mailman swore he'd delivered it; a brown envelope bearing the seal of the Embassy of the United States of America in Jamaica. Mr. Patwardhan said he'd never seen it. Martin, just back from a day's wiring on a condo block in New Kingston, charged into the store. Gerard went with him. "The Embassy send it last week!" Martin said. "They send it register mail. Let me see you register!"

"I don' have to show you m'register," Mr. Patwardhan said.

"I have a visa to live in America," Martin said. "Mam got the right to bring me there. And when I get there I'm gonna bring me three daughter. Me oldest daughter, she twenty, she a English teacher from the University of the West Indies. She get a good job in America. Me two little girls, they go to school …"

"You have big plans," Mr. Patwardhan said. "You have dreams of Hollywood! Maybe you forget who you are. I a civilized a person. My wife mother come from very high-caste people in India. I go to England on holiday in 1982. I see Buckingham Palace. Look at me and look at you. Look at you family. You not fit to say hello dog, hello cat to me family and you think you gonna live in America …"

"You a rude boy!" Martin shouted. "That all you are! You less civilized 'n m'arse!"

He rushed out of the store. In the garbage pile behind, swarming with ants, he and Gerard found the pig gnawing on a corner of green vinyl that had belonged to the cover of his passport.

He started his application again. He applied for a new passport and had it mailed to Cousin John's address in Kingston, made a new appointment at the U.S. Embassy, waited for four months until his day came, then went in and explained what had happened and asked if they could re-issue the visa, stamping it into his new passport, and mail it to his cousin's address. The official told him that in principle this could be done, but that they would need to investigate the original visa's disappearance. Martin waited and waited. The day after his funeral, a brown envelope arrived registered mail at Cousin John's tiny row house. "Patwardhan kill him," Rachel said. "If Martin get the visa, he safe in Miami. Patwardhan kill him as sure as if he shoot the gun."

⁓

"WHEN ARE YOU MAKING it official?" Renata asked, a teasing gleam in her eyes.

Philip took refuge from her challenge in the gloom of the wine bar. Renata had insisted on meeting here; it was *the* spot in Islington now. They'd had to wait to be admitted. As they sat down among the lozenge-shaped black marble tables where the waiters flashed past in thigh-length white jackets, Philip's first observation was that everyone was white. Renata, who was half Italian and half Tunisian and had grown up between London and Paris, was closer to being a person of colour than anyone else in the room. Their tall, blond waiter spoke with an accent that Philip took to be Polish. London might be racially mixed, but Islington wine bars were not. He wondered whether any bar in downtown Toronto would attract such a monochrome crowd.

"You're wondering how she'd feel here," Renata said, with the eerie intuition that had drawn him towards her every time they had met over the last ten years. Whenever she displayed this aspect of her personality — the last time had been during a conference in San Salvador — he resented and desired her. A few words from Renata could knock the foundations out from under his bond with Doreen by exposing their communication, in all its banal concreteness, as deficient in spontaneous understanding, intuitive affinity, and emotional depth. Each time he met her, he returned to Doreen ridden with doubts, which days of shared life slowly washed away.

"You start to see things differently," he said.

Renata nodded. "You went looking for exoticism and it's swallowed you up. You never really expected to see the world like a member of a racially oppressed minority, did you?" She sipped her wine. "Philip, when I see that side of you, I'm glad that you and I never had an affair."

For an instant, in spite of himself, he felt crushed. "I was hoping you'd have at least a few regrets," he said.

"I'll admit that in San Salvador I felt perfectly ready to shag you —"

"Weren't you with Arthur —?"

"It was very casual. I didn't have any commitment to him."

"San Salvador's a terrible place to have an affair," he said, suppressing a passing regret at having underestimated the seriousness of their flirtation there. "So utilitarian ... there was that time we met in Mombasa. That had more potential."

"Mombasa's lovely, but at that stage I was completely wrapped up in Jean-Paul." She leaned forward, her long brown hair, with its residual Italian curls, gathering around her face. "What I mean is that when I see you about to marry a Jamaican girl, I wonder how much of *me* you actually saw and how much your Canadian colonial soul was simply yearning for this frightfully glamorous crossroads between English and French and Italian and Arab."

"Doreen's actually more Canadian than she is Jamaican," he said, feeling defensive. "We've got that in common. The real difference is in her being an electrical engineer."

"She has no time for your complicated feelings about your feelings?"

"That's where I have my doubts," he conceded.

"I'm not convinced, Philip. Are you sure this isn't just sexual exoticism? I've had men interested in me for the wrong reasons. I've usually known enough not to let them get as close as you did."

Philip sat very still in his chair. He decided that, making allowances for Englishness, Renata's declaration was a compliment. "I'm glad you let me get that close," he murmured. "Sometimes I wish you'd let me get a little closer."

"Oh, it's so dismal that we're talking about this in the past tense! I don't want this stage of my life to be over."

"But you said that you and Sayid were trying to get pregnant."

"Yes ..." Renata advanced her wine glass across the table. Her index finger, curled around the stem, grazed the heel of his extended hand.

"Yes ... but ...?"

"Well —"

Philip's cellphone rang.

"Sweetie, we've got to talk. Something really serious happen."

"I'm having a drink with my friend Renata, who's going to be involved in the project."

"My brother's dead."

"What?"

"My brother Martin. They shoot him in Kingston."

"Just a second." He got to his feet. Holding the cellphone away from the table, he murmured, "Doreen's brother's been murdered.

I have to go outside." Renata's face smoothed into a blank expression that resembled hostility. Returning the cellphone to his ear, he dodged between the gleaming tables, aware of the glossy young Londoners regarding him with the disdain reserved for those who had failed to clear up business before leaving the office. He sidestepped the queue of people in expensive jackets and white dresses too skimpy for the evening chill waiting to be admitted to the bar. The brakes of black taxis screeching in his ear, he walked to the end of the picture window, where he could see Renata, alone at the table, staring straight ahead over her drink. "What happened? When did you find out?"

"About half an hour ago. Actually about three hours ago. My sisters phoned from Miami. The first news was that he was in hospital with a bullet in his head. He probably died just about when they were phoning me, but they only phone me back now."

"What did you do for three hours?"

"I watch TV. What was I supposed to do?"

"Why didn't you call me?"

"I wait to be sure. When Rachel said he was shot in the head, I figured he was going to die. I want to know for sure before I tell you."

Her reasoning confounded him. Weren't they meant to share...? He suppressed his anger, aware of her hurt and her needs, even if he didn't understand her way of dealing with them. "What happened?"

"Gerard said Martin had a fight with a guy over a girl, but I just talked to Cousin John, and he's a cop and he say it probably just robbery. In Jamaica if they rob you, they shoot you to make sure you can't tell who did it. I tol' Martin to stop goin' up Spanish Town Road wearing his fancy shirts. But he liked dressin' up, even if he did have a belly the last time I see him."

A long silence. Renata's face, visible through the muted lighting on the other side of the glass, receded into ghostliness. "It's horrible," Philip murmured.

"I'm going to have to go to Jamaica for the funeral, but Grenada is probably still on. Cousin John says for murder they do a autopsy.

It have so many murders in Kingston they have a waiting list for autopsies, so they put you on ice. The funeral might not be for three weeks."

"Do you feel okay about going on vacation at a time like this?"

"I booked my vacation. I might as well take it. If I have to go to Jamaica, Grenada's pretty close by."

"But if the funeral's in three weeks you'll have to come back from Grenada, then turn around and go back to Jamaica."

"I'll be jetlagged, but I'll be alive. My brother probably thought he still had his whole life ahead of him —"

"Look, let me go pay my bill. I'll come right over."

"No. Stay at your hotel. It don' have no reason for you to come over. The phone'll just ring all night. Mam tell me my brother's father's brothers all move to England —"

"Are they in London?"

"How do I know? Sweetie, they're not my relatives! I just have to call them. Mam give me three numbers, but nobody was home. I leave messages for them to call me back no matter how late they gets in."

"Doreen, I don't care if the phone rings! Really! I'm not far from the Northern Line. I can be at your flat in half an hour."

"Philip, can't you tell that I want to be alone?"

Fury and rejection made him turn away from the glass. He watched the taxis and red double-deckers and motor scooters hurtling through the darkness. A tall young couple in evening clothes stepped out of the wine bar to share a cigarette. The streetlights gleamed off the young man's white forehead, the cleavage exposed by the woman's gown. He hated their upper-crust accents, their unquestioning accord; they had never been put to the test by cultural difference. He wished he could express his anger with Doreen. His resentment mounted at the thought that Martin's murder gave her a licence to treat him as she pleased. "Do you think this is a good time for you to be alone?" he managed.

"I have to think about my brother's kids. The oldest girl, she's

twenty. Martin can bring her to the States until she's twenty-one.
By the time all this mess cleared up, she be twenty-one and she have
to apply on her own. It take seven years minimum to get her in ...
sweetie, you think if us get married and have a baby we could
hire her as a nanny? It's easy to get a nanny visa in Canada. You'd
like this girl, she go to university in Kingston. You think we could,
sweetie? The two younger girls, Mam's goin' to adopt them so they
can go to Miami as her kids. Their no-good mother's not interested
in them anyway. I got to figure out how to send Mam money from
here, she and Rachel and Minnie don' have money to go back for
the funeral —"

"Doreen," he said. "Doreen, you're going too fast. Slow down.
Do you not think it would be better if I came over?"

"How come? You're not helping me, Philip. Didn't you hear me
when I say I want to be alone?"

"All right, I'll call you in the morning. Maybe around nine- thirty?"

"At nine-thirty I'll be at work."

"You're not going in to work?"

"Why not? That's what I'm here for."

He felt exhausted. "All right," he said. "You've got my cellphone
number. Any time you need me, I'm here."

"Thanks a lot, sweetie. Now I'm gettin' off the phone. Martin's
uncles are probably tryin' to call me."

He stood still for a moment, breathing in the damp sooty London
air, then went back into the wine bar. "Is she all right?" Renata said.

"Doreen's invincible. She doesn't even need me to come over
tonight."

"She may be invincible now, but she's unlikely to stay that way.
Being independent is just her way of coping. She'll need you later....
You can't imagine how much she'll need you." She gave him a pallid
smile. "This may be your defining moment, Philip. After this you'll
have to marry her."

DOREEN FELT EXHAUSTED BY death. She, who rarely had spare

minutes, spent every spare minute on the phone or the computer. She made calls to Birmingham, London, Kingston, Brooklyn, and Toronto. She went on the internet to hunt for bargain flights and transfer money. In Miami, Mam had taken on an extra shift to pay for her trip to the funeral. Minnie, having decided to stay in Miami, took the bus to the domestic help agency to sign up for work. She asked the bus driver for directions, struck up a conversation with him, and got his phone number. She came home, having forgotten to go to the agency, and told Rachel and Mam that she had met the love of her life. Every time Doreen phoned to talk about flights or accommodation or the funeral service, Minnie diverted the conversation to love. Doreen had to call in the middle of the night London time to catch Mam and Rachel at home in the evenings. Rachel swore at Minnie for leaving her daughter alone at nights to go lie under some damned fat Haitian bus driver.

"Maybe that's her way of dealing with it," Doreen heard herself murmur, recognizing that the phrase came from Philip, that she was falling into middle-class psychologizing of the kind that had always irritated her. She felt her bond with Philip pulling her away from her family right when she wanted to be closest to them. She longed to push him away, even as her survival instinct told her to cling to him.

As soon as Cousin John phoned with the funeral date, she went to the boss of the British wing of the project to explain that she would need a second week off five days after her vacation in Grenada. "My brother died in Jamaica," she explained, uttering what she had decided would be her only words on the subject. "Please don't tell everyone."

"What did he die of?" the chief engineer, a sharp-featured man with dark hair and a North-of-England accent, asked.

She bit her lip, astonished to find herself crumbling into tears. The Brit looked vaguely disgusted. She felt herself absorbing his disgust, loathing herself for being trapped in a family that confirmed every stereotype of the racist British tabloid newspapers about how West Indians lived and died. She longed for Philip. He loomed up in her mind's eye, as large and soft and white as the snow-covered welcoming expanse of Canada. That night, she went to his hotel, and they lay side by side on his bed, holding each other in a light embrace. "My only brother's dead," she murmured. "It feels surreal." It took her a long while to tell him about her meeting with the chief engineer.

"Do you think you should see a counsellor?" he said.

"Don' you psychologize me!" Weakness sapping her bravado, she said, "I just want to be loved."

He squeezed her. In a repentant tone, he said, "I've told a few of my friends back in Canada what happened. I'm sorry, I couldn't help it ... the thing is, I can't believe the reactions I'm getting. People I would never think of as racist are saying 'He wasn't really her brother if they had different fathers,' or 'How much of a brother was he if they didn't grow up together?' All of them implying that of course you don't feel as much pain as a white person ..."

Doreen hugged him without meeting his eyes. "I'm really happy you're over here, sweetie. I wish I could stay the night, but I've got to go back to the flat and check my phone messages."

He looked as though he were about to protest, or offer to accompany her, but she could see in his eyes that he knew better. For a passing instant she regretted having trained him so well. Next morning at work she discovered, to her exasperation, that the personnel manager had made an appointment for her with a counsellor; she succeeded in forgetting about the appointment during a long meeting, and two days later she and Philip left for Grenada.

When they returned from their subdued week of listening to the waves thundering onto an isolated beach, there were thirteen messages on the efficiency flat's answering machine. The first one was from Cousin John. "Satty, I know who kill him."

She got through to him early in the morning Kingston time, after he'd come off an overnight shift. He told her he'd seen the records: Martin had been shot on a side street near the route taxi yard. He'd been out to the bars and was on his way home. Taxis to the countryside waited in the yard; at night thieves idled nearby, looking for easy marks among men who came back drunk. Martin had taken a wrong turn and stumbled into an alley where he had been shot in order to be robbed or shot after being robbed ...

"You said you know who kill him," Doreen said.

"The police are apprised of which miscreants frequent the yard," Cousin John said in the colonial-sounding officialese he adopted when questioned about his job. They knew these gangs, knew most of their members. "I make you a list of ten names and the rude boy that kill him on that list. But I got no evidence to tell me which one do the deed. It more like the place did kill him than the person."

⁓

SHE FLEW TO JAMAICA on a cheap charter from Manchester. Having overlooked the note on the ticket that warned passengers who had not chosen the meal option to bring their own food, she landed in Montego Bay whoozy with hunger, exhaustion, grief, and anxiety. Philip had returned to Canada two days earlier, having concluded his meetings. She had felt painfully close to him in Grenada, but once they were back in London his frustration with her rushed schedule and their failure to spend the night together prior to his departure, surfaced in his eyes as visible impatience, unsuccessfully covered up by polite Canadian consideration. She wondered whether she would ever teach him that he couldn't flirt with other women then expect her to damage her career by taking time off to be with him. Rachel and Minnie told her that a jake who flirted was better than a Jamaican brother who slept with three girls at once. She knew this, of course, and she saw that in her sisters' eyes Philip was an unimaginable catch — although not as good a catch, she insisted, as she was for him! "He didn't use to flirt," she told them. "I think it's just a phase he's going through since we started talking about getting married." It was when she spoke about relationships in this way, so alien to her sisters' experiences of men, that she saw

Rachel and Minnie stare at her as though she were a space alien. Their confusion reminded her of the distance separating her from Philip. As hard as she tried, she would never make him understand that he could survive an easygoing, unspectacular career because, whatever happened, he would always be a middle-class white man while she, unless she was conspicuously successful, would be a poor Jamaican girl who was suspected of being up to no good. She wasn't certain, in any event, that she had ever fallen in love with Philip or with any of the others. She recognized this as the obverse side of her life-saving brusqueness; there were certain vulnerabilities with which she wouldn't trust anybody, a distance she must maintain out of self-protection. If love was what turned Mam into a sobbing wreck at the mention of her first baby-father's name, thirty-two years after his death, she could do without it. If love, of a different strain, was what was made her feel this awful, heavy sickness every time she thought about Martin, she preferred not to feel it. She hated the way that her good memories of Martin kept being interrupted by bad ones. The summer she was fifteen, she'd woken up at night in Mam's house, with its tiny partitioned rooms, needing to pee. When she got to the bathroom, the door opened and Mr. Patwardhan's slutty niece came out. "I'm with Mar-tin," the girl drawled. In the morning Doreen called her brother a dog; they didn't speak to each other for the rest of her vacation. The next summer things were fine between them and he tickled her the way he always had. Yet, every time she thought of Martin's final moments — had he realized that his life was ending? — she saw life's appearance of eternity as an illusion and felt time pressing her to get married and have children.

By landing in MoBay, she was sneaking into Jamaica the back way. She had chosen the flight to avoid Kingston. She couldn't bear the thought of seeing middle-class suburbs of low Spanish-style homes such as those which Martin had wired, their drives spread with white stone and their windows caged with burglar bars; the downtown streets that were blocked by cops in flak jackets and semi-automatic rifles every time there was a murder; the gated embassies and business headquarters of New Kingston; or the aging grey English buildings near the port. She refused to stay in the city where she'd been born and she didn't think she could take the crowding and confusion up in the parish, where seven or eight people would be sleeping in every shack to squeeze in all the funeral guests. She didn't want to be around too many people, but she was equally afraid of loneliness. She had rented a tourist flat in Port Maria, on the north coast, near the road that led up into the hills and asked Minnie to share it with her. An old classmate of Minnie's named Ralph lived in Port Maria and worked part-time as a taxi driver. Ralph offered to drive them up to the parish on the day of the funeral. This suited Doreen fine. She regarded this funeral the way she thought about giving birth: as an experience to avoid, even if you had to go through it.

She arrived in Port Maria as dusk was sliding over the round blue bay, glimmering on the towers of the crumbling grey nineteenth-century English churches. On the way into town, skinny young men stood on the roadside offering spherical green guinea fruit to the passing motorists. The poor, crowded town centre shocked her; she took a taxi to the resort complex. She relaxed at the sound of British and American voices in the lobby, then felt angry. Shouldn't she feel more comfortable with Jamaicans? She watched television in her room, sticking to the Jamaican channels, while she waited for Minnie, who was being picked up at Kingston airport by Ralph. Minnie arrived at midnight, six hours late, her eyes bright, her large breast heaving. "Satty, I in love! I fall in love with Ralph. We go to his house." She laughed. "He a sweet man!"

"What about your bus driver?"

"Ralph the only man for me. M'come here, m'live with Ralph."

"You can't bring your daughter back here. Mam want the whole family out of Jamaica."

Minnie looked at her like a naughty child. The baby of the family, she indulged herself until Mam said no. That was the line she couldn't cross. With a defiant look, she said, "I go with Ralph. We come get you in the morning."

"You be here by eight o'clock, Minnie! If we don' leave at eight, we don' reach on time." To stress the seriousness of her command, she said the words that made her voice choke, "We don' reach late for our brother funeral. We show respect."

At eight thirty the next morning, fed up with pacing the lobby in her black dress, Doreen phoned a taxi company and negotiated a wallet-draining fare up into the hills. As the taxi climbed past bougainvillea so bright it hurt her eyes, she thought: My brother is dead. She felt helpless. The taxi turned off the blacktop at a curve above a gaping green valley where a sign warned: *Speed Kills! Don't Be in a Hurry to Enter Eternity!* Her anger with Minnie faded as the taxi hit the red earth of the side roads that wound through the bright green tropical vegetation. Her hands began to shake. As they passed through town, she saw Mr. Boom, the taxi driver, loading up his cab with funeral guests who sat on each other's knees. It was really happening. Her brother was really dead. She clasped her hands in her lap. "Miss," the driver said, "if I come to Canada you give me a place to stay? M'wan' see sweet Toronto! M' make my fortune there."

"You think a fortune all that matter?" she said.

Her heart clenched as the little wooden church, just down the road from Mr. Patwardhan's store, came into sight. The tropical canopy cast the spire, and the yard in front of it, into shadow. Doreen spotted Mam and rushed out of the taxi, almost forgetting to pay the driver. Relatives who had been put up by Old Man Austin and his sons approached from the other side of the clearing. Doreen hugged Mam; Rachel and Rachel's children; Gerard and Monique; and Martin's two little daughters, who didn't have proper shoes for the funeral because their no-good mother was too cheap to buy them; and his oldest daughter, the severe, religious, hard-working twenty-year-old who had lost the chance to be brought to the States by her father; and uncles and aunts from Kingston; and others from surrounding villages; and people who she used to see when she came in the summer but whose names she'd forgotten. They complimented her on having had her hair straightened for the funeral. Cars from Kingston were parked along the road. People from Brooklyn and Toronto arrived, carrying packages of clothes for relatives at home. Cousin John and his police brothers came in their uniforms. There were men from construction gangs and even a white man with straight grey hair who owned the company for which Martin had done most of his wiring. She was amazed by how many people her brother had known. She wished, for a moment, that she had asked Philip to come with her. Yet, Philip felt far away. Before she knew what was happening, the movement of the crowd was pulling her towards the tiny church. She hurried to catch up to Mam and Rachel so that Mam could enter the church in dignity, with a daughter on either arm. As soon as the three of them stepped inside, they saw the open coffin in front of the altar and began to cry. They kept crying when the pastor called for silence. He lifted his arms and started the service. Then Minnie and Ralph came in. Minnie's black blouse was open to the swell of her bosom, exposing a twisted white bra strap. She rushed to the front of the church and stared into the coffin. "Goodbye, Martin," she said. She turned around, looking at the astonished, disapproving congregation, then hurried towards Mam, Rachel, and Doreen for comfort, leaving Ralph stranded by the church door. In a whisper audible across the church, she said, "You see that, Satty? He got a exit wound in his forehead!"

"I don't want to see no exit wound," Doreen said.

The pastor started the service. Every time he mentioned Martin's name, Mam moaned. Doreen felt Minnie's weight growing heavier as her big little sister leaned on her shoulder. The pastor's words about Martin's diligent nature and support of his daughters made her cry harder. Different threads of misery wound together: the misery of Martin's death, the misery of being at this horrible event, the misery of being jetlagged and broke from all the money she'd spent for herself and others to get here, the misery of feeling the intrusion of bad memories as well as good.

When the service was over they went out into the clearing to find Mr. Patwardhan working at a portable stove. "I am cookin' assiduously," he said. "I make the best oxtail with rice 'n' peas in the parish."

"M' no' buy from that man," Rachel said.

Mam stepped forward. "M'wan' oxtail with rice 'n' peas."

The guests formed a line behind Mam. They paid Mr. Patwardhan and ate their oxtail in silence while overhead the breeze thrashed the tropical vegetation.

⸻

"TRY THE OXTAIL," PHILIP said.

"This is the first time you've bought me a meal as a married man."

"No doubt other married men have bought you meals."

"Don't be cheeky," Renata said. "I may be single again, but I want to see your photographs."

Philip, in London for three days to finalize the details of the rural violence project, had suggested that they meet at this West Indian restaurant on Wardour Street. They paid and took their numbers to a dark table in the back. The lunchtime crowd was a mixture of West Indians and white Londoners. Leaning close to him over the reggae music, she said, "Did you pop the question or did she?"

"She did. Though it wasn't so much a question as a command. When Doreen came back to Toronto, she took me to a jewellery store and told me I was buying her a promise ring. Three weeks later she mentioned she'd gone off the pill months ago and I no longer had a choice."

"Of course she knew you'd do the honourable thing," Renata said. "I never thought you'd be a parent before I was … show me the photographs!"

Philip lifted an envelope from the breast pocket of his jacket.

Renata opened it. He always felt a fullness, accompanied by a stroke of fear, at the sight of the pictures. "Sometimes," he confessed, "I think about how he wouldn't have been born — not now anyway, maybe not ever — if Martin hadn't been murdered."

"He's a fighter," Renata said, staring at the photographs. "You can see it in his eyes."

Leaning over her shoulder, Philip allowed his fingertips to graze Renata's silky blouse. His son's face scowled at him, his balled fists held high. Philip withdrew his hand, knowing there was no limit to what this boy would have done in order to be born.

11

A TIME OF RED EARTH

IN QUISSICO, WHERE THEY stopped for lunch in a yard of red dust, Philip realized that they were running out of time. Children ran and shouted among the families picnicking behind the white stucco municipal building and the lookout over the bay speckled with green islands. He touched Doreen's arm to draw her attention to the sight, but she continued to watch Françoise and Paloma hurrying around the market stalls, chain-smoking and gesticulating as they bargained for Tanzanian *capulanas*. The Petromoc station was out of gas and the staff at the roadside diner were surly, but miraculously the toilets were working and the *caril de galinha com arroz* was a perfect replica of the dish served at the Mozambican restaurant in Mouraria where Philip had eaten during his Portuguese course in Lisbon prior to being dispatched to the project to develop tourist skills in the populations of two villages on the coast near the Island of Mozambique.

After years of speaking Spanish in Latin America, he had been afraid that he would choke on Portuguese. Yet, a month in Lisbon and two months in the villages had made the archaic grammar, with its inflected infinitives and future subjunctives, a natural shape in his mouth. When Doreen came to visit him, he took ten days off and found a bus from the capital, where her flight landed, to Inhambane. From the covered market, patrolled by adolescent boys who walked hand-in-hand — "It's their culture," Philip had explained; "I'm sure that's what they tell you," she replied — they had ridden a packed *chapa* out to the coast at Tofo. A wide beach of brawling Indian Ocean breakers, deserted but for the occasional South African backpacker, spread in front of their thatched cabin, allowing them to ignore the malarial swamp that stretched back from the side road. The Mohamed family, who owned the cabins, hired the impossibly petite local men — Africans as fine-boned as the most delicate Asians — to stand guard at night. Getting to Tofo turned out to be easier than finding transportation back to the capital. They were down to the final days of their vacation when Françoise and Paloma, who were sharing the adjacent cabin, went into a huddle over a map, then walked across to the veranda where Doreen lay in her bikini. "We have a plan," Françoise said, "and we wonder if you would like to join us." It seemed foolish not to make the two-day drive back to Maputo with them in their rented Ford Fusion.

They drove past circular villages of thatched huts on low stilts — the chief's hut bigger than the rest — often overshadowed by a cellphone tower; girls squatting down to beat cassava while overseeing squads of tiny siblings. There were children everywhere. People at the roadside were selling woven reed stools, firewood, carvings, and polished mahogany furniture in front of billboards promoting the use of mosquito nets and condoms respectively to combat malaria and AIDS. Philip, accustomed to the country's impoverished north, sensed that they had entered the more prosperous, faster-moving southern zone dominated by the capital.

"Závora," Françoise said. "This is where we spend the night. A friend of mine say life begin on this beach!"

Paloma, sitting next to her in the front seat, clapped her hands. Françoise, who had left France to live with Paloma in Barcelona, made the decisions in their relationship. She was sixty; a no-nonsense financial planner who wore gold-rimmed glasses. Paloma, arching her sharply defined black eyebrows and stretching her legs in her narrow-hipped stovepipe blue jeans with the cuffs rolled up, acted younger than her probable age of thirty-seven or thirty-eight. She loped along in Françoise's wake with tomboy enthusiasm, calibrating the world through the older woman's finely ground lenses. The difference in their ages exempted them from the pressures of time. He envied them for being able to enjoy their relationship without needing to define it, make clear what it was for or decide where it would lead. He was older than Doreen, but, unlike Françoise, he was not in charge. Having paid down more than half of the mortgage on her condo, Doreen was settled; Philip was still renting. They revelled in their game of global tag, each taking off to work assignments in faraway places and daring the other to follow them. Power shuttled back and forth between their souls as erratically as it did when their lean bodies of dramatically different colours tussled on a bed. How long could this last? He wondered again what kind of couple Françoise and Paloma took them to be, what image of a black woman and a white man from Canada had enticed these two Europeans into inviting him and Doreen to accompany them on their road trip and whether anyone else in the Ford was as aware as he was of how fast time was passing.

⁓

IN MAPUTO, DURING DOREEN'S first days in the country, the police had tried to shake them down twice, right on Avenida 25 de Setembro in front of the old colonial post office. Each time an officer had demanded that Philip pay a bribe by threatening to arrest Doreen for prostitution. Doreen, fortunately, hadn't understood their accusations. As the skinny cops threatened, "*Vamos para a esquadra,*" she, not realizing that they were planning to take her to the police station, chanted in loud English, "I don't understand what you're saying!" The officers harangued Philip for corrupting an innocent

Mozambican girl. Doreen's Canadian passport shut down these accusations, reducing the policemen to making laboured claims that their visas were invalid and enabling Philip, after more arguments, to wriggle out of paying a bribe. In less menacing contexts, the comedy continued when they asked directions, or ordered meals in restaurants in the Polana district. People directed their replies squarely at Doreen, taking for granted that the black woman, not the white man, spoke Portuguese. The day of her arrival in Maputo, after they had made love, he had stared at their reflections in a mirror on the door of the hotel room's closet. Stretched side by side, they pressed each other into uncompromising molds. Had Doreen been with a West Indian man, she would have belonged to a mixed-race couple; Philip's pinkish hands, clasped against her ribs, made her black. His legs had never looked as white as they did tangled up with hers. Taking her in his arms, he ceased to be another guy from Kingston, Ontario and became a white man on a planet where most people were some shade of brown. The unitary identities they forced on each other were irrefutable because they were aware that these were the terms in which others saw them. Philip tried to dismiss this ruthless mutual reductionism as a public pressure from which their private emotional issues were absolved. Yet, racial dualism seeped into their conversations; sometimes race *was* their emotional issue. Confirming each other as black and white respectively defined their union as a challenge to others or themselves; it kept some people at a distance. Others, such as Françoise and Paloma, were drawn closer.

"ZÁVORA!" FRANÇOISE SHOUTED, WAVING at the sign for the turn-off.The Fusion left the two-lane blacktop highway, where sparse shrubbery grew in the light-brown dust. The side road that led to the coast was a belt of red earth. The dust, which looked like a fiery frosting covering a harder, more igneous bedrock, sifted with treacherous instability, hinting at the unsuspected beings that might be about to spring forth. They felt the dust drag at the sedan's tires as they rolled forward over the bright orange side road. Beyond a crooked baobab tree, the landscape was deserted. In the middle of this nothingness, he felt overcome with impatience and need. Doreen would be in Mozambique for only three more days. Bright green bushes closed in; the road gouged between them. Only the central band was firm enough to drive on; the edges — "shoulder" didn't quite capture their flat, tousled softness; the Portuguese word, *berma*, caught the amorphousness better — were as gently flaked as red-orange baking soda.

At the base of a long hill, a lone woman with a bronze-coloured scarf on her head was walking down the middle of the road. When she saw the sedan, she shuffled onto the soft border. Françoise stopped the car, Doreen opened the back left-hand door, and Philip leaned over. As the speaker of Portuguese, he handled communication. Françoise and Paloma were happy to expose their mangled English in the car in order not to exclude Doreen from conversation, but they didn't like being the sorts of tourists — Philip had met Spaniards and Italians like this in Maputo — who, not knowing Portuguese, spoke loudly in their own Latin languages and expected the locals to understand.

"Is it far to Závora?" Philip asked.

"Závora … *sim*."

"Is Závora close?" he tried.

"*Perto. Sim.*" The woman nodded.

"What's she saying?" Paloma asked.

"She doesn't know much Portuguese." Around the Island of Mozambique, where he was working, most people were bilingual, spiking their Portuguese sentences with Macua words. Surprised to find some-one this far south who barely knew Portuguese, he motioned toDoreen to close the door.

Fixing him with a stare, the woman said, "*Boleia*."

Her hand on the door, Doreen glanced at him. "She wants a lift," he said.

"All right. Give her a lift," Françoise huffed into the steering wheel.

Doreen slid over to make space. Setting a small, knotted bag in her lap, the woman stared at the upholstery. When Françoise slid the Fusion's automatic transmission into first gear to climb the hill, she gripped Doreen for dear life, an African woman seeking solace from a woman of African descent amid the supercharged madness of Europeans. The Ford's velocity reached the dizzying speed of twenty kilometres per hour. Philip wasn't sure whether it was a good or a bad idea for Françoise to drive this slowly. They avoided skidding onto the soft edges, but the car's momentum faltered. Two-thirds of the way up the hill, the wheels spun in vain.

"We must get out and *poouush*!" Françoise said.

Doreen opened the door and gestured to the woman to leave. The woman looked suspicious, as though stopping the car were a ruse to get rid of her.

"*Fora*," Philip said. "*Temos de empujar.*"

The woman shuffled out. He and Doreen followed. Philip joined Paloma at the rear bumper. They pushed as hard as they could as Françoise eased the Fusion into gear. The wheels spun, spraying red soil that felt heavy as it landed on his hiking boots. The car was going nowhere. They tried again. The Ford slewed towards the soft border. Françoise took her foot off the accelerator. Philip walked to the front of the car.

"I think we are not going to Závora," Françoise said.

"Where are we going to spend the night?" Doreen's voice was anxious. "What time is it, hon?"

The local woman stood gripping her bag, her eyes fixed on the Fusion's back seat.

"We've got time. If we get back on the highway we'll find something."

"Who would think such a small hill is so difficult to climb?" Françoise said.

She shut the door and backed the car straight down the hill.

The burnished band in the middle of the trench between the bushes was wider at the bottom. By tentative stages, with Paloma signalling when to reverse and when to stop, she turned the Fusion around. Glancing back, Philip saw that the woman, gripping her bag, had climbed to the crest of the hill and was gazing back at them as though unable to believe that the foreigners' car bogging down in the dust was anything other than a trick to avoid giving her a lift.

"How long till sunset?" Doreen asked.

He glanced at his wrist as though expecting to find a watch. "We have to hurry ... we'll be fine."

"Which is it?" Doreen said. "Will we make it or won't we?"

⌒

IF THEY HAD MADE it up the hill and spent the night at Závora, their lives would have been different. The conviction crowded in on him. This was his first trip to southern Africa in a decade; nowhere could be more different from "sunny Mozambique," as the Bob Dylan song went, than Johannesburg in the southern winter. Whatever he had expected, it wasn't this tamped-down, high-altitude greyness, more reminiscent of Mexico City or Bogotá in the rainy season than of anywhere he had been in Africa. The conference hotel was a fortress. When his London-based Nigerian colleague, Obi, asked at the reception desk where he could buy toothpaste, the attendant had insisted on sending someone out to buy it for him rather than allowing Obi to walk three blocks on his own. The control made Philip mutinous. On the afternoon of the workshop on micro-credit — a subject about which he had attended more than enough workshops — he took off into the old downtown. He had a Skype date with Désirée later that afternoon, but nothing to detain him in the meantime.

The business district had emptied out after the end of apartheid, white money fleeing to remote suburbs. As Philip walked downhill, exertion and the altitude stoking up his cold into a headache, the drab 1960s office towers reared in front of him, tarnished by the chilly smog. The ground-floor shops catered to the people who had moved in from countries farther north: cheap bulk groceries, fast-food joints specializing in mutton-on-pap, women dressed in boldly patterned robes searing meat on open grills in the street while others sold bananas and vegetables, a dark cove of a place offering *First-Rate Penis Extensions* next to a store selling wedding suits, as though it were a natural progression to move from the former doorway to the latter. Makeshift tarpaulins spread with belts, T-shirts, and watches filled every empty street corner; stalls spilled over the side streets that reached towards Newtown, a derelict industrial district with rough-edged aspirations to bohemian gentrification. The stalls boxed the traffic into a single lane. He saw no one else who was white, heard no English. Black and white: here in South Africa the old dualism remained unsettled. Rankled by the need to talk, he crouched down opposite a squatting man who was selling watches spread over a plastic sheet. "How much is the orange watch?" he asked.

INTIMIDATED BY JOHANNESBURG'S FEARSOME reputation, he had left his Bulova in Désirée's flat in Stoke Newington. In the old days he had never worn watches; they attracted thieves and discouraged equanimity about chronically late local transportation. He had bought the Bulova on Nathan Road in Hong Kong during a conference after he had moved to Ottawa and was attending a lot of meetings. He found it less intrusive to glance at his wrist than to tap his cellphone while someone else was speaking. He had brought neither the Bulova nor his cell, with its exorbitant roaming charges, to South Africa. Stashing some of his stuff at Désirée's place was part of his attempt to claim her, persuading her that a London-to-Ottawa transatlantic relationship deserved to be taken seriously. Long distances and lengthy separations had never troubled Doreen. Yet, now circumstances were different. "We have children who belong in different countries," Désirée had said when he had extended his London stopover to five days. Désirée's son, David — spurning his mother's acute-angled, tan-coloured face, which retained a hint of Morocco amid a certain lascivious French rectitude — was a blond English public school boy in a blue blazer, who took after his "something-in-the-City" father. She couldn't uproot him, even if that were legally feasible. Her concern for David stirred up Philip's guilt towards his own son, Martin, who also resembled his father, albeit with brown skin and dark hair that fell into fraying curls that he would no doubt twist into dreadlocks when he became a rebellious teenager. And, Philip thought, he would have plenty to rebel against. Since he had moved to Ottawa to hustle grants, he didn't make it to Toronto often enough to even pretend to be an involved dad.

When Martin was born, unplanned and unexpected (unexpected on his part: Doreen, in shock from the news of her brother's murder in Jamaica, had gone off the pill without telling him), the three of them had crammed into Doreen's condo. During the first year he had felt as though he were drugged; he had caught up on his sleep only when he flew to Colombia to work on the rural violence project, or hopped across the pond to London, where the project's funding agency was based. There, after months without sex, he recovered the despicable, indispensable illusion of radiating masculine allure by passing flirtatious evenings in Soho or Islington with Renata or Désirée. At home, even as Doreen boasted of how her hi-tech sisters in Silicon Valley envied her generous Canadian maternity leave, he could feel her chafing to get back to work at Micro-Transitions North. She resented his absences; not so much because he was absent, but because he was working and she wasn't. When he returned to the condo, she ignored him, or handed him the baby only to criticize the way he held his son, or the words he cooed at him, or to reprimand him for his shoddy diaper-changing technique. For the first eighteen months the baby was little more than a squalling annoyance. Even as Doreen often seemed impatient with Martin, she allowed his tiny body to drain away the current of her fascinated energy that used to flow straight into their sex life. As a tiny stranger, who also had a penis, sucked on her nipples for dear life, Doreen no longer confronted Philip as a lover — or even a breadwinner (for all his business travel, she made more money than he did) — but as a potential menace to her son's health; one more threat, if a well-intentioned, clumsy one, to Martin's well-being. She would not allow Martin to die a sudden, unexpected death like his uncle, whose name they had given him. Philip was never at ease with this name, worrying that it was a bad omen. Beneath his disquiet simmered their emerging power struggle over who Martin would be. By the time the tot started to walk, he realized that his son might grow up to be seen by others (by teachers, by the police) as a no-good Jamaican dude; about the most dangerously disadvantaged position from which to enter life in Toronto. Each time he tried to spare Martin from this fate by insisting that they clip his insurgent locks or, as he began to talk, by drilling him to pronounce the *s* on the end of the third-person singular verb — to say "he goes" instead of "he go" — she said, "Don't teach him to despise his culture." He replied, "His culture will be a hybrid culture." Even as he uttered it — hoping to win her over in the knowledge that she, too, was a partisan of cultural mixing, defining herself as a person of mixed race even though most people saw her as black — the rejoinder sounded weak, and, worse, suspect. Was he smuggling a racism he couldn't acknowledge in through the back door of parental concern? The most painful part of the experience was that it was when Martin reached the ages of two and three, transforming into a sharp-eyed, sassy little boy who capered to get his attention, mock-boxed with him and called him "Pappy" as he rolled Fisher-Price trucks across the carpet to the glass wall that gave onto a twelfth-floor view of Lake Ontario, that his long, intense, eternal-feeling relationship with Doreen began to run out of time.

⌒

THE SQUATTING MAN LIFTED an eyebrow. At the hotel reception desk the attendants consulted with each other in an African language —

either Xhosa or Zulu, Obi said — before answering guests' queries in confident English, but the migrants and refugees from other African countries who filled the downtown streets, where until twenty years ago white stockbrokers had held sway, spoke no English at all. Philip and the vendor mouthed at each other in mutual incomprehension.

"*Quanto custa o relógio?*" His query was greeted with a shake of the head. The man wasn't Mozambican. He switched to French: "*Combien?*"

"*Pour vous, mon ami, un très bon prix.*"

"*Vous venez d'où, monsieur?*"

"*Du Congo.*"

The man passed him a watch — not the garish orange one he had asked for, but a Bulova knock-off. Philip examined it. The vendor had offered the white man his most expensive merchandise. The second hand wasn't moving. He wound the tiny knob: the dials remained inert. He complained to the vendor, who seemed surprised by his objection. It didn't matter if the watches were broken, Philip realized, because the people who bought them had no jobs to get to, no schedules to meet; they purchased watches purely as adornments. As he was doing the same, it was incumbent on him to buy the Bulova. His purchase would be a form of direct foreign aid. He wondered what horrors had driven this man out of Congo. As they began to bargain, in a courtly way, Philip asked, "*Ça fait longtemps que vous êtes en Afrique du Sud?*"

"*Trop longtemps,*" the vendor replied with a grimace. "*Je déteste ce pays.*"

The eternally overlooked irony: as much as people hated having refugees on their doorsteps, the refugees hated being there even more. No country of asylum could ever match the familiarity of home. Observing how the wrinkles around the man's eyes dropped down to cut into his cheeks, Philip suggested a lower price. He bargained sufficiently to maintain his self-respect and the man's respect for him. Even if he didn't beat the price down very much, this was going to be the cheapest Bulova he would find, its price further reduced by the parlous state of the South African Rand.

He bought the watch and strapped it on his wrist. The pseudo-Bulova's ersatz extravagance added to his conspicuousness in the impoverished, shuffling crowd. "So where are all the white people?" Obi had asked, in a mocking voice, after their first day at the conference. "I thought South Africa had white people."

Philip walked into Library Square, where the stone Victorian buildings of long-dead colonial administrators were falling into ruins, the glass knocked out of the windows from street-level up to the seventh or eighth floor. Unnerved by the emptiness, he returned to the crowds of Newtown. Here every eye was on him and his stopped watch. He stood out glaringly as the only white hide in the clammy mist of the grey afternoon. He wondered how these people would see him if Doreen were at his side. How would they see Doreen? She had longed to visit South Africa. The stalls covered most of the street; the traffic in the single lane left free slowed to a crawl. A taxi stopped at his hip. The windows were down. He leaned over and asked the driver if he was free. The driver nodded and Philip got in.

Not knowing where to go, he made conversation about the weather. "It's damp."

"It rained in Soweto last night."

"Are you from Soweto?"

"Born and bred up there."

The driver was a wiry man with grey hair. Soweto must have been a very different place when he was growing up. "Take me to Soweto."

Once they had settled on a price, Philip felt that he was finally doing something constructive. As a student, he had cheered on the marches and demonstrations in the black township during the final years of apartheid from a succession of beer-stained couches in Ontario university towns. He had watched Soweto on television, never imagining he would have the chance to go there.

They drove south through the downtown. Billboards in glaring green and yellow urged voters to support the African National Congress. *Do It for Madiba!* ran the slogan next to the welcoming face of Nelson Mandela.

"You had better do it for Madiba," the driver said. "There is no good reason to do it for the present gentleman."

In the southern end of the city, a poor, run-down Chinese neighbourhood surrounded a large police station, yielding, as the buildings grew sparser, to more recent, better-financed Chinese installations; vast wholesale warehouses spangled with Chinese ideograms lined the highway that separated Johannesburg from Soweto.

"Which Soweto do you want to see? There is rich Soweto with the Nelson Mandela and Desmond Tutu houses, then there is ordinary Soweto for people like me. Then there is a very poor Soweto."

"Take me to the poor Soweto."

Giving Philip a wary look, the driver said, "You don't know how beautiful this city look when freedom come. Before that rabble move in. They're not like us. They have no culture of work! They just sit in the street with their rotten fruit and make the place ugly. It's a tragedy." He shook his head. "Congo, Zimbabwe, Mozambique —!"

"I worked in Mozambique. I liked it there."

Changing the subject, the driver said, "I know a girl who gives tours. We see if she there."

⁓

"NIGHT FALLS REALLY FAST here, hon," Doreen said. "You know it's dangerous to be on the highway after dark."

"There is another lodge that my friends recommend," Françoise said, relieving the pressure, though Philip knew that it was he whom Doreen blamed for getting them into this bind.

In the late afternoon sunlight the vendors along the roadside were selling cashew nuts. They stopped to buy a bag. Philip asked whether they were close to Chidenguele.

"*Está perto,*" the vendor said. "*Muito perto.*"

"It's close," he said, aware that this word's meaning was flexible.

"When we are near Chidenguele," Françoise said, "we must look for the sign."

The roadside turned bleak. For the next few minutes they saw no one. Philip munched the delicious cashews. Doreen, refusing them, leaned forward to scrutinize the road over Françoise's shoulder. "What it say there?" she said. "Sunset Beach!"

Françoise turned left off the highway. As they hit the side road, driving towards the ridges, they saw that the sun had begun to set. Time was short now. The slanting light, more orange than yellow, enveloped his forearm as he laid his hand on Doreen's wrist, drenching their skin colours to kindred shades. Doreen tugged him back into the Fusion's soft upholstery. "We need a four-by-four," she whispered in his ear. "How come Françoise don't rent a four-by-four?"

"Don't worry," Françoise said. "I take a dangerous driving course."

The Ford jerked and bumped. Thick bushes — less luxuriant, darker, and more bristly than those on the road to Závora — rasped against the car's doors on either side of the track. Philip gave Doreen a kiss in the hope of reassuring her. When he straightened up to look out the windshield, he saw that here the dust was not red but brown. The ruts looked hard and resistant.

"Why did you took a dangerous driving course?" Paloma asked Françoise.

"To be with a man I was in love with," Françoise replied. "Then, I was still foolish and fell in love with men."

"Men can drive you crazy," Doreen said. "But they have their uses."

"Men are a part of my life I almost cannot remember," Françoise said. "It feels like the memories of a different person."

Philip stared out the window at a glimmering lagoon that had appeared in an opening in the bushes. Clothes were spread out to dry on the brambles next to the shoreline. A tanker truck had dropped a hose into the lagoon; two men directed it as they sucked up water. He felt as gloomy as the sinking daylight. The present always became the past, inaccessible like Françoise's youth; only the beginnings of new lives mitigated this process. Since Doreen's arrival in Maputo a week earlier, he had seen that he needed stability. It had taken him a while, among the breakers in Tofo, to come to terms with this realization. He blamed his emotional delay on the way they had been received as a couple in Maputo. The need to understand how race was framed in Mozambique — where a Marxist revolution had demoted local languages and identities, enthroning Portuguese as the bearer of an ethos of egalitarian cultural mixing without erasing old suspicions about white men and black women — had distracted him from his own needs. The drive south was allowing him to concentrate. He wanted to fix their relationship in place in a way that long-distance global tag didn't allow. Their tussling had swayed back and forth for five years, one of them growing broody and sentimental just as the other became enthused with some new project. The truth, though, was that he was guiltier than she of compulsive evasiveness: her office was in Mississauga, most of her business trips lasted only days; his projects went on for months or years. It was his fault, not hers, that they had not settled down. The recognition coincided with the surge of a need to make this up to her. As the Fusion thumped over the ruts, going up and down the bumpy hills into the welling darkness that promised an ocean-front lodge, he resented the other couple's presence for preventing him from expressing all that he felt.

They came over the top of a ridge where sunlight flashed in their eyes. Philip pulled Doreen against him; she twisted away. "Hon, what do we do if the car stop again?"

"Look," he said, "there's another sign." As long as the makeshift signs that read *Sunset Beach* kept appearing, he remained hopeful. Yet, there was no denying that the road seemed to be inordinately long. Who would have guessed that the coast was so far away? Each time the Fusion hit the lowest point between two ridges, the windows sank below the level of the bushes. The sedan faltered, reviving the threat that a patch of loose red earth would ensnare them.

They bumped and bumped and bumped. The bushes dragging against the sides of the car turned from green to near-black.

"If it is not over the next hill, I turn around," Françoise said.

"How do you turn around?" Paloma asked.

"I don't want to be on the highway in the dark," Doreen said.

"The highway is dangerous at night, but it is better than being stuck here. In Xai-Xai there will be a hotel."

The Fusion's tires slipped in the dust, skidding in a way that kept the car moving. Suddenly, in the muted light, they saw hillocks of thick brambles growing over sand. At the top of the next hill stood a country manor of white Iberian stucco. They drove up the hill and into a deserted yard. Philip was surprised by the coolness of the air. The view made him gasp: thatched roofs of outbuildings that slipped downhill behind the manor, the tenacious gorse-like bushes, then the beach and the ruffles of foam that layered the distant waves one upon another so that they overlapped like a succession of molten grey plates that meshed without merging. He pulled Doreen against his hip and felt her relaxing. Her wide smile loosened. The thought of how badly he wanted to make love with her cleared his senses. He was attentive to every whisper of sand, to the crinkle of Françoise opening her pack of cigarettes and passing one to Paloma.

The front door of the manor was open. There appeared to be no one inside. Then, as they turned around, a huge white man with dark hair and dark eyes, wearing black slacks and a white shirt, came down the hill above the manor with a host of shorter, thinner black men following in his wake. Philip received the sight as a glimpse into the colonial past. Certain pasts persisted into the presents that succeeded them. He felt a surge of contradictory optimism.

Françoise and Paloma looked at him, urging him to speak. Surprised again by their insistence that he handle communication, he said, "*Boa tarde, senhor. Somos quatro pessoas—dois casais. Estamos a procurar quartos para a noite …*"

THE SAND-COLOURED RIDGES on the edges of the township soaked up the day's dampness. Streets and streets of box-like bungalows went past. "Four million people live in Soweto," the driver said. He parked on a sloping concrete square of massive, blank-faced concrete monuments. Philip paid him; they got out. The square was bordered by apartment blocks. In the passages between the blocks, people had set up stalls where they sold T-shirts, belts, and watches. The watches, Philip saw, as he stepped away from the driver for a moment, had the same garish plastic bands as those for sale down-town, though none was quite as fancy as his fake Bulova. Here the vendors were South African.

"This is Charmaine," the driver said, leading him to a short, energetic-looking young woman with supernaturally bright dark eyes who wore blue jeans and a tight white T-shirt that flattened her breasts. Charmaine stood at the core of a group of well-dressed people who wore black leather shoes that gleamed with fresh polish. She directed Philip to the woman at a nearby stall who was selling tickets.

"Are we ready?" Charmaine said. He bought his ticket and handed it to her. There were twelve tourists: Philip and eleven African-Americans. Charmaine welcomed them. She delivered a talk on South Africa's past: Dutch and British colonialism, the Boer War, the introduction of apartheid. She was intelligent and highly articulate, yet the potted history made Philip restless.

"Are there any questions?" Charmaine asked when she had finished her introduction.

A woman raised her hand. "When are you people going to get rid of apartheid? It's a terrible system. Can't you see you have to get rid of it? Back in the States we had the civil rights movement ..."

"So we did," three or four voices echoed.

"Madam, apartheid ended twenty years ago, in 1994. We got rid of it. I can assure you of that, madam." Charmaine provided a concise description of the anti-apartheid struggle, Nelson Mandela's release from prison, and the first free elections. As she was speaking, a man from the group wandered across the square, approached a local man, and held out his hand for a shake. The local man shied away. Philip saw the tourist take out his business card and brandish a pen. When he returned, Charmaine said, "Please don't stray from the group, sir."

"I just made me a friend!" the tourist protested.

"The fruits of democracy are sweet," Charmaine said, "but they are not shared equally by all. Even when you have your freedom, you must continue to struggle."

"Ain't that so," voices echoed.

"We are going to see some of that inequality now. What you are about to see is only a small part of South Africa today, but it is a reason to ensure that our vigilance never wavers."

As though leading a guerrilla platoon, Charmaine pivoted in her sneakers and marched down the slope of the concrete square. She led the group up the steps of a footbridge that crossed the railway line that ran along the bottom of the square. They straggled over the bridge, staring down at the railway ties below. When they came down the steps on the other side, they were in hell. Philip was shaken by the swiftness of the transition from the austere yet peaceful square. From the bottom step of the stairs, putrid, stinking sewage covered three-quarters of the dirt street. The shanties were dark and depressing. "Here," Charmaine said, as she hopped from one island of brownish dirt to the next, "every family is led by a single mother. Our constitution gives every child the right to an education, but most of these people never went to school themselves. If they decide not to send their children, nobody's going to come and look for them."

"We was poor down in South Carolina," an older woman in high heels said. "But not like this! Grampa always had his chickens."

Philip saw that the woman was right: these people had no livestock, engaged in no agricultural activity. The women huddled inside the dark, smoky shanties. The children ambled half-naked through the muck. The men hung out in groups on street corners, gathered around hookahs or scattered empty beer bottles. Some of the male tourists approached local men to offer a handshake and a business card. "It's a pleasure to meet my brothers," he heard one tourist say. "Send me an email anytime you feel like it."

He must have uttered a despairing sigh. A crisp voice behind him said, "They're only trying to make contact with their heritage. Why are you here?"

Charmaine was staring at him. "Do you get tired of explaining the obvious to people who know nothing about history?" he asked.

"I was fortunate to receive an education. If I were a few years older, I would have had a Bantu education and been forced to learn Afrikaans instead of English. I am a feminist! I do not wish to learn the language of my oppressor!" She drew a breath. "Since I have this education, it's my responsibility to share it. It's not my place to judge what they don't know, only to make them more informed." She turned and cranked her arm for the other tourists to follow her. She led Philip to a second staircase, at the opposite end of the slum from the first one, that would carry them over the railway line and back into the grey square.

They waited on the bottom step for two tourists in dark blazers to detach themselves from a conversation with a group of men who were responding to them with torpid gesticulations. The tourists offered business cards and friendship, but were asked for money. "This way, please!" Charmaine said. Once she had gathered her flock, she headed up the stairs. "This is your first time in Africa?" she asked.

"I went to a conference in Mombasa. Ten years ago I worked in Mozambique for six months." Unwanted, the coast around Mozambique Island pressed in on his mind, bringing back the villages full of ghostly hulks of Portuguese cottages that the Macua people refused to occupy out of fear that the colonizers might return, the tiny children who followed him down forest paths squawking, "*Branco! Branco!*", the Jeeps in which he had been driven over red earth roads that cut through the tropical greenery.

"You think you have some connection here, too." Charmaine's smile was cutting.

Before he could formulate a full-fledged denial, a metallic scream gashed the air. A freight train hurtled along the tracks, blurring past the landing at the top of the staircase. A half-naked man danced on the roof of a freight car, gambolling around and waving his arms.

Three steps below them, the woman who had spoken about her grandfather's chickens shrieked.

"People here like to risk their lives," Charmaine said. "That's all they've got to do with them."

Philip's eyes followed the train around a long curve that tilted the speeding rolling stock. The man teetered and danced. As the train gave a lurch, he was pitched into space. For a split second he resembled a cartoon hero, flying through the air with his arms spread like a Superman of the slums. Then gravity seized him, turning his gangly frame into spread-eagled ballast and slamming him to earth in a deserted lot a couple of hundred metres away. As the man smashed into the ground, Philip's heart compressed like a rubber ball clenched in a fist. He thought he was going to be sick.

"Your life can change in a second," Charmaine said. She reached for her cellphone.

"It doesn't even have to be an accident," Philip murmured, knowing she wasn't listening. Below him the tourist women sobbed. Local men gathered around a hookah uttered chortling whoops. He stared into the distance, trying to make out the shape of the far-off body. "Sometimes your life changes in a second and you don't recognize it's happened."

⁓

IN A FEW MINUTES, they were booked into a lodge at the top of the hill — the one with the best view, the owner said — and had ordered dinner. They were the only guests. "People turn off the highway looking for us, but if they don't have four-by-fours they give up."

"We have a good driver," Philip said.

Paloma smiled at Françoise through curls of cigarette smoke.

The owner gave orders to his employees, who tacked the word *patrão* — "boss" — onto every reply or question, while Françoise opened the Fusion's trunk. They carried their luggage uphill to the wooden lodge. Inside, two twin-bed rooms faced each other across a living room-kitchen stocked with copious cooking materials. A stout wooden balcony projected out over the green brambles, commanding a fantastic view over the greying ocean. Philip spotted stray fishing boats amid the swell. As he looked more closely, the tails and heads of humpback whales, announced by blossoms of white spray, butted up black between the boats. Françoise brought a pair of binoculars; they took turns watching the whales until the ocean's grey grew metallic.

Dinner was served on a huge wooden table in the front room of the manor before a fireplace hemmed by bright blue *azulejo* tiles. On the wall next to the reception desk was a logo of rifles crossing in an X over the pages of an open book; the emblem of Mozambique's revolution against Portuguese colonialism. Trim young men in white shirts swarmed around the room, as numerous as though there were twenty guests rather than four. The word *patrão* echoed from their lips; the boss directed operations from the kitchen. They were each sipping a local 2M beer when the attendants brought out the main course of barracuda steaks accompanied by French fries and rice. The owner emerged. Seating himself at the end of the table, he switched from Portuguese to a cautious English punctuated by thunking South African vowels.

"How long have you been here?" Doreen asked.

"I was born in Xai-Xai." Philip thought of the museum-perfect colonial town where, on the trip north, their bus had crossed the clear-flowing, bright, green-banked Limpopo River. "My father had a shop in Chidenguele. After the revolution we wanted to stay, but when the civil war started my father decided to leave. He never came back. But I did. I like Mozambique much better than South Africa. I can speak my language ... and here everybody is together. They say South Africa is a rainbow nation, but in a rainbow each colour is separate."

Françoise and Paloma kept their heads down, examining each bite of food with care before placing it in their mouths. Doreen was restless. She idealized South Africa as the slayer of racist apartheid. Anticipating her reactions, Philip guessed that she would be wondering whether the owner felt more comfortable in Mozambique because here his status as a white *patrão* went unchallenged. Yet, in one of those lapses indicative of his inability to anticipate the direction of her thoughts, just as he was congratulating himself on how well he knew her, he realized that her interest in the owner's political history was negligible; what gripped her was the resort the man had built.

"You planned this place, right? You built it all?"

The owner nodded. "There was nothing here before. This is my commitment to my country — to build something here."

"But there was no road, right? You found this place without any road?"

A faint smile creeping across his face, the owner nodded.

"You did it from the ocean? You went up and down the coast until you found the beach you wanted, and hills that were right for the buildings, and you worked back from there?"

"You are very intelligent." The owner's dark eyes kindled with interest.

"I'm an engineer," Doreen said. "That's why I ask a lot of questions."

"Please ask questions."

"I'm an electrical engineer, not a civil engineer, but I still like to figure stuff out."

"I trawled the coast from south of Xai-Xai up to Beira. I considered setting up in Xai-Xai because it is easy to get there from Maputo. I would have more visitors than I have here. But there is a problem with sharks in Xai-Xai. I came here because it was the most beautiful location I found. And no sharks, only whales. I built this house and the restaurant, and I added a campground. That was two years ago. I had to wait six months for the government inspectors to approve my licence. By that time I had started to build the cabins. I had to wait another six months for the inspectors to come back and license the cabins. It's only now that I feel like I am in business."

"I am sorry you do not get many tourists," Paloma said. "We will tell people about this *boo-tiful* hotel."

The owner stood up, shook hands with each of them and withdrew, scattering instructions to the young attendants.

"*Sim, patrão,*" they replied.

As Françoise and Paloma finished their 2MS, Philip laid his hand on Doreen's thigh. How he wanted her!

He took her hand as they got up from the table. The breeze made the bushes rustle. The air was cooler. Sliding bars of foam shimmered in the night. Philip, hopelessly aroused, slid his arm around Doreen's waist and kissed her on the mouth. Their clutch brought them to a halt. Françoise and Paloma, who had stopped to light cigarettes in cupped hands, caught up with them.

"I do not like that man!" Françoise said.

"How come?" Doreen said. "This is a pretty nice place he built."

"You see how he lives alone with those boys?"

"You can't know that for sure," Doreen said.

"I know for sure. I am one, I know one."

Philip wasn't certain that he accepted this logic, particularly across divides of gender and culture, yet he could see that Françoise's suspicion had made an impact on Doreen. She took his hand in hers as though both cooling him down and seeking reassurance. They walked to the door of the lodge, unlocked it, went inside, and turned on the watery lights. It was eight forty-five; the generator went off at nine.

They went to their room and closed the door. Françoise and Paloma were smoking on the balcony.

Doreen sat down on the bed closest to the wooden shutters.

"Françoise is right. There's something creepy about this place."

"It's beautiful."

"I don't feel safe here."

"I'm sure he has guards to watch the cabins at night."

"More of them boys of his ..."

"I don't think Françoise is right." Only he knew that in his introduction to the *patrão*, he had described them as *dois casais*: "two couples." The owner hadn't flinched at this description. Philip had taken his impassiveness as a sign of open-mindedness. But he feared that if he explained what he'd said to Doreen, she would place a different interpretation on the *patrão*'s acceptance.

He yearned to sit down on her bed and continue kissing her. She looked up at him with a wounded expression. Why did the room have to have single beds? He told himself to swallow his frustration, reassure Doreen, then go to sleep. Tomorrow they would arrive in Maputo, leaving behind Sunset Beach and Françoise and Paloma, and book into a business hotel in the Baixa where they would slip into the routines of their long companionship. He would get his sex; he would get his talk about their future.

A throbbing in the pit of his stomach that blended lust with psychic unease urged him to resolve these tensions right now.

"Doreen, when are we going to have kids?"

"When we get married, I guess."

"We should get pregnant now. You could tell your daughter she was conceived in Africa."

"Are you crazy?"

"No. I want us to settle down. I want certainty."

"We ain't got certainty until we're married."

"None of your sisters was married to the men they had children with."

"And look at them now. A bunch of single moms."

"You know I'd marry you if you were pregnant. But we're here now. Who knows how long —"

"Philip, what's got into you?"

"I want my life —"

The lights went out. Doreen's whimper of fear silenced him. The blackness was so thick that it strained his eyeballs. He couldn't discern the merest outline of Doreen's profile or the shape of her bed.

"Make sure that door's locked," he heard her say. "Put the chair in front of it."

He blundered across the room until his hiking boot struck the chair. He slid the chair to where he thought the door was, then found his bed again and undressed. Doreen's tensed breathing told him that it would be hours before she fell asleep.

THE POLICE CRUISER ROLLED up over the sidewalk onto the square. It stopped behind the stall and three cops got out. The two who hadn't been driving carried short-barrelled carbines strapped across their chests. Philip and Charmaine stood next to the ticket seller. The African-American women had huddled in a group, murmuring about the accident. The men roamed the square, offering their email addresses to passing brothers, until the van from their hotel had arrived to pick them up. With the Americans gone, Charmaine asked Philip to stay in case the police required a second witness. Now Philip watched the police question her. They were glowering and suspicious, their questions pompous aggressions that Charmaine met with sharp, clear retorts. They took down the information on her ID card. Charmaine presented him as a tourist who had witnessed the accident; the police ignored him. After ten minutes, during which the police treated Charmaine as though she were a criminal, one of the cops laughed. He switched from English to Xhosa or Zulu. The conversation was transformed. They joked and commiserated. The cop who had been driving detached a walkie-talkie with a BlackBerry-like screen from his shoulder and radioed another car. The police nodded to Charmaine, rhymed off a curiously upbeat farewell in their own language, got in the cruiser, and backed away across the square.

Philip walked to the edge of the square and bought Charmaine a strong coffee. When he returned, she asked him how much he had paid for it. "You would have got it for less if you hadn't ordered in English!"

"I would have got it for less if I weren't a tourist," he said. "I was surprised you spoke to the police in your own language."

"Apartheid," Charmaine said, "didn't just divide people by race. It divided Africans by ethnicity. But that preserved African languages." Soweto was cut into linguistic islands; most children did their schooling in their parents' language. English was a subject in school, not the language in which they learned. "I speak Xhosa. I am glad to speak English to meet the world, but it is not my reality. It is not my soul."

He wanted to tell her how different this was in Mozambique, where speaking Portuguese was an affirmation of national liberation and urban young people spurned African languages. Once, in Maputo, he had been crouched in a crowded *chapa* where an old woman had started speaking in an African language. "*Língua nacional, língua nacional!*" the passengers chanted, harassing her to switch to Portuguese. He kept the anecdote to himself, fearing that like other South Africans, Charmaine would seize on the neighbouring country's differences as proof of the inferiority of the migrants in the streets. He felt a wall of reserve, a wait-and-see caution derived from years working in other cultures, cordon him off from her as completely as though this were decades earlier and they were separated by apartheid laws. His desire to prolong their conversation faded. He finished his coffee, shook hands with Charmaine, tipped her in recognition that she had taught him about her country because she needed a paycheque, and crossed the square to the taxi stand. When he turned on his laptop in his hotel room, Désirée had written: *Did I get the time difference wrong? Must run to pick up David. Talk tomorrow?* He sent her a contrite apology. After a moment's hesitation, he added: *I'm out of time here in Joburg. Let's try again when I get to Cape Town.*

⁓

PARK STATION, WHERE HE bought his bus ticket, doubled as a gleaming split-level shopping mall with long escalators dropping down from the upper level to the lower. The signs were in English, yet among the hundreds of people who surrounded him — shoppers, people with incomes, South Africans rather than migrants — almost no one was speaking his language. He joined the queue at the Trans-Lux ticket counter. Sagging felt dividers suspended between steel uprights marked the head of the queue. When it was his turn to approach the counter, a skinny young man, ostentatiously playing with his cellphone, rushed up and shadowed him step by step, pressed in so close behind him that Philip could feel the boy's breath on his neck. Philip dropped his right hand to cover the pocket that contained his wallet.

"Back!" the woman at the counter shouted at the young man.

"Sis!" he beseeched her.

"Back!" she repeated.

"Sis! I got a right, sis! It's my country!"

"Back! Behind the line!"

The young man retreated with a deflated, "Aw, sis!" Philip glanced over his shoulder, then ordered and paid for his ticket. When he turned around, the young man was gone.

Late the next afternoon, when he checked out of the hotel, the clerks in their blue blazers were shocked that he was going to Park Station rather than Oliver Tambo Airport. One clerk deputed another to accompany him to a van. They made the two-minute drive to the station and entered a parking lot on the lower level. The driver manoeuvred to the edge of the TransLux waiting area. Philip grabbed his pack and over-tipped the man. In response, the man accompanied him into Park Station. It was late in the day. Hundreds of children in school uniforms poured across the lobby. The clerk led him to the TransLux waiting area, shook his hand, and left. A few minutes later a young woman in a red skirt and blazer with a TransLux logo on the breast, her relaxed, shoulder-length hair swishing as she shook her head, issued the boarding call. There were nine passengers for the overnight trip: Philip; a white-bearded old Afrikaner who understood Philip's phrasebook German better than he did English; a young, black-bearded Muslim from the Cape, who spoke to the Afrikaner in Afrikaans; and six members of a migrant family from another African country. The migrants arrived with bags and bags of produce that filled the luggage compartment. They carried more bags on board with them. The family's matriarch responded to the drivers' objections by brandishing a small, dark passport. Philip tried talking to one of the migrant men, but neither English, French, nor Portuguese elicited a reply.

The high-altitude mist was greying into evening as the Trans-Lux official came on board. She chatted with the drivers in Xhosa until, noticing Philip watching her, she snapped into English. "Who let these people go into the bus without showing a ticket? They must all show a ticket!" She waded to the back of the bus and bellowed rules and regulations at the migrants. Philip sensed that this performance was for his benefit, that the official was asserting her membership in the boss-culture of straight hair and English against the immigrants' mortifying backwardness. None of the migrants replied; no one called her sis.

Sisters. Brothers. Philip's cold had waned, but as the bus worked its way out of Johannesburg and onto the high veldt, his ears blocked up, immuring him in his past. Doreen had referred to her African-American women contacts in Silicon Valley as sisters; she confided in them more than she did in her own sisters, who regarded her with mystification or resentment. Her insistence on speaking to her siblings in Jamaican patois, though even Philip could hear that her accent and expressions weren't convincing, baffled them. Her sisters would have viewed Doreen as an object of ridicule had she not also been an object of awe; the only woman in the family to escape poverty, buy property, travel for business, have white boyfriends, not have an unplanned pregnancy. Her achievements cast her estrangement as superiority, causing her sisters to regard her as the migrants regarded the Xhosa woman with the relaxed hair and the short red skirt. (But who knew what the migrants thought? Who could imagine the culture they carried with them in their wandering?)

When Martin was six months old, the three of them flew to Miami, where Mam, Rachel, and Minnie, removed from violent Jamaica, worked for a domestic help agency. As he showed off the baby, Philip was astonished by how little attention the three women paid the infant. They liked the fact that he was named after their late son and brother, but, as a boy, he was irrelevant to the Jamaican matriarchy. Boys got into trouble, then were lured away by the first pair of hips that sashayed past; girls stuck around and became bulwarks of the family. They brought their paycheques, like their children, back to their mother or grandmother. Through the first five months of her pregnancy, right up to the second ultrasound, Doreen had spoken of "my daughter" and "when our daughter is born ..." When the technician pointed to a blurry protrusion on the screen and said, "Do you know what that is?", Doreen had fallen silent. The technician, Middle Eastern, assumed that a penis was good news. After they left the lab, Doreen was silent for over an hour. Finally she said, "We can name him after my brother." She said nothing more; he shouldn't have been surprised that Doreen's mother and sisters preferred to marvel at her waistline. "You not fat, Satty!" Minnie exclaimed in reproof, calling her sister by her patois nickname. Doreen's trim body was one more trait that divided her from her sisters' out-of-control lives; they had expected that having a child, even a half-white boy ("biracial," Doreen insisted; "son of a jake," Minnie giggled), would make her look more like them. Stepping into their apartment with a baby in hand, still as slender as she had been prior to her pregnancy, had supplied further proof that her essence, down to the fibres of her flesh, was of a different matter than theirs. The thought made him struggle to remember which forms of birth control he and Doreen had used at different stages of their relationship. His memories of their vacation in Grenada, right after Martin's murder, while Doreen was waiting for the funeral date to be set, included condoms. Soon after that she had gone on the pill, then, still in shock from her brother's death, had gone off it just as suddenly, without telling him. This was why Martin — his Martin — had been born late, as though some celestial stopwatch had already been running overtime when he had entered the world. If he had been conceived prior to his uncle's murder, if they had made love on Sunset Beach, when Doreen's brother was still alive, Martin would not be named Martin, bogging him down in the violent red earth of a Jamaica the boy had never visited. One night in her condo, when he had been about to get on a plane — he didn't remember where to — she had pleaded with him to find work in Toronto, "It's a big city. You can find a job here." He said nothing, his thoughts far away. "I need you here, hon," she murmured, barely articulating her words, as though embarrassed at not existing in perfect independence. "Just love me." That must have been when, without telling him, she had stopped taking the pill.

⁓

THE HIGH VELDT WAS a plain of bleached-yellow grass dotted with gnarled green shrubbery. In the grey light — which became dusk almost by osmosis — slag heap after slag heap and open-pit mine after open-pit mine rolled past. The earth's redness was rustier here, as though brushed with pyrites; it both was and was not the same porous substance that had snared the Fusion. The highway, a two-lane strip of blacktop, was crowded with sluggish trucks that hauled double trailers of heavy ore. The TransLux coach was overtaking all the way, perpetually playing chicken on the gloomy plateau with trucks lumbering in the opposite direction. Signs warned of "accident zones."

The blackness became impenetrable. The coach passed through shuttered towns with long Afrikaans names. The driver put in a DVD, a James Bond movie blasted at high volume from multiple miniature televisions. Shifting in his seat as he tried to catch some sleep, Philip wondered for whose benefit this entertainment was being provided. So far as he could tell, he was the only passenger capable of understanding the film's hokey dialogue. Bond sounded like Désirée's posh son in his school uniform. Grateful for the muting effect of his blocked ears, he thought of how he and Désirée had scrambled to get dressed, in her small upstairs bedroom with the hissing radiator, in time for her to pick up her son from school; he thought of his own son, whose skin, like Désirée's, was a soft, mixed-race brown.

When he woke, James Bond continued to leap and shoot and drive fast cars, except this was a different film and a different actor was playing Bond. The same man had different faces in different times and places. In the second film, Bond's leading lady was a beautiful mixed-race actress who resembled Désirée. Or did Désirée resemble the actress? His mind fumbled elementary logic. Accepting that he was awake, in spite of his profound wish to sleep, he looked at his watch. It had stopped at five o'clock — if it had ever worked. On the television, Bond was fighting a villain on the roof of a speeding train. The train swept through a valley, yet neither of the men was tossed into the abyss. *People here like to risk their lives. That's all they've got to do with them.*

Charmaine was right. But this wasn't true only in Soweto.

⁓

NO EXPERIENCE IN HIS life had sealed his understanding that race was a vile fiction, concocted to divide people, more powerfully than his sex life with Doreen. A white man and a black woman who went to bed together out of shared desire shed their pigmentation as quickly as they did their clothes. The yoking of their bodies, the sloshing of their tongues, their sweat, their whimpering, their drive towards orgasm, made them simply male and female, two copulating mammals of the same species. Yet, even in that moment of fusion, history burst in. From Mozambique to Jamaica to Mississippi, the threadbare history of black women fucking white men out of love or consensual lust was overwhelmed by centuries of plantation rape, backroom prostitution, poor women selling their bodies to rich men. Doreen, with her scrap of Scottish ancestry, was a product, an inheritor, a survivor, of this history. Her blue-eyed, brushed-copper-complexioned grandmother — "high red," they called that tone in Jamaica — was the daughter of a woman who had been a colonial British officer's "fancy lady." And who could say that Philip's ancestors, merchants in nineteenth-century Halifax, had not been involved in the Caribbean rum trade which had supported and maintained plantation slavery? If she had been created by a history of exploitation, so had he. His ancestors had been the beneficiaries, perhaps the rapists. When they clasped each other naked on a hot summer night he embraced the contradiction that the differences between them were not markers of division, but a levelling force that reduced them to man and woman. History, though, decreed that how they had sex mattered. They escaped the past only when their lovemaking acquired shapes unlikely to have been witnessed on the plantation. Until he had kissed all of her lips with equal care, until he had aroused then soothed her clitoris with his tongue, until he had acquiesced to her whispered, "I want to ride you," and let her pin his shoulders to the bed as she bucked in search of the satisfaction demanded by her unknowable fantasies, their blending would re-enact oppression even as it scoured away all history and asserted their unique existence as linked human organisms.

"Hon? Are you awake, hon?"

"Uh ... what is it?"

"It have somebody outside the window. I hear feet moving in them bushes."

"Go to sleep. It's the security guard."

"One of them boys of his."

"I really don't think Françoise is right about that."

"Takes one to know one ... she said that, not me!"

"What she knows is different from knowing stuff here."

"Then how come he live all alone? Tell me that, Mr. I-Suddenly-Want-to-Settle-Down."

"What if it's just one of them? What if he's just with one of the guys? Two consenting adults? Do you still disapprove?"

"He's rich and the boy's poor ... what do I know? As long as he not some old-time colonial master havin' his way with the whole bunch of them."

"We can't know for sure. Maybe if we stayed here longer."

"No way I'm stayin' here another night."

"Doreen? Can I come over to your bed?"

"And how you find a condom in this pitch-blackness? You stay where you are, mister, and go back to sleep."

—

THE COACH PULLED INTO a brightly lighted roadside gas bar where the down-angled surveillance cameras trained on them like stunted gun barrels as they stumbled out to the washroom. Philip bought a bottle of water at the counter and stepped outside. Under the lights, the Muslim guy and the TransLux agent were drinking coffee and talking. His English was broken; hers had a ringing lilt. Philip couldn't understand their conversation. Their code for bridging their cultural divide was unique, as each bridging of a cultural divide was original and unrepeatable. No cross-cultural friendship, flirtation, or love affair provided an idiom that could be adopted by any other; nothing learned in one such relationship was transferrable to the next.

The bearded, brown-skinned man and the black woman erupted into laughter. Philip missed the joke. Maybe it was his blocked ears. He returned to the coach, knowing he would not sleep. The bus pulled back onto the highway. The James Bond movies were over. His marriage was over and he still wasn't sure why it had ended. They had been married for only a few months, a hastily improvised civil ceremony once Doreen had confirmed that she was pregnant. It made him despondent to think that they had joined the ranks of couples who lived together for years only to break up as soon as they got married. No sooner were he and Doreen a societally sanctioned unit than Doreen began taking decisions without consulting him. That was the version he relayed to friends, until Obi, sitting in a Soho pub after a meeting for their violence project, said, "Philip, man, she's a Jamaican woman! She does what she wants! Don't tell me you didn't notice that for the first five years!" Philip's murmured amendment — "Jamaican-Canadian" — did nothing to change his colleague's opinion.

Once they were married, she expected him to stay in Toronto. She had got pregnant, he suspected, to hold a man close to her after the pain of losing her brother. When little Martin was two, Philip returned from a month in Colombia to discover that Doreen had bought a house and put the condo up for sale. Astute as always, she had got into the Toronto detached-house market just before it became unaffordable. The modest little place was on a side street off Lansdowne, north of Bloor, in an area that was Portuguese, Latin American, and Jamaican. "It's perfect for us, hon," she said in that coy, teasing, little-girl way that made it sound as though she were following some auntie's advice on how to talk to your man. "You can talk Spanish and Portuguese and I can eat really good patties!" The house's bedrooms were small, the floors creaked and the kitchen boasted the latest interior design accessories of 1975: Formica countertops, a hideous spice-rack that was fixed to the wall, a grease-grimed hood set too low over the stove. Yes, they were both to blame, but as Obi pointed out after loading his second Guinness onto a circular pressboard coaster emblazoned with a design of a crimson lion, apportioning blame equally was something people — men, usually — did when they knew that they were the ones who had crossed the line. That was how Obi expressed it, "You crossed the line." Philip knew what he was talking about; he knew that Obi knew that he knew. Their professional circles were small. It was common knowledge that he and Renata, after years of conference flirtations on different continents (Paris,

San Salvador, Mombasa), had finally had the affair that they had
postponed for over a decade. Yes, Renata, not Désirée, had been his
wrecking ball.

"They never stay with the ones they leave their wives for," Doreen
had murmured when she found out.

"I'm not leaving you for her," he had replied.

"You knew that fidelity was very, very important to me," she said.

———

ALL NIGHT THE SKY had been darker than the land. He failed to
perceive the moment when it began to grow lighter, as he had failed
to grasp the importance of a few minutes' disagreement on Sunset
Beach. He got a last glimpse of the high veldt before the coach
dropped into rocky cuttings. The driver had run out of red earth,
and he, like the inert Bulova on his wrist, had run out of time. The
phrase "out of time" rattled in his head, as he envisaged its meaning
as being not that of not having any time left, but rather of having
run so far as to have shed temporal boundaries.

The driver blasted the horn, waking up the dozing migrant family.
Baboons scampered away from the white line in the middle of the
road as the driver leaned on the horn again. Looping their overlong
arms around their young, suckling their infants, the baboons stared
up at the windows of the bus with the faces of humans mired in
bodies from a pre-human era. At the bottom of the winding cuttings,
enclosed by steel railings, the earth lost its burnish, passing from red
to brown. At six a.m. they reached the valley floor where workers
were lolling out of shanties with roofs made of scrap metal anchored
by rocks, men and women piling into the backs of trucks for the ride
to the vineyards. The sun climbed, revealing a wine-growing valley
and distant green hills. He had no reason for being here. It was he,
not his job, that required travel. To retain his mental equilibrium,
he wandered off, as Jamaican men wandered off.

Poor Doreen. She had sought stability by dating white men, yet
some atavistic coding in her emotional DNA had caused her to settle

on a white man who acted like a Jamaican, rambling from place to place, never staying at home long enough for his relationships to stabilize. The difference was fidelity; until Renata, he had been faithful to her. For Doreen, fidelity had been one of the benefits of his whiteness; it had allowed her to write off his perpetual wandering as evidence that he was a professional. Putting great stock in her own status as an engineer, she explained to her sisters that a professional's travel was different from the wayward itinerancy of the marginally employed men who got them pregnant. Yet, for all his campus activism and protesting of injustice in what back then had been called "the Third World," it wasn't politics that had led Philip into his present line of work. He had been drawn to international development by restlessness. Each project gave him a pretext for half a dozen deranged side trips. All his knowledge of the world did not help him to imagine Martin's perceptions as the only child of a single professional Jamaican mother in downtown Toronto; a brown kid attending grade two in a school full of brown and black kids, and white kids whose parents spoke laboured English, and kids with single mothers or two mothers or two fathers or blended families. It felt a hundred years from his own upbringing in sedate Kingston as the middle child of a Queen's University economics prof; in a family that had been in Canada for almost two hundred years; in a provincial redoubt that was thoroughly, stultifyingly Canadian, in a way that stoked up his urge to go elsewhere, nourished his conviction that life as authentic engagement, credible experience, existed only on other continents. Toronto's international population blurred the contrast on which he thrived, the blade-sharp line between home and away. Was this blurring of boundaries, as much as proximity to government funding, the reason he had moved to Ottawa? Had he abandoned his son to reassert the increasingly murky border between us and them, First World and Third World, wealth and poverty, aid donors and aid recipients? Had he left because Martin himself was blurring made flesh?

He wished again that his son had been safely ensconced in life, under a different name, prior to the night his uncle had fallen to the ground in a slum. Owing his conception to violence and grief would jinx him. If Martin had been born earlier, Philip would not have had to confront the uncomfortable realizations spoiling his pristine view of Table Mountain as the TransLux coach slotted itself into the Cape Town morning rush hour.

Out the window, he saw dozens of white people in cars. His headache returned. Glancing at the miniature televisions over the seats, he recalled his early days with Doreen, when she had taken her new boyfriend to meet her girlfriends at Lansdowne and Bloor or Jane and Finch, or in the West Indian enclaves of Kitchener or Stratford. Each of her friends was a single mother with children from one or more fathers. Each apartment was organized around the huge television in the living room that blasted day and night, producing kids — little boys, especially — who were hyped-up and clued-in and aware, yet lacking in serenity or confidence or respon-sibility. Even as Doreen caught up with these women whom she described as her closest friends — yet the electrical engineer was selective about how much of her life she revealed to these harried single mothers who did shift work — the television continued to blare at high volume, curtailing their confidences even when Philip stepped out of the room to leave them alone and talk to the children, who had never before spoken to a white man who wasn't a teacher or a cop. On a drive back from Kitchener, where they'd visited her friend who supported four children from three fathers by working in the Schneider's meat-packing plant, he had suggested to Doreen that, for the children, the TV screen substituted for the absent father. She had been silent for a long time, then murmured, "Men watch lots of TV, too. You don't, hon, but most guys do."

His son, too, had a television. When Martin was a toddler, Doreen's answer to the little boy's moments of defiance — when he turned off light switches and unrolled the toilet paper in the bath-room just to get a rise out of her — was, first, to say, "Do you want a slap?" and second, to sit him in front of the television. By now she would have trained Martin to turn on the TV during the long hours that she spent in front of the computer when she came home from work or, if she had reverted to not returning from Mississauga until eight o'clock, Martin would be latch-keying it, entering the little house to find a flatscreen instead of parents.

As the coach pulled into the station, the migrants gathered their bags. Philip grabbed his pack from the empty seat across the aisle and went to look for a taxi. The pellucid morning light was softened by a watery film that spoke of proximity to the ocean. He took a taxi driven by an elderly Afrikaner through a district of high-rise towers to the hotel he had booked at the bottom of Long Street. His room had a view of an upward jut of Table Mountain. He took two aspirins, a Sinutab and a Benadryl and conked out. By the time he woke up with an abrupt intake of breath, as though his body had dropped off a ledge, it was mid-afternoon. He showered and shaved. He climbed the undulating upward slope of Long Street, where late nineteenth-century arcades sliced the sunlight into sprawled shadows beneath second floors festooned with wrought-iron balconies and fronted by facades of metallic arabesques. There were cafés, antique shops, bookstores, music stores, bars, and back-packer travel agencies. As though in a parody of his self-image as a rugged independent traveller, he had landed in Lonely Planet heaven. Placards advertised tickets on transcontinental excursions by minivan, promising to whisk young people across an Africa that would consist only of animals, beaches, and waterfalls. Pasty-faced northern Europeans trailed in the wake of more burnished, purposeful-looking white South Africans in business attire. With the exception of a couple of in-your-face guys who sauntered up to tourists and said, "Walking tour of District Six, I give walking tours of District Six," and grabbed the arms of people who ignored them, most of the few black people visible were in service jobs.

He sat down in a café, in a wicker chair close to the sidewalk. Bypassing the Cape wines that dominated the menu, he ordered a glass of a wine from KwaZulu-Natal.

"Have you been here long?" the woman two tables over asked.

"I just arrived."

"You know this is not Africa? I worked in Kenya —"

"I worked in Mozambique."

They bantered for five minutes. He moved to her table. Eschewing names, they introduced themselves by nationality. She was Swedish, in her thirties, with a rumpled face that suggested a sense of humour and thick hair in which brown and blonde strands mingled. She wore a blue T-shirt; a leather satchel was draped over the back of her chair. "Europeans come here to pretend they are in Africa," she said, "and white South Africans live here to pretend they are not in Africa." She giggled, making clear that the glass in front of her was not her first of the afternoon.

Relaxing into a situation in which he knew what was expected of him, Philip listened. The Swedish woman spoke English with a naturalness matched by few people he had met in this country that he had imagined as English speaking. He watched the shape of her breasts beneath her blue T-shirt. His affair was Désirée was over. He must have been deluded to consider an Ottawa-to-London relationship with children tossed into the mix.

His companion noticed him watching her, no doubt imagining it was she, not his own gnarled life, that was dominating his attention. He was about to speak, to brake the growing intensity of her conversation, when a little boy slipped into the café. Tiny and wary, he asked for money. The boy was barefoot, he wore grubby, threadbare trousers, and a brown T-shirt covered with black stains. He carried a plastic toy AK-47. As he approached their table, the Swedish woman laid her hand on her satchel. The boy mugged a pose with the plastic carbine, pointing the barrel at Philip's face. Philip waved him away. The boy laughed, thrust his hand out for money in a derisory way, then scurried out of the café as the tall waiters in their white shirts stepped forward.

"That gun!" the woman said.

"It's a toy."

"I ask myself what kind of gun he will carry in ten years."

"That's a very good question," Philip said. He saw that the compliment pleased her.

The waiter who had run the boy into the street came to their table. "We are closing in ten minutes."

"Closing?" Philip said.

"Yes, sir, it is almost five-thirty."

The sunlight angling beneath the arcades had dimmed. The streams of South Africans in business attire were waning. The waiter brought them their bill. "By six o'clock the street is dark and there is no one here," the woman said, drinking the last of her wine.

Nightfall came too fast, as it had on Sunset Beach.

Philip reached forward and picked up the Swedish woman's bill as well as his own.

"You are very kind. We can go to Camps Bay in a taxi. There you can stay in the cafés after dark."

"Camps Bay?"

"It's on the other side of the mountain. The stars go there. Last week Prince Harry was at the beach." Her sardonic smile reassured him that in her eyes this was a dubious recommendation.

"So it's a beach ..."

"Not for swimming. Not at night ..."

"No, you usually go swimming in the morning," he said. They stood up. The compact curves of her blue jeans tweaked him with regret for the decision he had made. "It's been a pleasure to talk, but I spent last night on a bus. I'm going back to my hotel."

"I was pleased to meet you, too." The light in her eyes grew harder.

A quick handshake and he was out the door and descending the slope in the fading light.

The block in front of him was empty. Realizing it would be too dangerous to leave the hotel for supper, he stopped at the Nando's franchise that was the last food option on Long Street. He bought a Mozambican piri-piri chicken sandwich with wedges and coleslaw to take back to his room. Waiting for his food, he watched the girls who prepared and served the meals chatting in their uniform hats; poor girls who wore their hair with its natural curls and spoke to each other in dashes of colloquial English mingled with Afrikaans or maybe an African language. Unable to follow their conversation, he smiled at the girl who handed him his food. Outside, the street was dark. The light pooled in patches, the cool, salt air breezed in off the ocean. As he headed towards his hotel, the two guys who had been selling tours of District Six came out of the side street. One of them grabbed Philip's arm and pulled him close. As he recoiled, he smelled the smack of alcohol.

"Share your food with people who need it!" one man said.

Philip felt a dash of alarm in his chest even as he saw that the men were too drunk to do much harm. They pushed him back against a wall. One of them grabbed the Nando's takeout box and ran away, laughing. His companion stared at Philip. "Gimme my Nando's money."

"Get out of my way."

"I got no money for braaing chicken." The man sprang on him with a strength and coordination Philip hadn't expected. They wrestled hand to hand against a cement facing. Infused with outrage, the man rammed Philip back against the wall. His hair was unkempt, nearly an Afro. Philip heard the lunge of his breath in the deepening darkness. The office towers that surrounded them were empty. The man smashed Philip's hand against the concrete. "Your watch …!" He heard the watch's glass face crunch against the concrete. The man tried to knee Philip in the crotch and hit his thigh with a bruising force that made Philip groan. Pivoting, the man wrapped both of his clammy hands around Philip's right wrist. Let him take the watch and get this over with, Philip thought, moaning as the man bent his arm back at an unnatural angle.

A howl, a *ra-ta-ta-tat* of mock gunfire, a second whoop, distracted the man. The little boy in dirty trousers was cavorting barefoot along the sidewalk, mowing them down with his toy AK-47.

The man's grip faltered long enough for Philip to pull his arm free. He gave the man an ineffectual shove and took off running. His skin, liquid with sweat, greased his body to run faster.

He heard the man shrieking at the boy. He tried not to imagine what he would do to him when he caught him.

⁓

HE ENTERED HIS HOTEL room, ducking his head away from the flatscreen, stripped off his clothes, and stepped into the shower. As water beat into his head and chest, he remembered Martin's limbs scrambling against him as the little boy asked to be lifted up and shown the view of Lake Ontario. Hunger raked his stomach, expanding into a yearning that spread beyond the need for a meal. Doreen might not welcome a concerned father moving back to Toronto to meddle in her son's upbringing; Martin, by now, might prefer a flat screen to a dad. At first he would resent this white stranger presuming to set him an example. It didn't matter. Doreen, Renata, Désirée; these relationships were unsalvageable. Only his relationship with Martin could be rescued. Stepping out of the shower and drying himself with a towel, he decided to write to Doreen to tell her he was selling his Ottawa condo and would look for a job in Toronto. It was a big city; he would find something. Aware of his aimlessness vanishing before the rush of chores that awaited him, he glanced at the Bulova, which he had left next to the sink. Behind the scratched glass of the face, the second hand was sweeping around. The watch had started working and was keeping perfect time.

⁓

HE WOKE TO A cranny of light, got up and opened the wooden shutters. A warm breeze flowed into the room. It was five forty-five in the morning and as bright as day. Doreen rolled over. "Are we still alive?" They smiled at each other. The sight of his clothes on the floor, the chair jammed against the wall where he had thought the door was, made them laugh. He sat down on her bed as she sat up. He pulled her against him and gave her a long kiss on the mouth. He slid his hand along her inner thigh. She pulled her mouth away from his, then gave him another quick kiss and hung still for a moment as though pondering his offer from the night before.

Two quick knocks on the door. "We go to the beach," Françoise said. "You come?"

"Yes, just a minute!" Doreen jumped to her feet. "Come on, hon. Put your swimsuit on."

They took off their underwear, feeling the warm air surround their bodies. They scrambled in their packs for their swimsuits. Doreen looked at him and laughed. "Mister, you better calm down before you meet company. That thing there's not what two lesbian want to see!"

"What they want to see is you in your bikini," Philip said. "That's why they offered us a lift."

She threw a T-shirt at him. He kissed her, pulled on his swimming trunks, a T-shirt and flip-flops, then circled the room until his lust became less conspicuous. Doreen was wearing a cream-coloured two-piece that highlighted the darkness of her skin. She pulled on shorts and a T-shirt. They left their bedroom, took turns in the washroom, and joined Françoise and Paloma on the stroll down the hillside. The thatched roofs of the vacant tourist lodges were straw-coloured pyramids amid the blanket of brambly green that clung to the sand dunes. They were alone, as if history had evaporated, leaving them as the inheritors of this paradise. Doreen reached down and took Philip's hand. The mansion's front door, facing inland, was open, but neither the *patrão* nor any of the young men was visible. They circled around the Fusion. A sandy path cut downhill in a diagonal. The light brown sand was caked and soft at first, as rich with potential as the earth on the road to Závora; then it grew harder and grainier. The waves tumbled onto the sand with a roaring-and-sucking sound that would go on and on as long as the earth continued to spin.

"The Indian Ocean is always wild," Françoise said. She and Paloma were also holding hands.

They stumbled onto the beach. On their right, the high headland where their lodge sat blocked the view; to the left, the sand spread on and on into the blur of the sun reverberating off the coastline. The breeze beat salt air into their faces. Philip felt a delightful scouring sensation comb over him, waking up his nerve-endings. His stomach became alert to hunger, as the regions below his stomach exerted demands for the fulfillment of hungers of their own. "Let's go in," he said to Doreen.

As he stepped forward, he was aware of Françoise and Paloma holding back. He stopped. Paloma's eyes were bright beneath her etched black eyebrows. She gave him a smile that encouraged him to continue walking towards the surf. Over his shoulder, he heard her say to Françoise: "*Damos una vuelta. Quieren estar solos.*"

He was grateful to Paloma for this hint, though he suspected that she, as much as he, wanted to be alone with her lover.

"We will take a walk," Françoise said.

"I'm going to sit on the beach," Doreen said.

"Come in!" His mind feasted on thoughts of stripping off her bikini in the waves.

"Hon, you know how I am. I don't swim. I come to the beach to sit on the beach!"

He turned to appeal to Françoise and Paloma, but they had left. He watched them sidle along the sand, their hands joined, the heavyset older woman and the fine-boned younger one loping at her side. As they walked, the sun wreathed them in its glimmer, melting them into a single blob in the distance. Philip shucked off his shorts and his shirt. Aware of his trimness after two months in the northern villages, he revelled in the warm wind that hugged and celebrated his body's lines. He splashed into the water — chilly but bearable — and felt an ease that delighted him. He turned around and looked back at the shoreline. Far off on his right, Françoise and Paloma had merged into the sunlight, dwindling to a single fused grain of being in the hearth of the day's brightness. Doreen sat on the beach with her knees raised and her arms balanced on her knees. She had stripped down to her bikini and sat on a jumble of his clothes and hers. The sloping hills behind her, where patches of sand interrupted the flow of brambled greenery, made her look like the first woman in the world, alone on an African beach at the dawn of humankind.

He could not believe how alone they were. He splashed water all over himself, whooping, then ran up the beach to seize her hand.

"Hon ..."

"Come in, you'll love it!"

She let him tug her, stumbling, over the sand. He heard her gasp at the first cold kiss of the waves. They sloshed deeper into the water. He kissed her on the mouth in the warm wind. She pressed the length of her body against him. They swayed. She kept kissing him. His hands met behind her back to unhook her top. Receiving the wind on her breasts with shyness and boldness, she laughed as he bent over to lick the salt off her nipples. Her hands grew firm on his ribs. "Hon, tonight we'll have a room ..."

"Doreen, this beautiful place ..."

"Not in public ..."

"There's nobody for miles."

"You never know who's watching."

He cupped her breasts in his hands as they looked each other in the eyes. "Nobody's —"

"We don't have a condom."

"We'll get married. Imagine telling your daughter she was conceived on the coast of Africa!"

She laughed, and hesitated, and took a step back, then flung herself forward and kissed him. He reached down to lower his twisted swim trunks. She caught his hand. "No, hon ... when we get to the hotel."

He smiled at this momentary disappointment, absorbing it as an indiscernible ripple in the flow of their relationship. He gave her a quick kiss on the mouth.

He helped her slide her bikini top on. She reached behind her to close the clip, then swung around. Philip dived into the water's icy embrace, plunging his head beneath the ocean's surface and thrashing his arms against the waves until his body felt salt-scoured and at ease. He waded out of the water and sat down next to Doreen on the sand.

"It makes me so happy that you came here to visit me. Are you happy?"

"I'm happy," she said. A few minutes later, she said, "Let's go back to the lodge. I want to take a shower before Françoise and Paloma get back."

They pulled on their T-shirts and shorts over their swimsuits and climbed the slope between the brambles. Their flip-flops slipped in the sand. He took Doreen's hand. As they rounded the corner of the mansion, the *patrão* stepped out of the front door. A young man in a short-sleeved white shirt walked beside him. They headed up the hill. Philip and Doreen looked at each other, hesitating for a second, then followed in the men's footsteps, aware that, like the pair in front of them, they were similar and different, together and apart.

ACKNOWLEDGEMENTS

These stories were first published as follows:

"Three Fingers" in *Prairie Fire*. First Prize, 2016 McNally Robinson / *Prairie Fire* Short Fiction Contest.

"My Soul Will Be in Paris" in *The Antigonish Review*.

"Blue River Hotel" in *Ploughshares*.

"Terms of Surrender" in *Ryga: A Journal of Provocations*.

"Where Are You in America?" in *Prairie Fire*.

"La Santiaguera" in *Descant*.

"After the Hurricane" in *Grain* and *Numéro Cinq*. Nominated by *Grain* for the National Magazine Awards.

"Who Killed Martin Coombs?" in *The Malahat Review*. Nominated by *The Malahat Review* for the National Magazine Awards.

The author thanks Marc Côté for encouragement, confidence, and help in shaping this collection, and Sarah Jensen for her editing.